Who Wrote the Book of Death?

by

Steve Liskow

Mainly Murder Press, LLC

PO Box 290586
Wethersfield, CT 06109-0586
www.mainlymurderpress.com

Mainly Murder Press

Editor: Jack L. Ryan
Executive Editor: Judith K. Ivie
Cover Designer: Patricia L. Foltz

Mainly Murder Press
www.mainlymurderpress.com

Copyright © 2010 by Stephen Liskow
ISBN 978-0-9825899-3-9

Published in the United States of America

2010

Mainly Murder Press
PO Box 290586
Wethersfield, CT 06109-0586

**For Barbara,
who helped me actually finish it**

Thanks also to Suzanne, who gave me the idea,
and to the Guppies of Sisters in Crime,
who helped find it a home

One

No way in hell her real name is Taliesyn Holroyd.

Everything else about her strikes Greg Nines as unreal, too, from her energy level, which could eclipse a heavy metal band even if she were unplugged, to her clothes, *Sex and the City* meets *Pirates of the Caribbean*.

"I need to do this," Taliesyn-call-me-Tally says. Her stiletto boots make her Nines's six-one. He's offered her a chair twice, but she keeps pacing, her strut turning her calf-length leather skirt into a major event.

"Why?" He wonders how many baseball gloves died to make that skirt.

"*Love Insane* is a breakout," she says. Her face registers that he doesn't follow publishing. "My first three books sold enough for Isadora Press to keep me on, but this one's sold five times the others put together. *New York Times* bestseller, the whole deal. I've put together a Web site that's picked up a hundred thousand hits in four months, and my agent's convinced the publisher that it's time to tour." Her A's broaden slightly, and her R's flatten. Near Boston?

"Tour," he says. Somehow, an author touring lacks the impact of, say, The Rolling Stones at the Hartford XL Center. You don't need all the amps and a dozen roadies to set up. What does an author need? Probably a book to read from, a pen to write with, and clean underwear. "When you say tour, exactly how big a trip are you talking about?"

Outside, the wind along the Berlin Turnpike south of Hartford makes cheeks burn like broken glass. Tally's eyes get even brighter, and she finally takes the chair across from his desk.

"Locally I'm hitting R. J. Julia in Madison, Heather's Grove in New Haven, and Binding Agreements in Chester. Read a chapter, do a Q-and-A, sign copies. Borders and Barnes & Noble, too. Next month, the Southwest and a few stops on the West Coast. So far."

"You'd want me with you for all of it?" The woman's energy level could light up the whole county. A month with her would age him fifty years. "Why?"

"Security." Tally seems to hear the Hound of the Baskervilles panting over her shoulder. "Check out the places, keep autograph lines moving, make sure I'm not … bothered."

He hears the hesitation. "Do you expect you will be?"

When she crosses her legs, her thighs whisper like satin sheets. Her fingers twirl the silver ring on her left hand. If it were any bigger, she could use it as a hubcap. "I really need to do this. It's a step up."

"Uh-huh."

She stops playing with her ring and looks at him again, too-perfect champagne blonde hair floating to her shoulders and framing blue eyes that make him remember the big box of Crayolas he got for his fifth birthday. A thin silver bracelet circles her wrist, and a matching necklace glimmers gently over her breasts.

"The merchants push your books more when they've actually met you. That's really the best way to sell books, word of mouth. Besides, I'm local," she adds. "We're pushing around here, but the Web site's getting hits from all over the continent, Canada, a few from Central and South America. I didn't even realize the books were being translated until ..."

"Do you expect someone to bother you?" Nines repeats the question she hasn't answered, and she shifts in her chair to look at the sun glaring off the February snow.

"I almost got run down two days ago," she says, "in West Hartford. The guy didn't even stop."

"Did you report it to the police?" *Ultramarine*, he thinks. He's never comprehended the color before, but now her eyes make it a fact of nature.

"I didn't get the license number or anything. I thought it might be an accident until ..."

"That's a no, isn't it?" He's ready to wish her a nice day.

"Then someone tried to break into the house that same night."

"Did you report that one?"

"Yes, but the police didn't find anything." Her voice drips over him like syrup, but her eyes look like she still hears that hound howling. "Whoever it was, the alarm scared him off."

"So you don't know that the two incidents are connected."

She finds the ring again. "No, but when my agent called this morning, I mentioned it, and she told me to call somebody. You were close."

"Close. Gee, you mean none of the glowing testimonials from past clients had anything to do with it?"

Her cheeks darken. "I'm sorry, I guess I didn't notice them. Were they in the *Yellow Pages* ad?" She drips enough estrogen to stunt his beard growth.

"I can't do twenty-four-hour coverage alone," he says. "You need three or four people for that, and it's going to be pricey." He hears the mistake, and her eyes tell him that she has, too.

"How pricey?" she asks.

He doesn't want to do this. While he's standing around looking tall, he could be on line doing a background check without leaving the comfort of his office. Subway, Wendy's, and Burger King are within walking distance. He doesn't even have to cross the Turnpike. "I'm five hundred dollars a day plus expenses. For round the clock ..."

She doesn't need a calculator. "What if you do eight hours on, and I feed you?"

He can't help raising his eyebrows. "You cook, too?"

She shrugs, and the necklace shimmies on that cranberry silk blouse. "I do great eggs and coffee, and I know how to call for take-out."

"Where do you live?"

"New Britain. One of the old houses near the museum."

"How much will you travel before the tour?"

"I don't go out much. I write about eight hours a day and obsess the rest."

So if there's really someone after you, they'll know where to find you, he thinks. She seems to think of it, too.

"Then I talk with my researcher and webmaster, and we call out for Chinese or pizza or something healthy."

Her voice betrays what she thinks of healthy, but her body says she watches her diet with a microscope.

"When is your next appearance?" he asks.

"Thursday at the Borders in Farmington." She flashes a smile that feels more like a shield. "Getting my feet wet for the first time."

"Let me make a few phone calls and think about it, okay?"

She stands in a fluid motion that demands a harp glissando for accompaniment. Sure enough, she's eye to eye with him. "When will you decide?"

"I'll call you tomorrow morning." Her number's a New Britain exchange, not even a cell. He can hardly wait to go on line to look for her books—and to see if any mother in the United States has ever been cruel enough to name her daughter Taliesyn Holroyd.

Svetlana Melanova Thirst sits perfectly still except for her eyes, which slide down the page before her. Nines still expects her to tuck one leg behind her ear and groom like a cat. They've known each other since freshman comp at Central Connecticut State University, and she's never done it yet, but that's the vibe. She's folded her legs into a full lotus in the leather wing chair with Arnold, her cat, curled up at one end of the couch and Nines at the other. He eventually recognizes the flannel over her T-shirt as the one he left there when he and a couple of other guys helped her move her furniture in before her divorce.

Svet finishes *Love's A Game* in twenty minutes and picks up *Love In Vain* without missing a beat. She can read three thousand words a minute, and now she's only skimming. Nines grabbed the paperbacks at the

Newington library, along with *Love Insane*, the one Tally calls a breakout.

"You can check brat's dish if the mood should strike you." Svet's braid swings like Tally Holroyd's hips when she walked out the door.

Arnold's dish is half full. He's a picky eater. Nines brings back another slice of pizza and watches Svet pick up the hardcover. Across the room, her flat-screen monitor shows a tropical fish screensaver, and Arnold jumps up next to it, his tail across the keyboard. Svet's a computer genius who can find anything for the right price. For Nines, the price is an occasional dinner or concert ticket. She introduced him to Erin Cavendish and was her maid of honor eight years ago. It always seems longer when Nines thinks about it, but he tries not to do that too much.

"This one's definitely better." *Definitely* has a distinct T in it. Svet speaks French and English, as well as her native Russian, with only a wink of accent. She also has a master's in psychology, finishing that in the same four years as her lit major.

Nines watches the pages turning every ten seconds or so. "What do you mean?"

"The plot has more bite. Her characters have dimensions, but the men are deeper. The women all have big breasts and much feist. They say no for about two hundred pages, then come like train wrecks when the guy finally gets her pants off."

"Romance gets that sexy?"

"I read little of it. These stories feature subject and verb agreement. This new one, the hardcover, the plot is more involved, and her sex scenes are hot. She likes to talk dirty. I may actually finish this one."

"I've got the rest of the evening," he says.

"There's more Pepsi in the fridge."

Svet's been divorced for four years, but he still isn't sure which of the three G's she prefers, guys, girls, or groups. After not asking for so long, it seems awkward to bring the subject up now. He's never asked why she named the cat Arnold, either. He returns with more Pepsi and scratches Arnold's head.

"Well, I must be a better person now." Svet lays down the book. "What is she like?"

"Nothing real. Like an animé cartoon romance novelist."

"Tell me." She lifts Arnold's tail off the keyboard and goes on line.

"My height in heels. Pale blonde hair, amazing figure. A voice so sweet it would probably go right to your hips."

Svet scrolls down search results until she finds TaliesynHolroyd.com. She still takes her ex-husband out to dinner on his birthday. Her accent makes him "Zherry." All her J's have a little fuzz on them. She still uses the name Thirst because it's easier to fit on forms.

"Oh, my." On the screen, Taliesyn Holroyd's blue eyes look slightly smaller than satellite dishes. Her skin is porcelain, and her teeth are a testament to orthodontia or eugenics. She wears a filmy white blouse open to reveal the curve of her breasts and soft leather pants that make her look ten feet tall.

Svet raises her eyebrows. "She must have a stutter or lisp, yes?"

"Not that I noticed, but she's got an energy level that would make your face break out."

They scroll down the bio. Born in Japan where her father was in the Navy, then lived in Panama, Sri Lanka, Sydney, and Rome before she was ten. The family settled in New Orleans, and she went to Tulane, then got an MFA from Columbia. She has two cats and loves cooking and cross-country skiing.

"This is all bullshit," Nines says. "Her whole speech rhythm is from around Boston, and she told me she's not much of a cook."

"No other works listed here," Svet says. "If the MFA is legitimate, perhaps she writes under her real name, too. None of her books have a photograph. If she looks like this, they would, unless ..."

Svet's wearing no bra. Nines can look down the vee at her breasts, but it's like watching his sister. "She's not the writer, or not the only writer. She has the perfect look to do the tour, though. The romance readers would probably love a major babe instead of Miss Marple." In Svet's mouth, *major* becomes *measure*. "Late twenties?"

"Yeah, a few years younger than I am."

"Thank you for not saying 'than we are.' Why did you want to see me?" Svet resumes her lotus in the chair. Nines maneuvers around Arnold to claim part of the couch again.

"She wants a bodyguard for the tour, and I'm not sure I want to do it. I was hoping I, we, could find something bogus so I can say no."

"Her entire résumé is nonsense. Besides, Grusha, you can simply tell her you don't want to do it. You do not need a reason."

"I need to give her one." He sees the tropical fish screensaver pop up again and watches the orange fish drift down to disappear off the monitor.

"Hmm. Is this new?" Svet cocks an eyebrow. "Erin has been dead how long?"

"Five years this June." Jerry Thirst was a pallbearer even though he and his wife were already separated. The silence feels long enough for Svet to re-read one of the paperbacks, but she just flips it open to a page.

"She's definitely hetero," she says. "She notices men and likes them, probably has lots of hunky buds she can talk to for background."

Svet does computers because she hates the stuff in literary magazines, calling it narcissistic crap or worse. It sounds beautiful in French and even more demeaning in Russian.

"Her women, however, are all types. I suppose romance has its demands, all the genres do. But the women here are all a generic kind of pretty, and independent. They like men but aren't looking for *a man*. The guys, on the other hand, can talk about sports and cars and TV and still have brains. Some of them can even talk about feelings, and they're funny without any TV drivel."

"So you think I should take the job?"

She had helped him with his essays, and he had helped her understand guys fifteen years ago, but they've never dated. They can tell each other the truth about everything. Svet has even told him that her ex is thinking of getting married again. Jerry Thirst is dating a nurse. She turns it into a dirty limerick, but the line about coming first doesn't scan.

"Has she something beyond the beauty?"

Nines remembers the fear in those huge blue eyes and Tally's fingers twisting that ring.

"She's scared," he says, "really scared."

"Protecting a damsel in distress will pay your bills as well as a background check, Grusha, and perhaps she will put you in her next novel."

"You really think so?" Arnold melts on the couch, so relaxed his bones are jelly.

"Perhaps if you sleep with her." Svet sees the timbers crack, and lines appear around her eyes and mouth. "I'm sorry."

He finds his coat. "I'll see how it goes tomorrow, decide then."

Her eyes grow soft in a way he suspects no other man has ever seen, not even Jerry.

"How about the other thing?"

The Pepsi can on the coffee table looms big as an oil drum. "Coming up on three years."

"He said he'll let me know tomorrow."

Elizabeth Shepard hides behind the pinot noir glass on the coffee table. She wears a sweatshirt and jeans now, feeling more like herself and less like a Macy's Thanksgiving float. Her real self still feels afraid.

"What's your read on him?" Molly Pitkin chews one gold earpiece and stares at Beth as though she needs one more card to fill her flush.

"Okay, I guess," Beth says. "I only found a few investigators in the yellow pages. I thought there'd be more."

"Not in Hartford." Molly wears a crisp chocolate pants suit and little gold frames that make her look like a corporate lawyer. Beth reflects that she'd be pretty if she projected some personality, but Molly's a black hole, all her vitality turned inward and sucking the life out of the room. She designed the Taliesyn Holroyd Web site and updates it twice a week. She took the pictures of Beth that adorn it, too.

"L.A. maybe," Molly continues, "or the Big Apple, but not Hartford." Her voice is as crisp as shuffling cards. Her briefcase crouches on the coffee table, surrounded by printouts. "What was he like? Fedora, bottle of scotch in the top drawer, a gat under his trench coat?"

"Serious hunkitude." Beth falls into description mode, the stuff spewed across the pages of her first drafts before she replaces it with dialogue and restrained metaphors. "Probably a jock in school. Tall enough so I could wear heels and slow dance with him." His eyes remind her of someone. Her father?

"Do you think he'll take it?" Molly sips from her own glass without leaving any lipstick on the rim.

"He said he can't give me round-the-clock alone," Beth replies, "and it would run two thousand a day to bring in more people."

Molly shakes her head, and her spiky brown hair doesn't move. "No way Isadora will spring for that kind of money."

Beth wants to go stare at her monitor, try to put more words up there to delete before logging off. The words aren't coming now. She hasn't sent a story out since before Christmas or seen her byline since Halloween. Now it's February, winter wind slicing across Walnut Hill Park with a wind-chill in single digits.

Molly's eyes never leave Beth. "I still wonder if it wasn't just some guy late for supper, and you happened to step off the curb."

Beth's throat closes up. "I looked both ways. He came around the corner like a shot." She needs both hands to hold her glass. She's going to need a pill to sleep tonight, too, and she hates how they make her feel in the morning. When she puts the glass down, wine splashes on the copy of *Atlantic* under it. They rejected her last story.

Jim Leslie gallumphs down the stairs. He's got two speeds, manic and hyper.

"Hey, you're back. How'd it go? Hi, Molly." He's off to the kitchen to check the roast he's marinating for tomorrow, then reappears with an apple, another glass, and Beth's wine.

Beth had loved men until one raped her late in her sophomore year. Now she trusts only Jim Leslie. She met him less than five months ago before agreeing to be the public face of Taliesyn Holroyd. Jim bounces like an Irish setter. He says he's forty, but he'll look the same at seventy, maybe with less hair.

Beth repeats everything she's told Molly about Greg Nines with minor editing.

"Do you feel better after talking with him?" Jim's counting on the tour to boost sales. Personal contact sells books, but romance novelists are women, just like teachers. Jim taught history for twelve years, too.

"A little, I guess."

"If he says no, we'll try someone else." Jim's voice sounds like he's going to read her a story and tuck her in, but she still has trouble sleeping in a strange bed without a dead bolt on the door.

Molly holds up a print-out. "So far, we've got nine stops in Connecticut and eight more in the Southwest. More are still in the works. Then Frisco, L.A. and Seattle."

"Terrific."

Jim looks at the coffee table, pine with a soft varnish. The workshop in the basement helps him work out plots while he restores the house room by room. He makes ornate desks and custom CD racks while ten or twelve pages of *Love in Pain*, the fifth Taliesyn Holroyd novel, run through his printer every day. But *Love Insane* will only flourish if Beth Shepard signs his name in the books.

Beth tells him how much Nines would charge.

"Maybe we can hold a bake sale."

"A really big one," Molly agrees. Without her androgynous glasses, she's pretty. "Do you like him? I mean, as a person?"

What makes a man become a private investigator instead of a doctor or a stockbroker? Or a real police officer? Beth remembers Nines's eyes again, brown with something familiar under the frosting. Now, in Jim's warm, safe living room, she recognizes it.

"He gives off a vibe like he'd help a kid find a lost puppy. Like he doesn't like to see people hurt." Greg Nines hurts as much as she does herself.

"So maybe he'll say yes tomorrow," Molly says.

"Sure," Jim agrees. "If he were going to refuse, he would have done it today. I'll bet he's doing some background on me ... us."

"How cool is that?" Molly says. "He'll probably check out the Web site, see the pictures, read the FAQs and bio, see that you're really taking off." Her voice never changes pitch or rhythm. Beth wonders how often she changes her batteries.

"If he takes the job, we can interview him, too," Jim says. "He'd give me great background for a character."

"I've never known a Greg." Beth finishes her wine. "I've heard the name, but I've never met one."

"From the Greek," Jim says. "'Watchful.'" Both women stare. "I looked it up when you mentioned him this morning." He pours Beth more wine.

"Is he a sharp dresser," Molly asks, "as in dressed to the nines? I've never understood why it's not dressed to the tens anyway."

"I think it was something about nine as the superlative in early British contracts," Jim says.

Both women stare at him again. Beth wonders why she's surprised. Jim knows enough trivia to fill the Library of Congress.

"Watchful is nice," Beth says, "but maybe I'd feel even better if his last name was Argus."

"Hermes killed Argus, though." Jim finishes his apple and puts it on top of Molly's print-outs. "Put him to sleep and cut off his head. Remember the myth?"

Beth pours more wine. "Can we talk about something else?"

When Molly leaves, Jim pokes the embers in the fireplace until they stop glowing. "I'm going to fiddle with chapter ten some more, and maybe I'll see if Mr. Nines has a Web site." He gives Beth's shoulder a paternal squeeze. "You're going to be okay, Beth. This has all just been weird synchronicity."

"Maybe. Good night, Jim." She pecks his cheek and watches him trot down the hall.

Her room overlooks a tree-jammed backyard, but it has a massive closet. She sublet her apartment and moved in here four weeks ago to learn how Jim writes so she can handle questions on the tour. She has to study all four books, too.

She takes out her contacts and puts on the glasses she'll need to find the bed again. Maybe that was why her marriage tanked in under a year. She couldn't see what her husband was doing until she felt his hands on her, and that was like the dickhead spilling beer on her T-shirt and trying to lick it off.

She pulls a Huskies sweatshirt over her head, then returns to the room that contains nothing of herself except her laptop and a Spartan wardrobe, a few jeans and sweatshirts and the Tally costumes. She's lived here for a month, but the place still feels like a one-night stand. Pictures would help. She misses her cat, too, but Jim's allergic.

The magenta silk blouse she wore to Greg Nines's office peeps around the doorjamb. She can pull off Tally's funky look, but she feels her metabolism spike whenever she wears the stuff. She doesn't want to be Taliesyn Holroyd, bastard child of *Dynasty*. She just wants to be Beth Shepard. She misses her own bed. She'll go back after Greg Nines protects her through the tour—if she really needs protecting.

She hides her glasses in the drawer and slides under the covers. The sheets are cool, and the wind outside screams for fresh blood. She doesn't want to take a pill, especially on top of the wine. The wind keeps howling, and the room gets smaller. She stands it as long as she can, then pulls her glasses out of the drawer and boots up her laptop.

The two pages she's rewritten for the last week dance on the monitor, and she manages three more paragraphs in the next hour. She deletes them and goes on line to check her e-mail, bopeep77. Nothing but spam. She opens Tally's site and scrolls to the messages. Molly tries to delete the ones that the FAQs answer, but she's been over here today, so the usual half-dozen questions are more like twenty.

Where do you get your ideas? Is Love Insane autobiographical (Thanks, honey!)? *How do I get an agent? Is Taliesyn Holroyd your real name?*

Beth refers them all to the FAQs. A name catches her eye. Most of the readers have feminine New Age names or mythology allusions, but this one is Maddoggie4U. Mad dog? Beth opens the message and the animal in her chest starts racing even faster.

BETTER LUCK NEXT TIME BITCH.

Two

Call-me-Tally shows up at exactly 10:30 a.m. along with a smallish brunette packing a briefcase and a soulless stare who strides in like she's got a warrant. Nines knows a pain in the ass when he sees one, and he almost changes his mind about taking the case until he sees the tall blonde's eyes again.

She slides into the chair like she's been called into the principal's office for the first time, wearing a blue silk blouse the same color as her eyes. A pendant dancing in her cleavage and that huge ring are her only jewelry today, but her discomfort fills his office like fog.

"Molly Pitkin." Dawn of the Dead flicks her words at him and tries to crush his hand with her grip, which would be funny if she didn't take it so seriously. "I'm Ms. Holroyd's webmaster and general advisor, so I felt I should be here to make sure everyone knows what's what."

"I haven't said I'll take the case," he tells her. "Besides, if I do, I work for Ms. Holroyd, not for you."

"I approve any agreement we make," the brunette says. She's not used to someone telling her no. He can see it in the webbing that appears around her mouth. "I look out for Tally's interests."

"Then buy a gun, and guard her yourself." Nines sits down. "Hoffman's is just down the Turnpike. A gun is cheaper than I am, and if you pass the background check, they'll sell you a cannon. And maybe a new teething ring."

He turns back to his computer and feels Taliesyn Holroyd's eyes on him. Her companion stands in the middle of the room with her mouth open while he moves the ten of hearts onto the jack of spades and turns up the six of clubs. He starts through the deck again before the blonde speaks in that voice he could spread over pancakes.

"Mr. Nines? I'm ... Molly comes on a little strong. She's just... Well, I'm not ..."

"You're not starting off well," he tells her. "That's what you're not." He makes the mistake of looking at her face, and something ratchets in his chest. He may just have to shoot Molly Pitkin the next time she opens her mouth.

"I've got a few questions for you. If you give me the right answers, I'll work with you, but I can't do twenty-four-seven unless I have back-up."

"We can't afford that much," Molly Pitkin says. Her machismo fades, but she's far from cuddling up with him.

"Then I can handle your local appearances and check out where you live, maybe suggest ways to upgrade your security." He watches Tally process his words. "When you leave the state, you should notify the local police that you need an escort. But that's it."

"Could you guard the house?" she asks.

"What's it like?"

"One of the old houses in New Britain's West End, near Walnut Hill Park."

"Big old houses and lots of traffic," he says. "Joggers, dog walkers, kids. The hospital's just up the road, isn't it? Zillions of people around all the time."

"The houses on each side are business offices, a realtor on one side and a social worker on the other. That means less traffic after business hours."

"You don't cook." He watches Molly Pitkin slide to the other chair without calling attention to herself. "Your Web site says you love cooking. It also says you grew up all over the globe, mostly in the south, but your accent is Massachusetts."

"I put together the Web site," Molly Pitkin says. She has Massachusetts vowels, too, less obvious than Tally's. "Tally and her agent hired me last fall when the book took off. We invented a package we thought would sell."

If Taliesyn Holroyd were selling, he'd almost be tempted to bid. Thanks to his conversation with Svet, he saw Erin's face again last night. He asked her if she was happy, and if it hurt, but he couldn't make out her answer.

"What's your real name?"

"It's easier for us both if you call me Tally," she says. "That way, I stay used to answering to it."

"So it really is made up."

"Sure." She stops fiddling with that huge ring. Then her smile almost flattens him. "With a name so far over the top, I can get away with murder in my books. Right now, I'm thinking of naming a character Vanessa Libido in the next one."

It catches him off-guard, and he almost laughs.

"You said you don't go out much during the day?"

"Uh uh. I write and do research most of the time. Once in a while, someone makes a groceries run, but we do a lot of take-out."

"'Someone?'"

"Jim Leslie owns the house and lives there, too. He does most of the research."

"Are you and he …?"

"No. Jim's a nice guy and a good researcher, but there's nothing between us. It's a big old house with four bedrooms and four bathrooms and a full basement that he's restoring bit by bit. We each have our own room, and Molly crashes there once in a while."

Nines shakes his head. "I have to tell you, Ms. Holroyd …"

"Tally?" Her eyes go back to scared mode, which makes it harder.

"I don't think I'm the person you need for this. I'm not sure you really need anyone anyway." Molly Pitkin's eyes hold nothing behind them when he stands. "That driver might have just been a drunk, and you didn't report it to the police, so there's nothing anyone can do."

Erin died in a hit-and-run. He stiff-arms the memory away and plunges on. "That almost-burglary might have been a fluke. You're near the hospital, so maybe someone was looking for drugs or wanted to break into one of the offices to steal what he could find. Your alarm went off before he got in, so maybe you're safe enough already."

Tally's hands turn into pink knots, and tears roll down those porcelain cheeks. Her terror almost has a color. "He sent me an e-mail."

"What?"

"Th-through the Web site. I found it last night. Molly usually screens the stuff, but she was over yesterday, so she didn't have time, and I saw it when I went to bed. I couldn't sleep, so I started writing, but that wasn't working, so I …"

She unravels like a cheap sweater.

"Whoa. You got a threat?" He digs in his drawer for a box of tissues. Molly grabs them and passes them over, and they watch Tally pull herself back together.

"Slow down and try again, okay?" No mascara is running. She looks like an airbrushed fantasy, and she's not even wearing make-up. "Take your time."

She takes a deep breath, and her blouse probably registers on the nearest seismograph. "Someone sent it to the site, an e-mail."

"What did it say?"

"He was going to try to kill me again."

"The exact words?"

"I don't remember. I saw it, and I freaked. I started banging on Jim's door, and he came in and saw it, too."

An e-mail. It might have come from Alaska, Indonesia, or Mars, but probably not.

"Do you still have it?"

He hears Svet asking him again how long Erin's been dead. He couldn't save her.

"What if I come over and look at it and check out the house?"

"Does this mean you're taking the job?" Molly Pitkin asks. Her gold frames tame her eyes a little, but Nines still doesn't like her.

"Not necessarily," he says. They all pretend to believe him.

By the time Molly turns right on West Main, Nines knows she's still learning to navigate the area. They pass the Museum of American Art, the addition still gleaming and the landscaping buried under dirty snow, then follow the road another two hundred yards to a house with an enormous stone chimney and stone porch. The houses on each side display business signs, giving this one a quiet dignity like a once-beautiful woman who still carries herself well and chooses to ignore the liver spots.

Molly pulls into the driveway by a detached two-car garage, and Nines pulls up next to her. He could break the lock on the garage door with a good kick, and the windows are big enough to climb through. He'd have to check the place out every time someone wanted to open it. A three-year-old Toyota and a four-year-old Civic lounge inside.

Jersey barriers slow traffic to a crawl in front of the house so bikers and joggers can get a fair shake. Nines knows the park across the street gets heavy traffic in summer. The band shell faces the other way near the top of the hill, New Britain General Hospital beyond that. Constant traffic, even worse than he imagined. A platoon couldn't keep an eye on everybody. Four maple trees crowd Tally's back yard, bare in mid-February but enough to create cover for someone approaching from the rear.

He feels the women watching him circle the house. Heavy shrubs conceal basement windows on three sides, too, big enough for him to crawl through, and the wooden frames need replacing. He looks through dirty glass at a table saw and a rack full of files, awls, and a dozen tools he can't even pretend to name.

"Jim's got an alarm system," Tally says. Being outdoors dissipates some of her energy. "It's mostly for his tools."

"How extensive is it?" Nines sees a standard aluminum storm door that won't stop anyone, but the back door looks like solid wood.

"He can tell you better than I can."

Jim Leslie opens the front door for them, young eyes, slightly less hyper than Tally and about her height. He looks like he can wag his tail and chase a stick for hours.

Molly's crisp consonants perform the introduction. "Jim Leslie, Greg Nines. Mr. Nines is making up his mind whether he'll be our bodyguard. He wants to check out the house and … stuff."

"Come on in." Leslie drags Nines into a living room that looks like the stage set for *It's A Wonderful Life* with a hardwood floor, built-in bookshelves, and a magnificent stone fireplace with a mantel wide enough to accommodate a dozen Christmas stockings. A TV set awash in DVDs sits to the side, across from a worn but sturdy sofa and two welcoming chairs. A hooked rug covers most of the floor, and an old-fashioned radiator stretches across the front wall under a bay window big enough to admit Clydesdales.

That bay window opens onto the porch. A pile of fireplace logs sits right underneath it, too, in case someone needs to break the glass. Even in the cloudy day, the room hums with light and vitality. The park across the street provides no cover, but Nines worries about the porch with pillars that belong on Monticello.

Jim shows him a room opposite the fireplace with more windows on two sides. One window looks out onto the front porch, needing only a welcome mat. Nines follows him through what older architects would call a den, dark wood from a century ago, a half-bathroom abutting the kitchen.

The appliances and tile look new. The cupboards maintain the old look, but they're new, too. A windowless pantry lies beyond the sink, enough canned goods to feed a family for a month.

I could stash a gun in there, Nines tells himself. Then he notices the back door only two steps to the left and rejects the idea.

"That pantry's my next project," Leslie says, "when I figure out what I want to do with the shelves."

That pantry narrows the entryway. In a pinch, Nines could slide the kitchen table over and block it off. *But that puts the basement door behind me with those ground-level windows.*

The dining room has windows on two sides again but less light because it faces the back yard with its maple trees. Leslie points to the table with elaborately clawed feet.

"I refinished this last summer."

Molly Pitkin speaks up. "If I could handle wood the way Jim does, I'd be the most popular girl in New England."

It's the first time she's even attempted a joke, and it catches Nines by surprise. He follows the others back to the living room, central stairs to his left with a coat closet under them. *That might be a better place to hide a gun. Or the bathroom to the right?*

"Would you like coffee?" Tally asks.

Nines remembers that's one of her specialties. "That would be great. Thank you." He turns to Leslie again.

"Can you show me the basement? I didn't like the look of the windows from outside."

"They're wired." Leslie's already heading back to the kitchen. "I know, they're big and old, but you can't open them without letting the whole neighborhood know."

The water heater is new, next to a washing machine and drier. The circuit breakers live at the bottom of the stairs.

"I bought this place when I won the Lotto." Leslie runs a finger through the lint on the drier. "I had new wiring and a new furnace and hot water heater put in first thing. It's a miracle the place hadn't gone up in flames years ago."

His tools and workbench fill most of the front, every screw, nail, brad, and bit in its own little bin. What might be a piece of the banister lies next to the vise. An exercise bike sits on a rubber mat near the stairs, and an exterior door below the dining room has a shiny, double-key deadbolt.

"Who lived here before you?" Nines asks.

"Nobody. The last guy who owned it tried renting upstairs apartments and keeping the downstairs open so everyone could use the kitchen. It might have worked if there was a back staircase, too, but otherwise, it's just a pain in the ass. The only good thing about it is there are three decent bathrooms upstairs."

By the time they return to the kitchen, Tally is pouring coffee Nines can smell from the bottom of the stairs.

Leslie recites the specs for his alarm system in a monologue during which he doesn't seem to breathe, and Nines has to admit it's a good set-up. They all return to the living room and that beautiful fireplace. Ashes testify to its recent, and probably frequent, use.

"Upstairs?"

The central stairway has a tight turn at the landing, and the steps take Nines's weight with no creaking. The good thing about a central stairway is that it's easy to block off.

"The rooms up here were in decent shape but kind of boring." Leslie trots down the hall as if boring is the worst thing that can happen to anyone.

Nines can reach up and touch the second-floor ceiling. He guesses the big windows compensate for the closeness. Sure enough, light floods those two front rooms again, and the office has a door leading out to a balcony. No tree limbs hang within twenty feet of the second-story windows.

The room mixes chic history teacher and Boy Scout hobby junky. Maps, reference books, and old magazines threaten to spill from more shelves that share the space with a deflated football, a baseball glove, and a mounted fish that Nines can't identify. He sees a few model planes, too, probably as old as he is. A few old photographs of what appear to be Leslie and various other family members peep out from behind everything else.

A beautifully finished wooden desk holds a PC and a flat-screen monitor. A banker's lamp with its green shade hovers over a pile of printouts. In spite of the clutter, the room is spotlessly clean.

Leslie's bedroom has enough knickknacks to stock an antique store, too: coffee mugs, pen holders, pictures in frames, old toys. None of them look worth anything. His bathroom has a modern tub and shower, new cabinets, and for a change, a window so small only a cat could fit through it. Nines sees a connecting door on the far side.

"Does your alarm cover the windows on the second floor, too?" he asks.

"No." The guy actually slows down for two beats. "But you can't get to them except with a ladder, and somebody'd see that, wouldn't they?"

"Maybe not in back. What's back there?"

"On this side, two rooms I'm still working on. Molly stays in one of them once in a while, and you could use the other one. Tally's room's the other side of the bathroom."

Nines hears just the barest hesitation before he says "Tally" and feels her heat coming up the stairs to join them when they step into the hall.

"That's my room," she says. When Nines hesitates, she pushes the door open.

A purple comforter covers the bed, a matching mat on the floor. Primary colors wave from the closet, but nowhere near as many bright blouses and funky skirts or slacks as he expected. Two pairs of sneakers and a pair of moccasins lie on the floor along with brown boots similar to the black ones Tally's wearing right now. A few sweatshirts and jeans lie on a shelf, and a refinished dresser commands the far wall.

A geometric screensaver pulsates across the laptop monitor on the desk, and an iPod rests next to it. The walls are pale yellow, almost as light as Tally's hair. Even with her bright colors in the closet, the room feels sterile.

A hair drier and cosmetics sit on the bathroom counter, soft pink towels on the rack next to tan ones. *With three functional bathrooms up here, why do they share one, if they don't sleep together?*

Nines returns to the laptop and touches the mouse pad. A word document pops open on the screen, "BETTER LUCK NEXT TIME BITCH." He minimizes it before joining the trio in the hall.

The two rooms across the hall each have a bathroom and closet, functional furniture and a rug, but even less personality than Tally's room.

"If you take the case, you can stay here." Leslie moves on to the middle room, the one sharing a bathroom with his office. "Molly crashes here sometimes if she comes over late to talk about updating the Web site or something."

"Where do you live otherwise?" Nines asks her.

"Manchester." He waits for the click and a tape loop, but it doesn't happen.

He sticks his head through the trapdoor to the attic, an open space with a slanting roof leaving nowhere he can stand upright. Insulation foam covers most of the floor, but two floor fans and a few boxes rest near one of the ubiquitous windows.

Back in the living room, Molly sits with her ankles crossed and her hands hiding her winning cards. Leslie vibrates on the couch until Tally returns with more coffee for everyone.

"What do you think?" she asks.

Nines turns to Jim. "You said you won the lottery to buy this place?"

"Five years ago. I quit teaching at the end of the school year."

"What did you teach?"

"History. In Farmington."

Nines runs his fingers over the rough stone fireplace. "Tally, why did you move in here with Jim so suddenly?"

"Why do you think I did?"

"You share a bathroom, but you apparently have a platonic relationship. Jim had that room done, but he didn't have time to fix up one of the others for you. That means you just moved in here recently, and maybe quickly."

Tally sips her coffee and the others watch Nines'ss fingers stroke the mantel.

"We found more things we had to check on," Leslie says finally. "It was easier for her to stay here so she could tell me what she needed." His foot taps like a big dog's tail.

"All three of you are carrying cell phones," Nines points out. "You've got a router on your computer, and I wonder why Tally is only using a laptop instead of a full PC"

"Sometimes I travel," she says. "It's easier to take a laptop with me to write."

"You told me you almost never leave the house."

"I meant ..."

He interrupts before they get too sidetracked. "You only have a few clothes here, and only a half-dozen pairs of shoes and boots." He gave away at least thirty pairs of shoes, boots, sneakers, and slippers when Erin died. "You haven't even brought in any pictures to decorate the walls in that room. No gadgets, toys, animals, mugs, anything. The only personal item is your iPod."

She plays with her ring again. "I moved in here when I started getting scared."

"Last week?"

"Um, yes."

"That was the first attack, wasn't it? Saturday?"

"Yes."

"Mr. Nines," Molly Pitkin's clipped consonants fill the pause. "Will you take the case, or do we look for someone else?"

"Your upstairs is pretty secure," he says. "Your alarm system is good, but if someone comes through the windows, all it will do is tell you they're in here. It won't stop them. If you're upstairs, you can block the steps, but you'd have to move fast."

"The alarm alerts the police," Leslie says. He still looks ready for a run in the park, gray sweats and a flannel over a T-shirt.

"The Corbin Avenue substation is ten minutes from here," Nines says. "That can be a long time if someone wants to hurt you. Do you have a gun?"

"No. I hate guns."

"So do I." Nines has seen what they can do. That's why he's no longer a cop. "I don't like the location, either," he continues. "It's a great selling point, but the park, museum, and hospital are so close that lots of people have an excuse to be nearby."

Molly chews on her glasses. The silence in the room grows bigger and bigger.

"Does that mean you won't do it?" Tally's voice sounds like she's telling Santa Claus she really has been good, that someone lied about her. He feels his chest tighten again.

"I saw the message on your laptop," he says. "That driver wasn't a coincidence."

He holds up a palm before anyone can speak. "I want to talk to a friend of mine in the New Britain PD, but I'd like to have something concrete to discuss. Why would someone want you dead?"

Tally forces herself to drink from her mug. "I don't know," she says. "I don't have any enemies."

"Are you talking as yourself, or as Taliesyn Holroyd?"

All three people across from him look at their cards again.

"Um, Jim's found some stuff for the next book," she says. "We ... I'm changing it around, but it could be embarrassing if anyone recognized it, not to mention lawsuits."

"What is it?"

"Well," Jim picks up. "I did the research, so maybe I can tell it better."

A state politician allegedly had an affair with a married woman and got her pregnant. In the book, that politician is running for President, and the affair could come back to ruin his chances.

"In the book, I'm making the candidate color-blind," Tally says. "It's different enough so I don't think anyone will know what we're talking about, and I'm setting the book in Boston instead of here."

"The whole Kennedy mystique?" Nines asks.

"Uh huh. The politician is in love with a woman, and the old affair may come back to ruin their relationship. Love and power, what do you give up? That old dilemma. The illegitimate son is in college now, and he's color-blind, too."

Nines doesn't recognize the allusion.

"Neil Lexington, the state Senator who announced that he's running for Governor."

"Does he know you're using him?"

"We aren't," Jim says.

"But you got the idea from him," Nines says. "Is there any way he could know about it?"

"We've put a little teaser about the next book on the Web site," Molly says. "I don't think anyone could tell the truth from it, though, and he's never approached us."

Neil Lexington's reputation makes Bill Clinton look like a eunuch.

"We don't know if he's after me," Tally says. "Can't you just guard me through the tour?"

"What happens then?" Nines asks. "If someone's after you, he'll get you unless he's stopped. The best way to stop him is figure out who he is and get him first."

"What if it's not Neil Lexington?"

"That's what you're paying me to worry about. If it is Lexington, once the book is out, he can't hurt you. How long would that be?"

"Tally won't have it finished before fall at the earliest," Molly answers. "Isadora gets her stuff into print twelve to fifteen months after that. Maybe sooner since *Love Insane* is so big. They'll want to follow that up."

"Swell," Nines says. "Do you want to pay my rates for two years?"

He finishes his coffee and puts the mug on the magazine next to Tally's. "I won't stay here all the time," he says. "I'll come over for a day or two and get used to your routine, but I'll be out trying to find more about Lexington, too."

"Thank you." Tally's voice is even lower.

"I'd like you to tell me the truth so I know what I'm working with, okay?"

"Just what do you …?" Molly starts, but he silences her with a look.

"Did you miss something in the last half hour?" he asks.

Tally's force field diminishes slightly.

"I'll throw some things in a bag and be back in a few hours," he tells her. "In the meantime, the three of you make a list of anyone else who might want to hurt Taliesyn Holroyd. Maybe weird letters or e-mails, old boyfriends, problems on the job, whatever you can think of, no matter how silly it looks."

"What if there isn't anyone?" Jim asks.

"Then you wouldn't have called me, would you?" Nines thinks of one last question. "Tally, you had the message saved in Word upstairs. Is the e-mail still on the Web site?"

"I haven't gone to the Web site in a couple of days," Molly says. "It'll still be there."

"Then see if you can track where it came from before I get back."

The first thing Nines sees when he enters the Corbin Avenue substation is Art Tomasiewicz's round face break into the toothy grin he flashed while eating opposing quarterbacks.

"Sorry, we've already fed the animals." His handshake would turn a lesser man's hands to powder, and his corduroy jacket screams for mercy across his shoulders. "We might still have a few scraps." He and Nines roomed together at Central Connecticut State University, graduating fourth and sixth in the law-enforcement classes.

"Scraps are all I'm looking for," Nines tells him. He sees golf balls and a putter leaning against the wall in Art's office. "You know any scuttlebutt on Neil Lexington?"

"The senator?" Art's already a detective, off the street three years, fastest ever in the history of the New Britain PD

"No, the transvestite coal miner turned stripper."

Art settles into his chair, probably old during the Vietnam War. "Oh, that one. Nope. Nothing new on the Senator either. He is going great guns to add to the education budget and universal health care. Even the Ricans like him."

New Britain has the second-fastest Hispanic growth rate in Connecticut, people pouring in for the cheap housing and rare jobs, mainly midnight shifts at the convenience stores where half the patrons only speak Spanish.

"Does he still chase strange?" Greg asks.

"Are you kidding? For him, there is no strange left in the state unless you count dogs and sheep."

"Not slowing down now that he's running for Governor?"

"After Clinton, nobody gives a shit."

Nines looks at the sports clippings on Art's wall and the stack of memos covering his desk. If things had worked out differently, he might have the same thing going, nice medical and vacation pay.

"You didn't come here for a course in political science, did you, Nine-ball?"

"I've taken a case nursemaiding a writer. I'm trying to find out where the pieces are on the board, and she's leaving something out."

"A writer?" Art's face wrinkles. "That's not your usual style."

"Nobody's cheating, and nobody's hiring, but I've still got bills."

"A writer," Art says again. "Around here?"

Nines looks at the New Britain map on the wall. Even the natives have trouble finding their way around the town. After Stanley Street passes the college, it makes a Z-turn. Driving straight sends you up Martin Luther King Drive, across the Truman Overpass, and then somewhere else. If you get off at the Ellis Street exit from Route 9, Ellis becomes Monroe when you cross Arch Street. And the upper end of Arch Street, across Shuttle Meadow, which also curves, has changed its name to Kimball Drive. Houses have higher prices on Kimball, but nobody can find them. The natives still call it Upper Arch, even after going through the hassle of changing it.

"Yeah," Nines tells him, "a romance novelist. Her pen name's Taliesyn Holroyd. Just had a big seller."

"Never heard of her."

"She says some guy's trying to kill her, but I'm not sure. Did your guys get an alarm over on Ivy Street Saturday night?"

"Wait a minute." Art punches into his PC, fingers like kielbasa. "Um, an alarm went off at 12:40 Sunday morning at 241 Ivy. A black and white answered the call, but nobody got in. It looked like someone tried the back door, but the alarm scared him off."

"That sounds right. Name of the resident?"

"James Leslie. The guys who took the call said they thought he was gay. Frisky little fellow, very polite."

"That's the one." *So Tally's not making it up.* "No entry?"

"Nope."

Nines has never been in this substation before, built to placate the voters who want cops close at hand when they call. Low- to middle-income houses and a brick housing project from the 1950s sprawl up the street to the substation, then beyond until you hit gas stations, more banks, and the New Britain Diner.

"Can you get into the West Hartford board from here and see if there was a hit-and-run reported in a parking lot on Farmington Avenue the same afternoon?" he asks.

"Saturday?"

"Yeah. She says someone tried to run her down, but she was so busy ducking that she didn't get a look at the car." Nines watches Art punch his way through more screens, then shake his head. "Okay, she said she didn't report it, but last night she got a threatening e-mail on her Web site, and she's scared."

"She think it's Lexington?" Art's fingers twitch. Nines finally realizes he's practicing gripping a golf club. He'd be more natural with a sledgehammer.

"I told her to think of anyone who might have a reason to hurt her, and he's the only person she and Leslie came up with on the spur of the moment. I guess they've based a character in the next book on him."

"The guy cheat? In the book?"

"I don't know any details. I figured I'd see about the break-in first."

"Who's the writer again, Tasmanian what?"

"Taliesyn Holroyd. Don't worry, it's not her real name. She hasn't told me that yet."

"An attempted burglary does not mean anything."

Nines tells himself that if the woman's eyes didn't hurt so much, he could still walk away.

"How does she fit in with this Leslie fag?"

"He does her research. I've talked with the woman who runs the Web site, she's going to try and trace the e-mail. If it came from somewhere in Alaska, I'll tell her to suck it up and look both ways before she crosses the street."

"What does a woman—it is a woman, yes?—named Taliesyn Holroyd look like?" Art digs through his desk and finds a roll of Lifesavers.

"Unbelievably beautiful. Tall, blonde, big blue eyes, body like a sailor's wet dream."

Art's eyebrows move like a caterpillar stretching. He cuts his dirty blond hair in a buzz cut to hide his widening bald spot.

"Married?"

"Uh uh. Actually, I'm assuming. I've got to get her real info so I can look at other possibilities."

"Single," Art says, "and beautiful. She gay, too, like the research guy?"

"I don't think so."

"Um, Shasta has a friend who just got dumped a few weeks ago. Nice woman, smart. Likes basketball."

Art's caterpillars move up another notch. Nines hasn't had a half-dozen dates since Erin died, and Art or Svet set up most of them. A couple of the women called him back, but he deleted their messages.

"What does she do for a living?"

"The usual. Breathe, eat." Art shrugs, and his corduroy screams again. "She's a cop."

"You know what they say about dating a cop."

"You are not getting any younger, Nine-ball."

"Thank you, Dad."

"I'll bet your cooking is still for shit, too."

"I know how to nuke."

Three

Nines's condo in Newington would be three hundred yards from his office on the Berlin Turnpike if he could walk straight to it, but the vertical drop off the hill means he has to drive around for a half-mile. They've actually plowed the parking lot by the time he pulls into his parking space, and Svet stands by his steps while he pulls the fliers out of his mailbox.

She wears jeans that hug her curves like a lover, and he feels her eyes behind mirrored sunglasses. "You are going to protect her, aren't you? Her writer's imagination is not merely running wild."

"Someone did try to break in Saturday night," he says. He sorts through the mail while Svet loads the coffee maker. Her coffee can give him X-ray vision for two days running, but maybe that's good. "And she got a threatening e-mail last night. Her webmaster's trying to trace it."

Svet pushes her shades above her forehead, and her eyes turn serious. "Does she have any idea who might be doing it?"

"She gave me a name, but I don't think he's our boy."

"Who?"

"Neil Lexington."

"The gubernatorial aspirant?"

"She's basing a character on him for the next book. Her webmaster tells me they've put a teaser on the Web site that he might understand. I didn't notice it last night, and I can't picture a man checking out an unknown romance writer's Web site."

"Nor can I. Has she told you her real name yet?"

"Uh uh." He sticks the Visa bill in the holder by the couch and tosses everything else into the wastebasket. Coffee drips into the pot, and the smell fills the downstairs.

Svet gets two mugs from the cupboard and turns back to him. "Secrets will not help you do your job, especially if the malefactor is not after her for her persona."

"She's giving me little bits." He makes a mental list of what he'll take back to the house. "Like breadcrumbs so I can find my way back. She's scared, and I think she has reason to be."

He's only been a fool for a pretty face once in his life, and the face was the least of it. Tally's pain sings to him like the Sirens holding a case of bourbon.

"She hurts," he says. "In person, you can see it cover her like a shawl."

"Misery may love company, Grusha, but it takes years off your life."

He tosses socks, underwear, and his shaving kit into a duffel bag. A sports coat will cover his gun at book readings. He considers taking the Sig Sauer, too, but it's too bulky to wear concealed, and he never found a good place to hide a back-up weapon at Jim's. Erin's wedding portrait beams at him from the bureau.

When he returns to the living room, Svet is flipping through the swimsuit issue of *Sports Illustrated*. "I have not tried this," she comments. "Body painting. Do you think I could wear black and red to Max Downtown and get away with it? Perhaps the shoes and bag make the difference."

"You'd have to shave," he says.

"I do, darling. We have never been intimate, so you wouldn't know. I wear jewelry, too." She puts down the magazine and stretches languorously on his couch. "I am going to check Columbia's records for Taliesyn's photograph. If she won't reveal her true name, we will find it for her."

"I haven't asked you to do this, Svet." He tries to joke about it. "Besides, business is slow right now. I can't afford many dinners or concerts."

"Valentine's Day is tomorrow. Business will pick up. Cheating spouses. Besides, I want to do this. Were you joking before about her beauty, or is PhotoShop justifying its price?"

"She's breathtaking," Nines says.

Svet finishes her coffee and goes to the kitchen for a refill. "Her beauty is natural, isn't it?"

"I didn't think I should ask."

"No woman would rebuild herself so extensively and expensively unless she planned to be either a film star or a model. She works in a solitary and mostly invisible profession. An agent or publisher would not make cup size a condition of publication."

Nines forces his mind back to the job. "The house is easy to reach. Easy to get into, too. You could block off the upstairs, but you'd need a half-dozen rifles to keep someone from getting inside. Heavy traffic, a back yard with trees, big windows all over the downstairs."

"Where is it?"

"New Britain, near the museum. The guy, the researcher, bought it a few years ago and is restoring it little by little, but Tally's room looks like she just goes in there to write. No pictures on the walls or even her own coffee mug."

"'Tally?'" Svet does her motionless cat pose on the couch, waiting for prey to make the first mistake.

"It's what she likes to be called."

"You know, of course, that the original Taliesyn was a man. King Arthur's bard."

"No," he admits. "It sounds like a feminine name, though."

"It does, doesn't it?" Svet stands. "If the first attack on her was in West Hartford, how do we know that the target is Taliesyn Holroyd? Perhaps her true identity is the target."

"I know, but someone tried to break into the house when she was there."

"Perhaps she was still the target. She may have moved in with the man for more security. Is he formidable?"

"No way." Nines pours himself more coffee. "Fortyish, about her height. Cheerful, pleasant, looks like a Boy Scout leader."

"Darling, I know a Girl Scoutmaster who moonlights as a dominatrix." Svet finishes her coffee. "Bisexual, too."

Nines tells Tally three times that he's not moving in, and she won't have to cook for him, but she doesn't hear it. He finishes unpacking in two minutes, then finds her in her room, keys clicking on her laptop. He stands by the door watching.

"Oh." Those blue chips of summer sky widen when they see him. She's wearing a UConn T-shirt and has a blue-and-green-plaid flannel open over it. That and the well-worn jeans seem to lower her energy level to something more human.

"Sorry," he says. "I'll stay out of your way as much as I can, but I'm trying get a sense of your routine. Do you usually write now?"

"Uh huh. From breakfast until three or four." In civvies, she wears no watch or any other jewelry, and he sees no alarm clock in the room. She probably tells time by her computer.

"No lunch?"

"I do coffee or something when I've written four pages. Otherwise, I don't stop. It's part of my rewards system. I need at least eight pages before I can stop for the day. Then I do half an hour on the bike in the basement. At least, I tell myself I should."

He understands now how she maintains her figure. "So you finish a book in how long?"

"The first draft usually takes about three months." She runs her hand through that glorious hair. "But the outline's six or eight weeks before that. Jim and I talk about the research, figure out how the characters will work, try to put it all together. It all changes when I write, though. Some stuff doesn't work, and I need to fix it."

Nines steps into the room, and she immediately minimizes her writing to a blip at the bottom of the monitor. The sky looks like it has more snow in it, and the backyard already has a foot.

"Do you write every day?"

"Uh huh, but those eight pages? Sometimes I look at them the next day and hate every word."

"So you delete?"

"Not until the first rewrite. Everything sits here on a flash drive for a month. You have to get away from it so you can see what's really there."

"How about Jim?"

"He goes to the library sometimes, but you can find most of what you need on-line now. Except interviews. He's a fantastic interviewer. He's so enthusiastic that people open up to him like their favorite uncle."

"Phones?"

"Just the one downstairs with an answering machine. Jim and I have cells, but Molly and Trish know better than to call unless it's a real emergency."

"'Trish?'"

"Trish Pierce. She's the ... my agent. She calls to see how things are going or fill me in on figures sometimes, but Molly does most of that."

"How often does she come by?" He's still trying to figure Molly out.

"A couple of times a week, I guess."

"How often do you go shopping? Groceries, things like that?"

"Um, I've never really thought about it." Tally's eyes flick past him. "What made you decide to take this case?"

"The e-mail."

Her fingers touch where she wears that huge ring when she's dressed for show. In her casual clothes, she's even more beautiful, a Ming vase with a pulse.

"Why that especially?" He can see how hard she's trying to keep her voice steady.

"Because the car in the parking lot could have been just bad luck, and the attempted break-in that same night could have been a coincidence."

"You really believe that?"

He wants to read what she's written. No, that's not true. He wants to sit in that chair and feel the warmth from her body.

"It's possible, but the e-mail's deliberate."

"Oh, God."

"No, it's okay," he says. "If someone really wants to hurt you, he's got a reason. That means we can figure out who he is and stop him."

"Nobody would want to hurt me," she whispers. "I don't ..." She stands suddenly. "Shit. I can't do any more today."

"I'm sorry," he says. She swings by him and through the door.

"It's not your fault." He hears her feet on the stairs. When they reach bottom, he moves over to the laptop and brings up the double-spaced lines:

I can't think of anything to write. I can't think of anything to write. I can't think of anything to write. I can't think of anything to write. I can't think of anything to write.

He minimizes it again and walks down the hall to find Jim Leslie staring out the window and sucking on a peppermint stick.

"I seem to have distracted Tally for the day," Nines tells him, "so maybe we can all just put our feet up and toss ideas around."

"Sure." Jim closes his files and steps toward the door. "Um, Molly tracked that e-mail. She didn't tell Tally, but it's from a Hotmail account that was opened at the West Haven Public Library."

The New Haven suburb lies half an hour southwest of where they sit.

They find Tally hugging herself on the couch, her eyes watching the steam rising from a cup of tea until Jim puts a hand on her shoulder. "Are you all right?"

"Yes, thanks." He sits a few feet from her. Nines takes the chair facing the front door.

"Tally, tell me more about the book, the one with Lexington."

"It isn't Lexington." Leslie's voice picks up a slight pedantic edge like he's warning someone not to split an infinitive. "But the rumors about him were the germ of the idea."

"'Germ?'" Nines has heard the term, but he never believed writers really use it.

"Yes. You know, the inspiration, if you'll pardon it. You're always working with something real, but if you alter it, you can work with it better because it doesn't have the limitations of a real place or person."

Svet can probably talk shop with these two for a week. Her psychology thesis was on creativity caused by psychosis and trauma in early childhood.

Nines sees Leslie falling into lecture mode, the teacher's default. "The philandering politician is almost a cliché now, but it has a very real basis in the connection between power and sex. Look at the famous statesmen who were sexually profligate: Franklin, Jefferson, Jackson, Harding, F.D.R., certainly the Kennedys."

"Sure."

"The Greek tragedies often deal with the warrior king as a fertility symbol, and his death leads to a rebirth."

"Jim," Tally interrupts gently. She sips from her cup of tea.

"Oh, sorry." Leslie still seems to bounce in the chair. Nines reminds himself to bring the guy a ball to chase next time or handcuff him to Tally's bike for a couple of hours. "Um, I'm … we're looking at a politician who had an affair years ago, and he's color-blind. So are the children, but the mother has let them grow up believing they live with both their parents."

"'Children?'"

"Twins, a boy and a girl. The girl will get involved with the politician's son, and the boy will try to assassinate him. The mother has to tell the truth even though it will remind her husband of her affair years ago."

"How was Lexington the … germ of this idea? Just because he has a reputation for chasing women?"

"More than that," Tally speaks up. She's still playing with the ring she no longer wears. "Neil Lexington has mismatched eyes."

"Excuse me?"

"Yeah," Leslie says, "one brown and one blue. It's really rare. There's a boy at a private school now in Woodbury who has them, too. Rumors say that he's Lexington's illegitimate son."

"Does Lexington say he is?"

"No. The boy's mother doesn't either. She claims his father also had mismatched eyes and died when his son was an infant."

"That would be easy to check," Nines points out.

"I have," Leslie tells him. "There's a death certificate for a man whose name matches the name of the father on the boy's birth certificate, in New Hampshire. There's a marriage license for that man and the boy's mother, too."

"So the story is really bogus?"

"Yeah, apparently, but for some reason, it still has legs. Lexington doesn't go out of his way to deny it, either."

"Why not?"

Leslie's rearranging the magazines on the coffee table. Tally's posture is so erect Nines wonders if she's modeling for an Easter Island statue. "My guess is he knows there's proof that it's wrong, so it's not worth worrying about. Or maybe he figures that with the mismatched eyes, nobody will believe him anyway."

"That doesn't sound like he's a very likely suspect, does it?"

"Maybe not." Leslie puts the magazines down and glances at Tally, who's still twirling that phantom ring.

"He's just the start of the idea," she says again. "We've put a little teaser on the Web site about the next book, but lots of stuff may change before it goes to press."

"Next fall, you said?"

"The deadline is October, yes." Without moving off the couch, she seems to pace. Nines wonders how long she hasn't been able to write.

"How much of your plot do you work out in advance?"

"Most of it is character work," Jim answers. "Once the characters are in place, they help show where the story's going to go."

Nines remembers Svet's comment about Tally's males. "Your men seem to have lots of complexity."

"Eighty-five per cent of my readers are women," Tally says. "They want a female who's a little generic so more of them can identify with her. But I'm writing contemporary stuff, so the guy has to have some substance. A sense of humor is worth about two inches."

"I'll try to be funnier." It pops out before he knows he's going to say it.

"Do you need it?" Tally seems to catch herself, too. She sips her tea and puts it back on the same *Sports Illustrated* swimsuit issue that Svet critiqued.

"Frankly, Lexington doesn't seem like a really strong suspect," Nines tells her. "How about the family of this boy with the mismatched eyes?"

Tally sips her tea again and avoids Nines's gaze.

"The boy's at Lexington-Lancaster," Leslie says. "The parents are in Glastonbury."

"Plural?"

"The mother remarried when the boy was two. He probably doesn't even remember another father."

"Does his stepfather have money? Lex-Lan's pricey."

"Corporate law in Hartford."

Nines looks at the meticulously arranged logs in the fireplace. "Anyone else you can think of? Editors, critics, whatever?"

"Critics don't kill writers," Jim says. "It's usually the other way around."

"How about editors or agents?"

"They need us as much as we need them," Tally says. "Without writers, the agents and publishers don't have anything to sell. Then they'd have to find a real job."

"Do you really need an agent?"

"Well, Trish Pierce, my agent, rejects about ninety-eight percent of the queries she gets, and she's pretty typical. Those are all books the publishers don't have to reject, so it saves them time. I had how many rejections before Trish picked up, Jim? You'd remember."

"About a hundred and fifty. Two novels got rejected completely, and thirty-some agents passed on *Love's A Game* before Trish decided to look at it."

Nines shakes his head. "I don't think I could keep going that long." Tally shrugs, and he realizes she's managed to sidetrack him again. "Okay, so no critics or agents. What about in your own life when you're not Taliesyn Holroyd?"

"I'm always Taliesyn Holroyd, at least until the tour is over. That way, nobody's going to slip and call me by the wrong name in front of people."

Nines wants to pace. "If Taliesyn Holroyd doesn't really exist, she can't have any enemies. That means someone wants the person who's pretending to be her. Besides, you said someone tried to run you down in West Hartford. Is that where you really live?"

The woman rearranges the magazines on the table.

"What if Taliesyn Holroyd isn't really the target?" Nines continues. "What if this person who doesn't like you didn't know where you were until he saw your picture on the Web site?"

"But the bio's all nonsense," Leslie blurts. Tally glances at him, and Nines watches the duo commune telepathically. Then Tally slides her finger up the handle of her teacup.

"I'm divorced, but that was years ago."

"Is your husband still in the area? Your ex-husband?"

"Um, yes, but it was friendly, no adultery or violence or anything. We had a bad idea together. We admitted it and moved on."

"Do you get alimony?"

"I did for two years, but that was over about two and a half years ago."

"Did someone else want to marry you? A jealous boyfriend or someone?"

Tally's eyes match the UConn T-shirt, and Nines realizes he's jealous of the smiling Husky on her chest.

"No. We met in … no. There wasn't anyone else in line."

"How about since then? A more recent break-up."

"I haven't been seeing anyone."

"What about work until the books started to sell? A co-worker, a boss?"

"I did temp work until last summer when *Love Insane* took off, but I was usually only at a place for a week or two. I never dated anyone from any of those places, and nobody gave me any hassle that I can remember."

Nines knows it's time to quit. "Sleep on it, okay? And will you give me the name of your ex-husband, just for a start?"

"Do I have to?"

"No," he says, "but for the money you're paying, I'd feel better doing more than sitting around watching your DVDs while you write."

"He's right, Tally." Jim Leslie touches the woman's shoulder, and she bites her lip.

"Drew," Tally finally says. "Andrew Brennan. He's a teacher in Hamden." Nines sees Leslie's head turn. "I haven't seen him in at least three years. I don't think we've talked on the phone since he stopped paying alimony. He doesn't even know I'm the author of the books."

"So your name is Brennan?"

"It was," she says.

"Your Web site says you have an MFA from Columbia. Is that made up like your globe-trotting childhood?"

"What makes you believe that's not true?"

"Tally, you've got as much New Orleans accent as I have."

"We didn't settle there until I was ten."

"Okay," Nines says. "Now that you mention it, I hear traces of Japanese, Italian, and Indonesian. I guess I wasn't paying attention before."

The woman bites her lip the way she did in his office that first day when he knew he was going to work for her.

"No, you're right. The travel's bogus. We thought people would like it. But I do have an MFA from Columbia. It's in creative writing, and I've published about twenty stories."

"Okay, so Svet will probably find you when she's digging."

"'Svet?'"

"An old friend. She was going to check Columbia and see if she could match your picture to the Web site. We're assuming you haven't had a sex-change or anything else that'll throw her off."

Leslie reaches over and squeezes Tally's hand, like a dog licking a crying child's face. "It's all right, Honey. You've always been her. The Web site's only a few months old." When he hugs her, Nines realizes he only seems short because her beauty makes her larger than life.

"Elizabeth Shepard." Her eyes study the fireplace.

"One P or two?"

"One."

Leslie waits until she pulls her hand away, then turns to Nines. "Now it's your turn, Mr. Nines. What makes a man decide to become a private investigator?"

There's the long answer, then there's the short answer. "I used to be a police officer. When my wife died, I was pretty fucked up for a while."

Naturally, they want more.

Four

Harold and Roberta Winstead live in a beautiful colonial off the New London Turnpike in Glastonbury, and even in winter Nines can tell that their landscaping bill runs more than his mortgage. The sidewalk and driveway are impossibly clear. Someone has a good snow blower, and Nines suspects it lurks behind the doors of the two-car garage to his right. He's still discarding bad plans for how to handle the questioning when the door opens.

Roberta Winstead's brown hair resembles a helmet over a face that's memorable only for her wide mouth. Her eyes are brown, too, both of them. She demands his identification, then closes the door. When she hands it back, she doesn't invite him in.

"Ms. Winstead," he says, "I'm looking into some allegations about Neil Lexington, and I was told you might be able to help me."

"Who sent you?" The woman's eyes scale over.

"I'm looking into claims that Mr. Lexington may have …"

"Will this never stop?" The woman can't be over five-six, but she feels a foot taller when she lets loose. "Jesus, this is about Terry, isn't it? The same old bullshit. What do I have to do with you people?"

"Ms. Winstead? I want to make sure we're talking about the same issue."

"My son's father is dead. He had a stroke in 1991. If you people could read, you'd know that. I've heard this for …"

"Ms. Winstead," he tries again. "I know you have proof of what you're saying, but I'm looking into …"

"Just go away and leave us the hell alone."

"Ms. Winstead, Tally Holroyd sent me."

It stops her long enough to look at him. "Who?"

"Taliesyn Holroyd is writing a book about Neil Lexington and wanted me to verify certain, um, claims."

She steps back to let him in, and he sees her tan slacks and brown sweater. Her hands look forty, but her face and body seem ten years younger.

"I've never heard of… What is it, a campaign biography or a smear? I know the man's running for Governor, but I've …"

"Taliesyn Holroyd is a novelist using Mr. Lexington as the basis for a character in a book but wants to avoid embarrassing anyone."

He's swinging wild, but the woman's eyes say he's still in fair territory. The room's furniture matches so perfectly that he knows he's looking at the good stuff. A beautiful, glass-domed clock gleams on the mantel next to a pair of trophy cups that display old-fashioned flintlock pistols. A sixty-inch TV looks out of place in the far corner.

"I know there have been rumors about your son, and I understand they're false. I'm just wondering how they may have affected Terry's growing up."

When he mentions the boy's name, she grows taller again.

"Don't you dare bring my son into this. He's taken enough grief to last ten lifetimes already."

"I understand that, Ms. Winstead, but I'd like to talk to your son, interview him. Get his take on things."

"Never. My husband, Terry's stepfather, is a lawyer. If you or this Holroyd man even breathes in Terry's direction, we'll have you in court before ..."

"Ms. Win..."

"I mean it. Leave us alone, or your grandchildren will be paying for my grandchildren's graduate school."

Jim Leslie and Tally-Beth are upstairs writing. Nines sips coffee and watches Molly Pitkin open her laptop. Her screen has enough icons to fill a Latin American dictator's uniform, so thick he can't even distinguish the picture behind them.

"The Web site's set up so Jim, Beth—Tally—and I can get into it with passwords," she says. "That's it. I update the pictures and graphics every two weeks and the tour appearances every week. I look at the questions and send the unusual ones on to Tally so she can answer them."

"How many is that?" Nines asks. He watches Molly open the "Ask Me!" link, and dozens of e-mails pop up. The names suggest women: "Teddybear19, cowgrrrl, kellibriars, surfchik."

"We're up to about twenty-five hundred hits a day, and a lot of them seem to look at the FAQs. We haven't had any interesting new questions in a while, so Beth doesn't need much time to handle them. I've set this up so they post for a week and expire on their own. Saves me the hassle of having to go in and delete them. Otherwise, the site would get so bloated nobody could navigate it."

"How often do you check them?"

"Two or three times a week. I was running around and shopping Monday, so I didn't see the threat until Beth told me about it Tuesday. Then I went in and tracked the cookies. Whoever sent it is local. That's bad, isn't it?"

Molly's voice sounds like she's asking if he has a match. Her eyes are dark chocolate chips behind her gold frames. Her fingers are long, but her nails are short like Beth's. A small gold watch on her left wrist and a small rose stud in her left ear are her only adornments, and they seem separate from her. Beth wears no watch, either as herself or as Tally.

"Well, it means I have to be alert," Nines says. He still doesn't like the windows, but he's glad Beth spends most of her time upstairs. He's already told them to draw the drapes before turning on lights in the evening. "On the other hand, if the guy's around, he's going to leave tracks. He's already done it once."

"You say guy," Molly says, "but Tally's readers are female. The e-mail names tell us that, and the mailing list is almost exclusively women. Not many men read romance, and most of them won't admit it."

"Threatening is a more masculine pattern," Nines tells her. "If they sent it from the West Haven library, that means they were using a new account and name. They could have driven in from somewhere else to do it."

He looks at those big windows again. "Whoever he or she is knows about the Web site and probably visited it before. Is there any way you could track down the hits?"

"No. Like I said before, they expire in a week. I'd only have a way to track them if they left a message anyway. Stuff comes in faster than I could trace it, too. By the time I checked out what's here right now, I'd already be another week behind."

"Shoot," Nines says. Molly Pitkin is attractive, but she projects nothing. He might as well be sitting next to a cardboard cutout. "How did you become the webmaster?"

"I saw an ad on line," she says. "I talked to Trish Pierce, the agent, in August sometime, and she hired me."

"You're not from right around here, are you?" Greg says. "Your accent is more Massachusetts, like Tally's."

"I grew up in Springfield and moved down here last summer."

"Any particular reason?"

Molly closes down the Web site and looks at his mug. "You want more coffee?"

He follows her to the kitchen, where she finds another mug in the cupboard and fills that along with his. She sips slowly before she answers.

"A relationship went really bad." She looks out the window. "I needed some space to get things back together."

"I'm sorry."

"It isn't your fault." She disappears back into the living room. When they're both on the couch again, her shoulders rise, then sag. "Beth is really sweet, and she's as innocent as a kitten."

"Divorce tends to toughen people up," Nines says. "Bad things do."

"Look at her, Mr. Nines. I don't know anything about her divorce. She never talks about her past. We made up the stuff for the Web site, and I could tell she was just pulling it out of her ass. I don't have a clue about her family, brothers, sisters, anything. I'm guessing she went to UConn as an undergrad."

"You've noticed her sweatshirt, too, huh?" he says.

"Yeah." Molly chews on her earpiece. "A couple of times I've come over at night, and she's watching UConn women's basketball on public television."

Nines absorbs this little tidbit. Maybe Svet can find something at UConn. A professor, another student. If Beth Shepard really has an MFA, maybe there was a problem getting a recommendation, or even a plagiarism charge somewhere along the line. Anything. Molly's talking again, that same monotone that seems odd when she's talking about something that most people would find urgent.

"She doesn't have a lot of defenses, and she can't lie to save her life. She's too damned sweet. If I got a cold, she'd go on line to learn how to make chicken soup for me."

"I get that same kind of vibe," he says.

Molly slips her glasses back on. The lenses don't distort her eyes at all.

Nines looks past her shoulder toward the stairs. "There's nothing personal in her room," he says. "Does she always travel light?"

"Like I said, I only met her a few months ago when I came on board to do the Web site."

"She says she just moved in a few days ago so she and Jim could communicate on research stuff more quickly."

"But?" Molly prompts him.

"But they're working on her fifth book. They should have this down to a science by now. If Beth just moved in here recently, what changed? She said she has a place in West Hartford. What made her leave it?"

"I don't know," Molly says. "What are you thinking?"

"Did something happen that scared her?"

"Someone almost ran her down last week, remember?"

"She was already living here then, wasn't she? Or is that when she moved in? It keeps changing."

Molly puts another log in the fireplace.

I can't think of anything to write. I can't think of anything to write. This has never happened before, and I don't know why I can't just write junk to get through it like I usually do. If I just put enough stuff out here, something usually gives me an idea I can go with even if I make a few false starts. It's like the letters appear on a wall, and I can just copy them out. But now this shit has me so worked up I can't sleep, and I can't focus. The detective thought it was just some silly girl overreacting in his office, I know he did. Then I got that damn e-mail.

At least he believes me now. I wonder what else is going through his mind. He seems kind of nice, but his wife died a few years ago. He left something out. I still don't understand why a police officer quits to become a private detective unless something has really gone wrong. Well, I know about that, don't I?

Greg Nines. Nice looking, about six one, really nice eyes, dark hair. Straight, too, no question about that, girlfriend. If I were on the market for a boyfriend, he'd be the first aisle I'd walk down. But I still can't be with a man. Drew and I found that out for sure. Whenever he touched me, I thought my heart was going to ram right through my rib cage.

I couldn't even tell him why, even Mom and Dad don't know. It was my own damn fault, Little Betty Tease, going to that party dressed like that. Shit, Rick and I'd made out a couple of times, he knew I liked it. But then we started back to his place when he spilled beer all over me. Okay, I was a little buzzed, too.

I knew better, but I trusted him. When he started licking the beer off my boobs, it was funny at first, then my bra, God, I threw it away the next day, probably still smelled like Budweiser.

But when he went south and found all I had was that little pink string between my ass cheeks, I was too wasted to stop him. I tried telling him no, and I think I even cried, I don't remember anymore, it was so long ago. God it hurt it hurt it hurt it hurt. I could never tell anyone. What would Mom and Dad say? Or Mark, Tina, and Tori? I can't even think of being with a man again. I thought I could with Drew, but our honeymoon was a disaster. It's a wonder he didn't leave me in San Francisco and fly back alone. I wanted to make it work, I really did. But if a man even looks at me now, it's all I can do not to throw up.

It's Valentine's Day. Nobody's sent me flowers or even called me up in years. Drew took me to dinner when we'd only been married, what, seven, eight months? Wine, dessert, the whole deal, and I couldn't even undress in the same room with him when we got home.

We tried counseling, and I finally told Jessica — the therapist — about it, but she couldn't help. Bless Drew for taking the divorce so well. I'm just a fucking doll — make that an UNFUCKING doll with broken parts.

And now I can't even write. I've always been able to go somewhere else, invent someone who hurts more than I do, make up stories about them. Maybe I could make up a story about Greg Nines. What did he leave out? And why? Actually, that's my job. Maybe I should ask Jim to look him up. No, I don't think I want to know.

Jim's a sweetheart. Makes sure I'm OK, never demands anything. He cooks, and he does that great carpentry, I can't even imagine how you make a chair, he's fixed up most of this great old house. Neat neighborhood, too. There's a museum in walking distance, I haven't been in it, but it looks great. He told *me they just finished the addition last spring, lots more space for the stuff, and a patio out front, you can sit there in the sun and sip tea or wine. Not me, though.*

Molly's downstairs talking with Greg. She's really sharp. Takes the pix, put together a truly hot Web site, lots of graphics, pix, the whole harem. The whole Taliesyn gig sounded like a perfect deal until last week. What if Greg can't take care of me? Who'd want to do this to me?

Greg Nines. I've never known anyone named Greg, not in real life. I wonder if there's a story behind his name. I'll ask him. Maybe he'll tell me something that gives me an idea.

Does he have a girlfriend? It must really suck being stuck here for Valentine's Day instead of being with her. Maybe that Svetlana he mentioned. Svetlana. She probably has eyes like black diamonds and cheekbones that could chill a drink. Little fur cap and nothing else, lying on a bearskin rug for him when he comes to pick her up and they make love on that rug in front of a roaring fireplace until their moans drown out the flames. Then they dress and go out to a dinner and he drinks champagne out of her slipper. They go home, he pours it all over her breasts, licks it off, then she pours it all over him and licks it off him, too, and they make love again. Maybe I can write a story about a woman named Svetlana. What the hell do I know about Russia? Let Jim dig into that, too.

God, I haven't had an orgasm since That Night. I've forgotten how to please a man. I'll never get the chance again. Maybe I should try another therapist.

So why do I still like sexy underwear? So the men don't know what they're missing? Because I'm a masochist? Maybe so every day when I undress, I remember what a monster did to me. Maybe I'm really crazy.

It's Valentine's Day. God, I'm miserable. I should call someone. Maybe Mom and Dad in Arizona. But they'd ask how things were going, and Mom can smell bullshit long distance. Why upset them, too?

Beth Shepard closes the file without saving it and turns off her laptop. When she hears Molly leave, she walks downstairs.

Nines spends the next hour walking around the downstairs and basement with his eyes closed to get used to where everything is. He moves the throw rug in the living room slightly off center so the corner that sticks up is closer to the normal path from the door, then moves the chair at the end of the couch a foot to the left. If someone comes in at night, he wants to keep the lights off and have an advantage. He walks the whole place fifteen times, stopping only when he knows that he's two steps from Jim's table saw, a step from the TV set, or four steps from the fireplace without opening his eyes. His footfalls echo differently in the small parlor and den.

Now all he has to do is convince Jim and Beth to stay upstairs.

Beth. She wants him to call her Tally, but Beth fits her better, more vulnerable, her eyes full of something that makes him vibrate like a tuning fork. Taliesyn is a swashbuckler, like the image on the Web site. Tally is a tornado scattering broken-hearted men in her wake. Beth Shepard is a lovely woman carrying a burden so heavy she can barely walk.

When he emerges from the basement for the last time, she's watching the oven pre-heat. Her eyes say she hates having him here with the drapes closed, and for the first time he realizes that it's Valentine's Day. Svet's probably out with Jerry or her dominatrix scoutmaster. Or both.

"How's it coming?" he asks.

"Okay." The red light clicks on, and she strides to the bottom of the stairs. In her dark blue sweatshirt and jeans, she looks nine feet tall, and her hips turn the Levi patch into a thing of rare beauty. "Jim? The oven's ready."

"Be right down." They hear footsteps above, then Beth continues to the living room couch. Nines sits across from her while she studies the unlit fireplace.

"Jim makes a great roast," she says. "He won't tell me what he puts in the marinade, but I keep hoping I can catch him at it."

"Your Web site says you enjoy cooking, but you said you only do coffee. Where's the truth?"

She plays with that phantom ring again. "Somewhere in between."

"You're through writing for the day?" He wonders how many times she can type *I can't think of anything to write* in eight hours. She runs her fingers through her hair, pale strands picking up the amber glow from the lamp.

"I've got all Jim's research, so I have to decide how much of it to leave out. All I need is two or three really good details."

"I thought all the science or technology details helped sell the book."

"Maybe, but I hate writing description and technical stuff. It just lies there and gets boring."

Her foot twitches rhythmically, and he can't help watching. "Jim's really good at figuring out the least amount of detail you can get by with," she says. "Readers want to know about the hero's cruel eyes and the room's ambiance, and the sunset coming through the window like whatever. It bores the shit out of me. It's hard to do without stopping the whole story for the slide show. I'd rather get to the dialogue." Her eyes flicker to the dried flowers in the pewter bowl on the table. "And the sex."

Nines clears his throat. "I'm a little surprised an attractive woman like you doesn't have a date tonight."

"I was going to say the same about you," she says. Her voice is still that low purr, so rich he can almost see chocolate frosting. "I know you said you were married once."

The ceiling seems to sink lower until he has trouble breathing.

"What was her name?"

"Erin."

"It's a beautiful name."

"She was a beautiful woman."

"How did she die?" she asks. "Or is that none of my business?"

He feels his voice die, too. His chest hurts. She seems to pick up on it, and her foot jerks more quickly.

"Greg's an unusual name, too," she says. "Is it a family name, your grandfather or something?"

"My mother's maiden name was Louise Gregory. She and Dad thought it was a good way to combine their names when I was born."

"What does — did — your father do?"

"He was a cop, too." *He retired within a month of his son's leaving the force.*

Jim returns from the kitchen and joins them, so much energy that Nines can almost hear the hum. He explains the rules that he's decided they need.

"You don't answer the phone, period. You've got an answering machine, so let it screen everything."

"What about cells?" Beth asks.

"Let your voicemail pick up. That reminds me. Put my number on your phones." He watches them punch buttons, then asks for their numbers, too.

He points out the minor shifts in the furniture. Beth cocks an eyebrow.

"But won't they see them?" she asks. It's dark outside, but mild for Connecticut in February.

"Not if the lights are off," Nines says. "I don't expect anyone to try anything during the day, so I'm going to loosen all the light bulbs when you go upstairs for the night. I've practiced finding my way around here with my eyes closed."

"Like that old movie," Leslie says. "What's it called, about the blind woman in the apartment? I think it was Audrey Hepburn."

Nines tells them to stay upstairs once they've gone up, or to speak when they come downstairs so he knows who it is.

"You'd shoot that quickly?" Beth asks.

"If I think you're in danger, yes."

They move to the kitchen, and Nines watches Beth sprinkle chopped almonds onto green beans while Leslie ladles gravy over his roast. The aroma permeates the room. Leslie moves with his usual hyper energy, but Nines notices that none of his motion is wasted.

"Beth, you have the reading at Borders tomorrow night," he says. "Will you have anyone else with you besides me?"

"Molly wants to take more pictures for the Web site. If any good questions come up, we'll post them, too."

Borders in Farmington has a corner entrance, far from where authors usually read. It's a comparatively easy place to control traffic. They'll be done by eight o'clock, but Beth will autograph any books that don't sell before she leaves.

"I talked with Terry Winstead's mother this morning," Nines tells them. "She thought Taliesyn Holroyd was a man."

"You believe her?"

"Yes. I'll talk to Lexington, too, but I wanted her side first."

Leslie arranges canned potatoes around the roast and watches them soak up the gravy. He touches food the same way Nines suspects he touches his tools, like they're extensions of himself. Art said the cops thought he was gay, but Nines is less sure. The guy's mannerisms are definitely masculine, but his and Beth's eyes lack that intimate spark that even bad sex leaves behind.

"Beth, have you thought of anyone else who might want to harm you?" Nines asks.

"Tally," she corrects him. "I've got a gig tomorrow night, remember. We should stay in practice."

"Right. Tally." He shakes his head. "Where did you come up with Taliesyn?" He remembers Svet's comment.

"King Arthur's bard," Leslie says. "Sometimes he's associated with Merlin, but we figured the name could be a woman, too. Unique, lyrical, exotic."

In her sexy clothes, Beth Shepard sure as hell fits that template. She and Nines set silverware and paper napkins on the table.

"I want to talk to your ex-husband tomorrow, Tally. What does he do?"

"History teacher." Beth sips a glass of wine. "Let me know how he looks, will you? He's a nice man. He could have made things a lot uglier. I hope he's happy."

"You aren't."

They transfer the food from the oven to serving dishes and move into the dining room. Even with the oven open, it's chilly in the kitchen, and Leslie makes sure the basement door is closed tight. The roast reminds Nines of his mother's cooking. He doubts that she does much baking in Florida, even though Dad is still a meat-and-potatoes kind of guy.

After they clear the table, Beth-Tally retreats to the living room, and Leslie pours coffee.

"How long have you known Beth?" Nines asks.

Leslie dumps the coffee grounds into the trash. "Let's see, the first Taliesyn story was done about five years ago."

"Did you know each other before she started writing the novels?"

"Uh uh. We just sort of hit it off. I like working with her."

"Anything beyond the work?" The question has overtones nobody can ignore. Leslie's mouth twitches.

"She's the most beautiful woman I've ever known in my life, but she doesn't like herself very much."

"Why is that? Do you know?"

Leslie's mug thumps on the counter. "She doesn't talk about herself at all. Hell, Molly and I didn't even know she was divorced until she told you last night."

But Beth's divorce took place after they'd already been working together for two years.

"How did you two agree to work together, if you know so little about her?"

"Just a feeling, I guess. We just looked at each other and realized we were what the other one needed. It's hard to explain." He shakes his head. "Are we lovers, that's what you're asking, isn't it?"

"Yes."

"I don't think she's on the market."

Nines wonders if he should introduce Beth to Svetlana. Svet could pick up a gay vibe if it's there.

"Geez," Leslie continues, "you're around her for a while, you can feel her misery, but she seems to like hanging around here. Like she's hiding, but I don't know from what."

"Maybe from someone who's trying to kill her."

Leslie refills their mugs and rinses the empty carafe in the sink. "If someone's trying to kill her, why wait until she moved in here?" he asks.

"I don't know," Nines admits. "I hope she'll think of more names, give me more to go on. Is there anything else in the book that might upset someone?"

"Not that I can think of." The carafe clatters in the dish drainer, and Nines sees knowledge in Leslie's face.

"I looked you up, Mr. Nines. I hope you'll forgive me, but it's what I do. Everything is potential material."

He dries his hands and leads the way to the stairs. In the living room, Beth has her feet curled under her on the couch and stares at the TV with the sound off. Nines recognizes a Connecticut Public TV announcer and decides they must be doing a pitch for contributions. Beth's probably watching a basketball game in between the commercials. He makes sure the dead bolt is on the front door and the drapes are drawn.

Leslie stands on the fourth step, suddenly looking much taller. "I think I understand why you left the Hartford PD," he says.

Nines feels tightness in his chest, but he follows Leslie up the stairs and down the hall toward his office.

"Two incidents," Leslie says, "and the second one involved a shooting?"

He steps into the room and reaches for the banker's lamp on his desk. When he touches it, Nines sees the spark from six feet away.

Five

They're still working on Jim in Emergency, and Beth's stomach is doing a world-class rumba when the big man walks in like Moses probably walked through the Red Sea. He spots Greg Nines sitting next to her with the cup of water her hands can't hold steady.

"What happened?" he says to Greg. No preamble, no how are you, just the question, and she feels his voice cut through the polylingual hum around her. Greg hands her the cup, and water sloshes over her knuckles.

"Art, this is Taliesyn Holroyd, the writer I told you about yesterday." The man puts out a hand the size of a brick, and she hastily wipes her own hand on her jeans. His gentle grip surprises her, and Greg finishes the introduction. "Detective Art Tomasiewicz."

"How do you do?" she says mechanically. *When will they tell me about Jim? Oh, God, what if he's dead?*

"Probably better than you at this moment. Can you tell me what happened?"

"He tried to turn on a lamp in his office and got zapped," Greg says. "I told Tally not to touch anything electric, and we brought him over here. I don't think it was an accident."

"Where's his office?" People swirl around Art Whatever-his-name-is like a rock in the center of the river.

Even though his eyes are on Greg, she feels his attention enfolding her.

"That house over on Ivy. The same one that had the break-in last week."

"So someone tried to fry him," the big man says. Beth's breath stabs in her throat.

"Me," she hears herself say. "I got a threatening e-mail Monday night, and someone tried to run me down Saturday in West Hartford. Someone wants to kill me." Her voice spirals out of control, and Greg leads her out into the hall, Art a step behind them. Greg wraps his arms around her and holds her until she knows she won't scream. His stubble prickles her cheek.

"Where were you when this happened, Ms. Holroyd?"

"On the couch downstairs. Jim and Greg, Mr. Nines, went upstairs, and a minute later I heard Jim fall, and Greg shouted at me not to touch anything."

"Do you have any idea who would want to hurt you?"

Beth feels like she needs the right answer. "Nobody. Well, nobody I know. I'm working on a book, maybe someone's worried about that. We, I'm, using a real person as the basis for a character, but nobody ..."

"Lexington," Greg says. "I asked you about him yesterday. And the Winstead family, they're in Glastonbury. And Tally has an ex-husband, I'm going to talk to him tomorrow."

"Let's talk to him tonight. Where is he?" The man's eyes sweep across Beth, and she has to step back.

"He teaches in Hamden, but I don't know if he lives there. We haven't seen each other in years."

"We might as well start somewhere," Art says. "What is his name?"

"Drew, Andrew Brennan. He teaches at the high school."

Art tells someone to find an Andrew Brennan in or around Hamden and have the locals question him. He asks Greg about the Winsteads' address, too, and repeats his order, then closes the phone and turns back to Beth. "Why would these people harm you?"

It feels stupid when she tells him, but she can't think of anyone else. She can't believe Drew would want to hurt her either, but Greg's right. She's not dreaming it. Someone shocked Jim into unconsciousness. The detective takes a deep breath, and the room contracts.

"You said he was upstairs. Did you also lose power downstairs?"

"No," Greg tells him. He glances at Beth, and she nods automatically. The TV set and the lamp never flickered. She hasn't thought about that before. "The house was rewired with circuit breakers instead of a fuse box when the guy moved in a few years ago."

"Circuit breakers do not short out." The detective looks at Beth, and she realizes that she's biting a fingernail, which she hasn't done in years.

"Don't you have an alarm system?"

"Um, yes. I hadn't turned it on yet because I was still downstairs."

The two men look at each other. "Let me call an electrician to look at your wiring."

An orderly wheels Jim out of Emergency. Before she can think about it, Beth dashes over and throws her arms around him. The only safe man she knows, a whisker away from dying.

"Wow," Jim says. "If I'd known this would happen, I'd brush my teeth with a cattle prod."

"Oh, God, don't joke about it. You could have ..." She's fighting back tears when Greg wraps his arm around her shoulders and leads her toward the exit.

They finish Jim's paperwork, load him into the car, and drive home. A panel truck with Torelli Electric stenciled on the side sits in front of the house, and two uniformed officers stand on the porch. They guide Jim up the steps. Then they let the electrician, who's nearly as wide as he is tall and doesn't reach Beth's nose, unlock the door just in case the house has any more surprises. It doesn't. Beth sits Jim on the couch and hugs him tightly. Greg shows the others the basement. He returns before her pulse rate is back to normal.

"A basement window was open a little," he says. "Now that I think of it, there was a draft in the kitchen before dinner. Stupid, I should have checked it out."

"Would you have found anything?"

"There might have been puddles on the floor. If the guy really came in the window, there's snow on that side."

"Does the electrician know what happened?" The writer in her wants this all to make sense.

"Yes." Tomasiewicz and Johnny Torelli reappear. "Someone tampered with your circuit breakers. The whole upstairs was hot."

"The whole ...?"

Greg glances at her then back at his buddy. Beth understands that they are buddies. They've spoken a telepathic shorthand again that means they know how the other thinks. She remembers again that Greg was a cop in Hartford once.

"That means our boy knows the routine or at least has some idea of it. He knows the layout of the house and that Tally writes upstairs. He didn't know which room, so he rigged them all. Jim just happened to go up there first."

"If you hadn't ..." Beth tells herself she won't cry again. Maybe this time she'll throw up.

"How long would it take to do what he did?" Greg asks, and the little electrician shrugs.

"If he knows what he's gotta do and he's got the tools, he can do it quick."

"But he did it while you were all here," Tomasiewicz points out. "What time did you have dinner?"

"Um, Jim came downstairs to put in the roast a little after five." Beth remembers. "It was getting dark."

"So he was nearby and saw the lights go out upstairs, then moved in. By the time you ate, he was gone again." Tomasiewicz meets Greg's eyes. "There aren't any prints on the circuit breaker. You want me to have someone patrol outside?"

Greg shakes his head. "The guy's probably miles away by now. He won't try again tonight anyway."

"Makes sense. Ms. Holroyd, you listen to what Mr. Nines tells you. We'll talk to your ex-husband, and here's my card in case you think of anything else."

When the police and the electrician leave, Beth and Greg help Jim upstairs and into his room. He insists that he's fine, damn it, and closes the door behind him.

Beth turns to Greg and feels herself shake again.

"Oh, God, oh, God," she whimpers. "S-someone almost killed him."

"Shhh," Greg says. He's nuzzling the top of her head. It's new, a man holding her. It's almost nice, too. "I was going to leave tonight, but I'll stay here and keep an eye out."

She can't say anything. She'll still sleep with the door locked. If she can sleep.

"You need to rest, Beth," he says softly. "Big day tomorrow. You're going to rock their world at Borders, so you've got to be even more beautiful than usual, and bright and funny and entertaining."

"Yeah, right," she says. "What are you going to do?"

"Tomorrow morning, I'm going to look at Lexington a little more carefully, and we'll wait and see what Art finds out about your ex."

Beth Shepard takes out her contact lenses and gropes her way to bed before she remembers that it's still Valentine's Day and that Greg Nines has told her she's beautiful.

The next morning, Nines tells Leslie and Beth to set the alarm as soon as he's out the door, then walks two blocks in each direction writing down the make and license plate of every car he sees. Even as he's doing it, he realizes that there's a bank two blocks down on West Main, and two churches within fifty yards of that, not to mention two fast food places. The museum won't open for another hour, but there's already enough legitimate traffic to camouflage a marching band.

He expects to hit Svet's voicemail, but her chilled purr picks up on the second ring.

"Grusha."

"I didn't expect you to be up yet," he jokes. He's not sure she ever sleeps.

"I just arrived." He doesn't ask, and she doesn't explain. He summarizes the previous evening and tells her to dig into Lexington and Brennan as fast as she can, and look at Jim Leslie, too, just in case.

Six

Molly Pitkin ignores Borders' parking lot and pulls up in front of the door so Nines can scoot Tally inside. It's four-thirty, and a line to the cash registers stretches clear to the calendars. The manager pastes on an automatic smile that goes with her white blouse and corporate suit. Her necklace looks like she dusted it off for a New Age get-together.

"Ellie Sanderson," she introduces herself. "Ms. Holroyd, we're thrilled to have you here. Can I get you anything, coffee, tea?" *Champagne? Caviar? A massage?*

"Um, just water, please." Beth's energy is spiking, that same full-arena concert level Nines remembers from his office. She's not Beth Shepard now but Taliesyn Holroyd, glamorous darling of the romance set. Her eyes look bigger and bluer, and when Nines looks into them more carefully, he sees that the role isn't just a way to sell books. She uses the huge persona to hide her terror.

About forty people huddle expectantly in chairs near the nonfiction section, mostly women, mostly young, and mostly wearing bulky winter coats. They could be hiding guns, but nobody avoids his eyes or looks twitchy. When someone spots the tall woman with pale blonde hair and soft leather coat, all the heads turn on the same string. Her flowing stride could paralyze an avalanche, but Nines sees her hesitate for an instant.

"They love you," he murmurs, "and I'm here. You're going to kick ass."

"Oh, God, I hope so." She touches her briefcase for the fiftieth time. He knows it contains a dog-eared copy of *Love Insane* with marked passages, two roller balls for the signing, and laminated bookmarks featuring pictures of the earlier covers, the URL, and a picture of Taliesyn Holroyd with more teeth than a pack of Cub Scouts.

Molly catches up. "This is great," she whispers with more animation than usual. "You're going to lay them out like firewood."

"You really think so?" Tally chews on lips that remind Nines of red licorice whips. The fluorescent lights fight her natural skin tones, and he decides that he prefers Barnes & Noble across the street, not just because of the name, but because they use warmer, incandescent lighting.

"I know so. They've got two hundred copies of *Love Insane* and fifty each of the others. I'll bet every single one of them goes out the door tonight."

Nines helps Beth out of her coat and drapes it over a shelf displaying new romances. Ellie Sanderson materializes with a sweating pitcher of water and plastic cups, then goes to the podium. Nines pours two cups and drinks from one first, not that he's expecting arsenic in a bookstore, but they're paying him for something. The water's cold as diamonds. He hands a cup to Tally, who takes a deep breath before she sips. She wears just a hint of eyeliner and lipstick, but it's enough to make her the template for beer posters in the Connecticut Beverage Mart across the street. Her crimson blouse pulsates, and Nines forces himself not to think of her in a bikini.

Ellie Sanderson introduces Taliesyn Holroyd and steps away as applause peppers the corner of the store. More people drift over, again mostly women, a few dragging husbands or boyfriends. The men look less bored when they get a look at the Major Babe, and Nines wonders again why such a beautiful woman is alone. Writing's a hard job, but you've got to recharge the batteries. Svet thinks she likes men. Where does her fear come from? Did Drew Brennan beat her? Nines reminds himself that Drew's on tomorrow's agenda.

Tally starts speaking, her voice a fuzzy blanket that makes Nines want to curl up with his thumb in his mouth. She gains confidence with every word, looming over the lesser mortals in the chairs. The audience sinks into the kind of trance Nines hasn't seen since Bruce Springsteen played the Hartford XL Center, only quiet. No Bics flick, but Tally works the crowd like The Boss, moving from behind the podium to use the whole space in front of her crowd, her hips showcasing a gentle ripple that makes him swallow.

She gives them a two-minute summary of *Love Insane*, then reads a passage that introduces the main character, the female surgeon who must deal with her mother's Alzheimer's. It's wrenching in its spareness, no gushing description, just observations of a woman who can't decide what to wear to a P.T.A. meeting that happened twenty years before. By the time she finishes, several women surreptitiously dab at their eyes, and even some of the men are wilting.

She shifts gears before everything turns into a wake, reading the first meeting with the arrogant lawyer representing a patient who's bringing a trumped-up lawsuit against the lady doctor. Her voice grows stronger, and she looks even taller. When she finishes, seventy people applaud softly.

"Okay," she says. "You don't read these for the medical background, do you?" When she gets a laugh, she nods, and that pale blonde hair sweeps her shoulders. "You want the nitty-gritty." She sweeps the crowd with her eyes, and her voice turns to rich syrup. "Oh, come on, admit it. You want to see his birthmark and her piercings, don't you?"

She launches into the first sex scene, the one Svet described as the woman coming like a train wreck. It tells who puts what where, a half-inch beyond what even the cable networks can present. A few of the men shift carefully in their seats, and a woman in the front row leans forward. The scene is very hot, and Nines forces himself to keep watching the crowd until Tally finishes.

"Hoo, boy," she says. "Anybody else need a cigarette?"

The crowd roars with approval. Taliesyn Holroyd steps back to pour a cup of water, and a dozen hands go up for the Q & A. A man in a corduroy car coat moves around the crowd and slides his hand into his pocket. Nines feels his own muscles tense and moves to cut the guy off before he gets any closer.

"How do you get your ideas?" a girl in the front asks. She looks sixteen, probably came to this for extra credit in her English class.

"They're everywhere," Tally says. "I read the newspaper, watch CNN, listen to people talking in stores. Everyone has a story. You just have to find one that excites you. If it seems happy, you invent problems so that the happy part doesn't happen until the end."

The man pulls something out of his pocket, and Nines tenses. It's a Blackberry.

Other questions fill the air. *How long do you write? How much of this is real? How do you handle bad reviews?*

"I cry a lot," Tally says, and everyone laughs sympathetically. "Seriously, you have to tell yourself that you wrote a whole book, and maybe the person who doesn't like it hasn't done that yet. Look at what they say, too. If someone says, 'Character X wouldn't do that,' it means that they believe Character X is a real person, but you haven't given her the right motivation for the scene."

How much do you know about psychology?

"I had a couple of classes in college, but I think we all understand how people tick at a basic level. It's just a matter of chipping away until it feels like you're telling the truth."

Does anyone read your work before you send it out?

"My agent," Tally says, "and she's brutal. She has to be. If the book doesn't fly, she doesn't eat either. And I have a couple of close friends who know me well enough to understand where I'm coming from."

A middle-aged woman with short hair and enough jewelry to make you dim your headlights raises her hand. "You write such interesting men. How do you make them so real, especially their feelings about love?"

"Research," Tally says quickly. There's another laugh as people read whatever they want into it.

"Are you married?" a man asks from the back.

"Is that a proposal?" When the laughter fades, Tally bites her lip again. "I was."

"Are you seeing anyone?"

Tally smiles gently. Ellie Sanderson tells everyone there will be a short break and points out the table where Taliesyn Holroyd will be autographing books in a few minutes.

Ninety minutes later, the last woman clutches four signed books to her bosom and floats away on a cloud of sheer bliss. Tally leans back with a sigh that threatens to take all the air out of the room. Molly squeezes her shoulder.

"You were absolutely amazing." Ellie Sanderson's face beams toward the cash register. In the last two hours, over two hundred forty copies of Taliesyn Holroyd's books have moved through the scanners.

Ten minutes later, Molly pulls up in front. Nines hands Tally into the back seat and slides in next to her. She sags, and he feels his arm pull her shoulders against him. Her hair smells like honey.

"God, I was scared." Taliesyn Holroyd drains away, and Beth Shepard takes her place. Nines squeezes her tighter, and she doesn't fight it.

"Anyone hungry?" Molly demands from the front seat.

"Starved, "Beth says. "Thank you."

Fitzgerald's in West Hartford Center has leather booths and soft lighting, the crowd thin on a Thursday night. Beth melts in the corner of the booth, and Molly sits across from her. She sorts through the nearly sixty pictures she took with her digital camera and shows them the ones she likes best. Tally handing an autographed book to a woman with silver hair and an aluminum walker. Tally reading from *Love Insane,* her eyes sinking into the character. That one has a tall man with dark hair hovering behind her.

"This one will be great for the Web site," Molly says. It shows Beth's blue eyes and clean cheekbones as she hands a book to a teenaged girl who looks at her like she's a goddess.

"Where did you get that walk?" Molly asks. "My God, you could have told the men in the audience to bark like dogs, and they would have done it."

"What was I doing?" Beth asks. When Molly tells her, she blushes. "Oh. I was a majorette in high school. I guess it all comes back when you need it."

Nines congratulates himself for not asking about her pompoms.

The server asks about drinks. Beth orders pinot noir, Molly a vodka martini, and Nines a ginger ale.

"Ah," Molly says. "Still on duty."

He feels Beth's eyes on him. "The twenty-fourth's next Saturday," he says.

"Okay," Beth agrees. "So?"

"On that day, I'll be three years sober."

The guy is holding his wife and two kids in a bedroom, but the third kid made it next door, and the neighbor called the cops. Nines and his partner are the first car on the scene, and the negotiator tries to talk the guy out for three hours. It's hot out there, and the cable news trucks have the whole fucking street tied up.

The wife's called in for three domestic disturbances in the last two years. The husband has a habit of coming home shit-faced and taking it out on her. The last time, he blackened both her eyes and loosened three teeth. Naturally, they made up before he even made bail, and she dropped the complaint. Again. They won't go to counseling.

This time, the kid says, Daddy's got a gun.

Nines and Davey Charles watch the bedroom window from behind the garage, but they haven't seen anything move in half an hour. Joey Fortuna's stag finally ended at two-thirty last night, and Nines stayed around to tip the stripper and finish off the last of the beer. Now the sun is cooking his brains like spaghetti.

Six other units seed the streets. You want to hit a bank in Hartford, now's the time to do it. They've had Connecticut Light & Power cut the power to the house, so there's no air conditioning. The June sun feels like a blanket, and everybody's sweating to death in those fucking Kevlar vests. Nines is afraid his badge is going to melt.

The SWAT boys have a crosshair on every door and window. Domestics are the worst. More often than not, the wife changes her mind when all the cops gang up on her husband — like this chick's done before, thank you very much. Everyone here remembers that cop who died in Torrington last year, too. The wife grabbed him to stop him from hurting her husband, and the son of a bitch pulled a shotgun out of the closet.

If the crowd gets any bigger, they'll have to call in more traffic control, and someone's probably going to call out to the guy just to get some action. They tell Nines and Davey to get closer. The back yard has a picnic table under a tree, but it's open grass for thirty feet to the back door.

The negotiator calls the guy's cell phone again to distract him. Jaksina waves them on, and Nines tears like hell for the corner, Davey two steps behind him. They've got their weapons out, and the Glock .40 feels like a truck. They reach the house, and Nines slides down the wall to the back door. It's locked. He could kick it, but that would alert everyone inside.

Davey whistles softly and points to a basement window. When he leans against it, the whole frame swings in.

The basement smells of mildew and mouse droppings, cobwebs festooned over the beams. A washer and drier sit on the far side, but most of the place is filthy. Davey holds his torch away from his body and points it at the floor so they don't trip over something until they find the stairs leading up to a closed door. The landlord says it's a kitchen up there, then turn right to the dining room and living room. The stairs to the second floor will be on their right.

They take the stairs one at a time, Nines five steps ahead of Davey so the weight's distributed more evenly, and nothing will creak. The doorknob turns, and he opens the door a quarter of an inch. It's quiet, so he tries another quarter, then another. Then he's in the kitchen, leading with his Glock and moving to the far side so Davey can come in, too. The refrigerator whirs, and they both jump. Nines stops himself just before putting a shot into it. His head still hums from the beer. What was that stripper's name? She offered to go home with him, but he knew he couldn't do anything with her except puke.

They negotiate the dining room and see the banister beyond a recliner with a yellow and orange throw over it. The sunlight outside looks like an explosion. They can hear the crowd, but Nines doesn't look at the windows now. His eyes have adjusted to the dimness. He zigzags around the furniture step by step and prays to God none of the steps has a squeaky board. Davey's three steps behind him.

The front door has a chair jammed under the knob, and it's right in front of the steps. Nines moves it out of the way. Davey holds his own piece in both hands and points it up the stairs, which take a ninety-degree turn at the landing. Then there are six more steps to the top. The guy's in the bedroom at the end of the hall.

Nines listens for nearly three minutes, hearing nothing but his own blood pounding in his temples. Except for that damn refrigerator, they haven't heard a sound since they came in. He wipes his right palm on his thigh, then does the same with his left. He looks back, and Davey nods up the stairs.

Nines steps to the far wall, and Davey moves up. The stairwell can't be more than three feet wide. If someone gets caught there, he's fucked.

They hear a chirping upstairs. Jaksina must be calling the guy's cell again. Nines has a bad feeling about this; it's too quiet. What if the guy's killed everyone already? But they haven't heard any shots.

He moves to the first step, close to the wall where it might not creak. He gently shifts his weight, one ounce at a time, and it stays quiet. He tries the second one. The guy's cell phone is still chirping. Nines moves to the third step, then the fourth. The phone stops. Has it gone to the guy's voicemail? Nines tries the fifth step, and it feels like Davey's gun is pointing right up his ass.

Suddenly, the guy is on the landing above them, and he's got the wife. His eyes widen and his mouth opens, but Nines sees the woman has short dark hair and huge, terrified eyes. Jesus, it's Erin. Somehow, the bastard has taken his own wife hostage. The guy's gun is coming up, and Davey doesn't have a clear shot. The motherfucker is going to kill Erin.

Nines fires three rounds, and his ears ring with the explosions. The guy's chest gushes red, but he's still upright and lifting his own piece. Nines fires twice more, like a fucking bomb in the confined stairwell, but the guy still doesn't go down. Erin's screaming something, Nines's ears are gone from the shots, and he can't believe the guy is still standing there. A Glock .40 at this range should stop an SUV, and the guy's gun keeps coming up to center on Nines's chest. He fires three more rounds, Erin screaming her lungs out, and now he feels Davey charging up behind him, and he keeps shooting, all fifteen rounds, but the guy's still standing there and Erin's still screaming, and Davey grabs his arm and tries to pull him back so they almost go ass over badge down the stairs.

Davey wrestles him down, and Erin's still screaming, and before Nines's eyes, her face changes, and she's not Erin anymore, plump, her hair longer than Erin's, turning blonde before his bloodshot eyes. The front door implodes, and SWAT guys pile in and over him, and the guy's not standing anymore, he's splattered all over the wall at the top of the landing and some little kid is standing over him screaming. Slowly, Nines's ears sort out the sounds. Davey saying "Jesus, sweet Jesus," and Jaksina yelling something about "You fucking idiot," and "Get those EMTs in here now," and he still can't figure out where Erin went.

The little kid is still screaming "You killed my daddy."

Then Nines pukes all over the stairs, and you can smell beer and whiskey even through the smoke and shit.

At his hearing three months later, five officers testify that Gregory Nines consumed at least a fifth of Jack Daniel's and a dozen beers the previous evening. The thing is, that's not unusual for the last year. Then Davey has to testify that the guy's hands were empty when Patrolman Nines opened fire. When the Hartford Courant gloms that he's the same officer who beat a suspect into a coma less than a year earlier, there's no way they can keep the shit off the fan. Seventy-two hours later, he turns in his badge and weapon.

As soon as they get home, Beth scurries upstairs and peels off her Tally armor. She isn't Tally, she's Beth, and even though she used to love dressing up to pull in guys like albacore in the Gulf Stream, now she feels more real in jeans and a T-shirt. But she's more vulnerable, too, Beth Shepard without the mask.

Greg Nines's agonized monotone still chews on her heart, and she knows she won't have the second glass of wine she thought she'd have when she got home. She's already asked Jim to brew her a cup of herbal tea, and it sits steaming on a magazine when she returns to the couch.

Greg sits in the chair facing the stairs, and his eyes make her want to hold him. Molly stalks the length of the living room, finishing her play-by-play for Jim. Her camera rests on the coffee table. She's probably already shown him all the pictures of this strange woman everyone worships.

Jim smiles at her, his energy bouncing him off the couch. She squeezes his hands and sags on the couch next to him. She plops her feet on the coffee table while Molly slows down. Then Jim's back upstairs, and Molly's en route to Manchester to download the best pictures onto the Web site.

Greg turns on the alarm and replaces Jim at the other end of the couch. He doesn't look at her, but his partial revelation has made him less frightening. They should have a fire in the fireplace, but it would be forcing things. So would music, especially since Beth's looked through Jim's CDs. Most of it is '80s pop stuff: A-ha, Flock of Seagulls, Tears for Fears, Crowded House. She can put up with Dire Straits and U2, but the rest of it makes her curse the MTV that used to play music. Her iPod spills over with Billie Holiday, Ella Fitzgerald, and a host of jazz angels, music you can dance to. She used to dance, but not since her wedding.

She wonders how to reopen the conversation now that Molly's gone. She can feel Greg's pain gnawing through him.

"Were you drinking when you shot that man?" she asks. He leans forward like he's going to be sick. Before she can think about it, she moves closer to him and touches his face. "I'm sorry. That's none of my business, is it?"

His cheek feels as cold as the monkey bars at the park across the street.

Then he tells her about Erin, who kissed him good-bye the morning of her appointment with the obstetrician. She was five months pregnant with their first child when a drunk ran a red light and didn't stop. Cops who had been at their wedding fought to be pallbearers, his and Erin's parents taking turns holding each other up through the eulogy. He remembers throwing dirt on her casket and falling to his knees by the grave while his partner Davey and two other men kept him from leaping in after her. Erin, whom he was going to love forever and have babies with and watch them grow up. Maybe a son would be a cop too, like he was. And his own father.

Jim does the interviews, Beth tells herself, *but Jim's enthusiasm won't unlock Greg Nines's agony. He needs someone invisible so he can spill his pain to himself. It rips her own chest like rusty wire.*

Five days later, the lab identified paint samples so they could cross-match the partial license number to a guy with four DUI's in three years. He lived in Rocky Hill, and Greg got to him first. The man claimed he didn't remember how he got the mashed-up fender, so Greg helped him, beating him into a coma that lasted for nearly two weeks.

Internal Affairs suspended him for sixty days, and the guy's lawyer got the case thrown out of court because of police brutality. During that sixty days, Greg built up his tolerance to nearly a liter a day.

The stag was just after the anniversary of Erin's death. The next day, he was still carrying a little buzz, and he saw Erin's face on the woman. He shot the guy fifteen times in front of his kids.

"The papers remembered the guy from the year before," he says. Beth feels like she's pulling the words out of him on a tangled rope. "The one who killed my wife and baby. They started screaming for my head, so the department decided to cut their losses."

Beth knows he won't cry in front of her. Maybe she'll do it for him.

"My father left the force a month after I did," he tells her. "He had his twenty-five years in, and he and my mother decided it was easier to bag it than listen to shit about their screw-up of a son day after day."

"Are they around here?"

"Florida." He stares at the fireplace like he's watching a movie.

"I still see her face some nights." His voice feels like cardboard. "She tells me it doesn't hurt, and she misses me, and she wishes ..."

"Where is she buried?"

"Litchfield." His grip tightens on her hands. "I haven't been there since her funeral." He turns, the pain bleeding from his eyes. "I can't. If I see her grave, it means she's really dead. Then I won't see her face anymore."

Beth Shepard has pitied herself since she was raped, but this man makes her feel selfish. Now she understands why he decided to take her case. And now she feels safe.

Seven

An old brick building with white woodwork, Hamden
High School guards the exit from the Merritt Parkway onto
Route 10 just north of New Haven. The school's closed for
winter recess, but Nines finally tracks Drew Brennan there
anyway. A secretary who's delighted to have something to
do besides play computer solitaire gives him impenetrable
directions to the Audio Visual Department where Mr.
Brennan is updating the equipment. Nines thanks her and
spends the next half-hour wandering halls that lead to
dead ends, floors that go down two steps for no
discernible reason and rows of doors with no room
numbers. By the time he blunders on the door that says
"AV," he's ready to charge Beth Shepard for an entire
day's work.

"Help you?" Even sitting down, Drew Brennan looks
huge. He takes Nines's ID with a hand the size of a leg of
lamb. "Private investigator. What's up?"

"I'm just asking a few people questions," Nines tells
him. "You know—knew—an Elizabeth Shepard at one
time, is that right?"

"Beth?" Brennan's eyelids go to half-mast. "What's this
about?"

"Where were you Wednesday night?"

A dozen computers jam a windowless room smaller
than Nines's dining room, and he feels confined. Brennan
seems used to it. "My wife and I went out to dinner for
Valentine's Day."

"Where did you go?"

"You know, the cops asked me this stuff too, and they wouldn't tell me anything. What's this about?" The monitor flashes "installation complete." Brennan removes a disk from the computer and turns to the next one. He inserts the same disk and the installation wizard flashes its blue screen.

"Your ex-wife's being harassed by someone," Nines says.

"She actually thinks I'd do shit like that?" The guy's eyelids droop even lower. He resembles a crocodile waiting for prey to draw closer.

"Your name came up."

"What's happening?"

"Where did you and your wife eat?"

"Why does Beth think I'd do anything to her? Shit, I never missed a payment, and that was years ago."

Nines looks at the jewel case on the table. PowerPoint. Brennan picks up a clipboard and checks something off. "So, you going to tell me what's going on?"

Nines watches the guy's enormous hands. "Your ex-wife received a threatening e-mail a few days ago. It came from West Haven, and you're the only person she can think of who lives in the general area."

Brennan's eyes open wider. "Who the hell would want to hurt Beth?"

"Like I said, your name came up."

"Horse shit. She broke my heart, and *I* don't even hate her."

"Where did you meet her?"

"In grad school. Columbia." *Okay, so that part of Beth's story is true.* "We were in the same apartment complex and started dating."

Brennan clicks the screen, and the computer ejects the CD again. He moves on to the next one. "Well, anyway, we got married. It was a disaster right out of the starting block. We weren't together a year."

Brennan runs his hands through hair that's already thinning in front. Nines puts him at about thirty.

"When was the last time you spoke to her? Or saw her?"

"Years. When the divorce was final —"

"When was that?" Nines reads the body language. Andrew Brennan's unhappy, but his breathing rate hasn't changed, and he doesn't fidget.

"October, 2003. I paid alimony for two years."

Nines wonders where else to go with this. "Has she mentioned anyone she's dated since you two split? Anyone that gave her a bad time and might want to hurt her?"

"I don't even know if she's seen anyone since. She was really …" Brennan watches the blue dots track across the monitor. "Look, I still care about her, okay? But she had enough baggage to slow down the Amtrak."

"Family maybe?"

"They came down from Massachusetts. I don't know if they're still there, but I liked them." Brennan's hands lie on the desk. "I talked to her mother on the phone a couple of times while we were separated."

"You can't think of anyone else that might want to hurt her?" Nines is going in circles like the CD "Anyone she dumped to date you? Or later?"

"Not that I know of."

The clock in the room stares back at Nines. "How long have you been remarried?" he asks.

"About a year and a half." Brennan makes another mark on his list. "We're expecting our first child this summer. A girl."

Nines can't decide whether *congratulations* is the appropriate comment or not. "Just to humor me, can you tell me where you ate dinner Wednesday?"

He recognizes the place. Brennan says he paid with a credit card, too, easy to verify. He was thirty miles from New Britain when Jim Leslie was being electrocuted.

Everyone was getting shit-faced. The guys in the apartment complex were famous for their parties, and they had three kegs and who knows how much of other stuff, including E and weed and probably a little coke. Beth was a little high, which was unusual. Normally, she limited herself to two beers, but tonight, for some reason, she lost count. When Rick spilled a full cup all over her T-shirt, everyone laughed, even her, even though the chill made her nipples stand erect. She even laughed when Rick tried to lick the beer off her boobs. He filled another cup, and she was wasted enough so when the guys suggested the girls have a wet T-shirt contest, she egged them all to get up there with her. She won, like she knew she would.

They all wanted her to take her shirt off when she won, but she wasn't that buzzed. Then when they left, Rick walked her into the shadows away from the Quad and started kissing her. She kissed him back at first, but then he slid his hands under her shirt and pulled it up to see the soggy little spider web holding those boobs at full attention. He started kissing them, and she told him to stop, but maybe she was a little too mellow to sound like she meant it.

"A babe wears something like this over her tits, it's because she wants everyone to see what she's got," he said, "and if she wants people to see what she's got, she wants them to enjoy it, too."

She told him no again, but he pushed her down and kissed her harder. She felt his hands ripping that bra off, and suddenly she was afraid. She'd made out for the first time when she was fourteen, six years ago, with her brother Mark's buddy from the basketball team, the first boy she ever dated, and she'd slept with a few guys, but she'd always known them for a while first. She'd even given a boyfriend head in a movie once. This time was different, and she didn't remember Plan B. She'd never needed one before.

"Look at those tits." Rick's growl turned her insides to ice. He started sucking her nipples, then biting them, and it hurt. When she told him to stop or she'd scream, he clamped a hand over her mouth so hard that she tasted blood.

"Shut up, bitch. You know you really want it. What you got under your jeans?" Then he found the thong, a little pink nothing like the bra. "See?" he snarled. "You're a little fuckbunny, aren't you, little porn princess, wrapping that pussy in nothing so it's easy to get to. I'll bet that ass is fantastic, too."

He flipped her over like a coin, his fingers tearing the fabric so she felt the cold air on her ass. She was afraid she was going to wet herself. Looking back later, she realized that maybe she should have tried it.

"Please, Rick. No. Not here. Not now. I'm – "

"Shut up. You're a fucking tease, aren't you? Well, this time, a real man's going to teach you about teasing."

She tried to scream again, but he stuffed her soggy T-shirt into her mouth, almost choking her, then rammed her face into the dirt. She felt his hands spreading her behind, and then the warmth pushing at her little opening, forcing it wider, tearing her until she thought he'd split her in two. She almost choked on the T-shirt filling her mouth with beer. She closed her throat before she could vomit and drown in her own bile, but the pain seemed to go on forever, burning and ripping until she was afraid she was going to die. She clenched her fists so hard her nails cut her palms, but her terror kept her from feeling it until the next day.

She felt him withdraw, then he yanked her T-shirt from her mouth and wiped himself off. When he stood, she couldn't look at him, but she heard him zip himself up. Now that her mouth was clear, she sobbed helpless tears, huge gobs of snot pouring from her nose. Her breath felt like bloody chunks fighting their way free.

"Listen to me, you little cunt." He almost broke her neck turning her face to his. "You wanted this, you know you did. You wear that little cock-teasing underwear, you really want a man to fuck you good. So I did. You tell anyone else, they'll say the same thing."

When his footsteps faded away, she grabbed the beer-soaked rag that had been her T-shirt and vomited up all the beer and hamburger and salad until she wondered if she would ever stop. She could feel her sphincter dripping, too. She crawled to her feet and pulled her jeans up to hide her savaged rear, but she abandoned her shirt, and her bra was in tatters.

She stumbled back to her dorm, avoiding the sidewalks and hiding in shadows, waiting until the lobby was clear before she staggered through to use the stairs instead of the elevator so nobody would see her naked.

Her roommate was away for the weekend. She lay in the tub and scrubbed herself until dawn and cried until her throat was raw. She couldn't stop shivering.

Maybe Rick was right, and she really did want it. Maybe that was why she wore thongs and lace. She could never ask anyone because it was just too horrible.

The most horrible part was that she'd had an orgasm.

Eight

Svet wears a silver blouse that Nines can see through and has her hair pulled into a ponytail that suggests she just crawled out of bed after a long night with the New England Patriots. She sits cross-legged at the computer, and her brown eyes sweep Nines for clues.

"I have found very little concrete information on Neil Lexington," she says. "There is lots of gossip, but none of it goes beyond that level. No names or verifiable dates."

"Jim Leslie must have talked to someone, then," he says. "Roberta Winstead says she's never heard of Taliesyn Holroyd and doesn't look like a reader. Jim says he found paper that supports her claim that Lexington isn't the father, too. And the step-father backs it up."

"You have been busy."

"But none of it goes anywhere. It's all just eliminating people without giving me anywhere else to look."

"It's a big world, Darling. We call it progress." Svet vanishes into the kitchen and returns with a can of Pepsi.

"I talked with her ex-husband earlier." Nines sips from the can. Arnold finally looks up from the couch long enough to yawn, then turns his head upside down and falls asleep again.

"Who?" Svet's fingers poise over her keyboard.

"Tally's real name is Elizabeth Shepard, and she grew up in Dedham, Massachusetts. Her ex-husband says they haven't seen each other in years."

"What is his name?"

"Andrew Brennan. He's a high school teacher in Hamden. He and Tally, Beth, divorced in October of 2003, and he remarried about eighteen months ago."

"You said the threatening e-mail came from West Haven?"

"That's what Molly Pitkin told me, but Brennan looks like he's got an alibi for Wednesday night when Jim got zapped."

"I'll look at him anyway." She types the name into her computer, then frowns. "This electrocution that nearly killed the woman's researcher. Was he the target, or did the assassin make a mistake?"

"The whole upstairs was booby trapped." Nines reads over her shoulder. "I think the guy knows where they live and may know the routine, but he's isn't sure of the layout. He's seen lights in the upstairs rooms, so he loaded all of them."

"That may also mean he wants both people dead."

"The e-mail said *bitch*," Nines remembers. He watches Arnold turn his head right side up again. Svet moves like a cat and has the same self-absorbed quality.

"Do you think the researcher could be the real target?"

"I doubt it." Nines puts the Pepsi can on the table. "Art said the cops that called last week thought he was gay, but I don't. He's told me he likes Beth, but she's so beautiful he doesn't stand a chance."

"Why do men always think that?"

"You're the psychology major, not me."

"But I lack empathy. I love men and figures in the abstract, but I cannot stop analyzing them. Tell me, Grusha, would you ask out a woman of such beauty?"

"She's a client."

"Don't evade the question. You have been around her for a couple of days now. What is she like beyond the beautiful façade?"

"She was really upset about Jim Leslie," he says. "She feels responsible and doesn't like to see someone else hurt. It's like she's had enough pain of her own, but I don't know what it is. Was."

"Hm. She sounds like someone else I could name."

He ignores that. "The threats are getting to her. She's trying to write every day, but I got a look at her monitor the other day, and she's blocked up, writing the same sentence over and over and not going anywhere."

"That is work ethic behavior. It's commendable in her job, but what is she like as a person?"

He remembers Taliesyn Holroyd leaving the crowd for dead at Borders, then Beth Shepard in jeans on the couch.

"She hides in the Taliesyn role, so big you can't see her behind the sexy clothes and the incredible smile. She can work a crowd like you wouldn't believe, but she really seems to like people. She was great with the teenaged girls who showed up at Borders the other day, took time with them, answered their questions, wrote notes to them when she autographed their books."

"Isn't the point of the book tour to convince people you are nice so they will purchase your wares?"

"Yeah, but she really *is* nice. When she's not performing, she just hangs out in jeans and a sweatshirt, and she pays attention to everyone else. She doesn't seem to care about herself at all, and she doesn't want to talk about herself either."

"Have you learned enough for me to investigate at all?"

He ticks off what little he knows. "Oh, she did go to Columbia, that's real."

"Excellent, and with her real name, I can find her Social Security number. That means family. Do her parents survive?"

"They've retired and moved to Arizona," he says. "I don't think she mentioned her father's name."

"Shepard is not unique enough to narrow things down. I suppose I could try to cross-index Social Security numbers from Massachusetts with current ones from Arizona, but it would be cumbersome."

"I'll see what else she'll tell me."

Svet does her motionless number again.

"She sounds like a very desirable woman, Grusha."

"She's a client."

"You have never protested before, Darling. I find this auspicious."

"Jim Leslie likes her, and she obviously likes him, even if it's not romantic. Most guys don't think they're good enough for a really lovely woman unless they're hot, too."

"You are hot, Grusha."

He feels his chest turn to taffy. "The only reason I could work up the guts to ask Erin out was because you introduced us. I figured you'd already run interference for me."

"I knew you and she would connect. I did not know how quickly or deeply."

He remembers Erin telling him that after they met, she told Svet that she was going to marry him before they had even gone out on a real date.

Svet clicks her tongue and backtracks. "How did our assassin arm the house?"

"Nobody turned the alarm back on when Molly Pitkin left. Art Tomasiewicz and I think the guy got in while we were getting ready for supper. I remember feeling a little draft in the kitchen while Jim was cooking, but didn't think anything about it."

Svet still hasn't moved. "Was it an intricate process?"

"No. The electrician who fixed it said that someone who knew his stuff would only need a few minutes, but it means there's someone watching the house. I'm trying to get used to the cars in the area to see if someone doesn't belong."

"He could park somewhere else, or maybe there are even two of them."

"That's what really bothers me," he says.

"Tell me more about Mr. Leslie."

"He used to be a teacher in Farmington. He's about forty, but he comes across as younger. Bounces around like a big playful dog. He won the lottery a few years ago, so he had enough money to buy the house and retire. He does lots of woodworking and carpentry, and he's good. "

"What exactly does he do for the books?"

"Research. Beth says he does great interviews because he's so enthusiastic that people open up for him."

"Perhaps he found out something else that is damaging beyond this Lexington gossip, or he failed someone as a teacher. That happens."

"Yeah, maybe." Nines clunks the empty Pepsi can on the table.

"I will check him out, too. You don't think he has been married or been in a nasty relationship?"

"No, but that doesn't mean rule it out."

Her tongue pushes out her cheek. "You are approaching three years sober, and now you admit that you are attracted to this woman. That's healthy progress." Before he has time to worry, she continues. "I would like to meet Mr. Leslie and Taliesyn. Are you going over there soon?"

"Soon as I leave here."

"I will follow you."

The scary woman's hands flick over Jim's keys like she's enticing him to a shell game. He stands behind her left shoulder, so mesmerized that Beth can feel it across the room. They're discussing mega-search engines and primary sources and all the things she knows from her own writing, but she feels like someone's strung a rope between her and the deep end. Greg leans against the doorframe.

"Have you a sequence?" Svetlana asks. Greg introduced her as "Thirst," which doesn't sound Russian. Beth wonders if the woman shortened it, or maybe her parents, something like Thristokova. Wouldn't fit on the school forms, so they said, "Fine." She has only a slight accent, more in her clipped rhythm like scissors than pronunciation, so her slang sounds syncopated. Beth can almost chew her sexual vibe and considers looking for her on porn sites later.

"I start very general," Jim tells her, "then narrow it down as I find where I need to go." He's in his glory talking shop, so pumped that Beth can see his tail wagging. Most people couldn't care less about it, except maybe someone from the Library of Congress, but this brunette hangs on his words like he's telling her she has eyes like the ocean and skin like silk. Beth catches herself biting the inside of her cheek.

"I started looking at colorblindness, then went into the heredity factors. Twins, we have twins in the book. Then abortion and adoption practices. Then the political background, that kept me busy for a while. We needed the politics in Greenwich, political action committees, campaign fundraising practices, methods of tampering with election results."

"Devious." Svetlana Thirst gives Jim a smile that Beth pictures on a shark.

"Oh, and the backgrounds of the schools, Choate Rosemary Hall, The Gunnery, Philips Exeter Academy, places like those."

"Record-keeping, of course," Svetlana says. It feels like the bitch just told him she's going to slip into something comfortable and pour two snifters of brandy.

"Of course," Jim says, "and more lethal material: sniper rifles, how to sabotage a plane. There's tons of stuff about that and security after nine-eleven."

"I have explored much of that, too." When the woman stands up, Jim holds her chair, and she actually lets him take her hand. Beth forces her chin not to go slack.

"Anything interesting?" Greg asks. The Ice Queen glances at him and shrugs. Beth sees her breasts bob behind that translucent blouse and bites her cheek again.

"Nothing we did not already know," she says. "As your webmaster said, the threatening e-mail came from the West Haven library."

"I can't believe Drew would have sent it." Beth needs to neutralize the spell that's wrapping around Jim like a python. She's never seen him like this, and it's embarrassing. In another minute, he's going to roll over and let the woman scratch his tummy.

"Me neither," Greg agrees. *There! Someone's on her side.* "I talked to him a few hours ago, and he felt okay. Besides, he's got an alibi for Wednesday night."

"Perhaps he hired someone?" Jim is already ushering Svetlana Thirst out and offering her coffee. He watches her braid like it's a watch on a hypnotist's chain, and Beth wonders if it's a lingering effect of the electrocution. Greg offers her his arm, and they go downstairs, too.

"Where have you published under your real name?" The woman transforms the couch into a throne, and Jim sits at the other end.

"Literary magazines," Beth answers. Maybe she can distract the woman long enough for Jim to escape, but he doesn't look like he wants to escape. "Um, *Glimmer Train, Zoetrope. Missouri Review.* I had a story in *The New Yorker* last summer."

"How many stories altogether, and over what period of time?"

"Around twenty. The first one got second place in *Glimmer Train's* new writers' contest. That was in July of 2001."

"Could any of those have material that anyone would wish to avenge?"

"Not that I can think of. Why would they wait so long, if they did? My last story appeared around Halloween, and the first attack was only a week ago."

Greg lets Molly Pitkin in. Even though he doesn't leave her sight, Beth feels his absence. He introduces Molly to Svetlana Thirst, and the two shake hands like they're waiting for the referee's instructions before they dive for each other's throats.

"Svetlana Thirst," Molly says in her machine voice. "Intriguing name."

"I retained my ex-husband's name after our divorce," the Ice Queen tells her. "We parted on amicable terms. My maiden name is Melanova and too many people mispronounce it. Freudian, perhaps, but only my birth sign is Cancer."

Her eyes flicker to Beth. "You say your divorce was also friendly?"

"It doesn't make it any easier."

"No," the brunette agrees. "It is painful, perhaps more so when you feel it is your fault, and I certainly contributed to the situation."

"That's hard to believe," Jim says. She lobs him a smile, and he grows taller before Beth's eyes.

"No, I am an impossible companion for more than a few hours at a time. I am selfish, and sometimes I forget that humor can be a weapon." It feels like she's reading the warning label on a pack of cigarettes.

Molly tells them that both Binding Agreements and R. Julia have Taliesyn's readings on their Web sites, and she's sent them pictures from the Borders gig. She and Svetlana Thirst discuss DreamWeaver and alternative web design programs the way Beth's brother talked about basketball.

Cancer Woman finally stands and stretches like a panther. "I must leave. James, thank you for explaining your work to me. I can see that Elizabeth has a priceless resource." She doesn't quite bat her eyes at him.

Jim rushes over to help her with her coat, which has enough buckles and straps to supply a group S & M session. Greg keeps Jim out of the doorway, so he escorts the woman through the kitchen and doesn't return until her car has pulled away. He opens his mouth to say something but sees Beth's face and gallops upstairs instead.

When Molly leaves, too, Beth pours herself a cup of tea and moves to the couch, still warm from Cancer Woman's ass. Greg moves to the other end, where Jim paid court.

"How long have you known ... her?" Beth reins back the bitch in her voice.

"We met in college," Greg says. He's wearing jeans and a corduroy jacket over a white shirt.

"Date?"

"Uh uh. But she introduced me to—"

"Erin," Beth finishes. "How long were you two married, if you don't mind my asking."

"Not quite four years." He moves to the fireplace and lights it. Beth feels pain squeeze him like an orange.

"That's a long time until it's over," she says. "Now, it probably feels like nothing."

"Uh huh."

"You were on duty when she died, weren't you?" *God,* she wonders. *What would it be like to hear that accident report come over the radio in your squad car? Your own wife and baby.*

He nods, and she wants to pull him into her chest and stroke his hair.

"Greg, I can't even pretend I know how you felt, but you couldn't protect her."

"I didn't." He returns to the couch on knees that don't bend.

"No," she says. "You *couldn't.* It's different. No matter how much you love someone, you can't protect her from everything. All the old religions have myths about loss. Even the Old Testament. You can't stop people from getting older. Or dying."

"I didn't protect her." His voice burns her ears.

"No," she says again. "You couldn't do anything, Greg. Even if you'd been there with her, you couldn't have stopped it. What would you have done, thrown yourself in front of the other car? Then you'd be dead, too, or instead. Would you rather she lived without you? Would she have wanted that?"

His eyes fight, but he's listening. *This is what I do best,* she tells herself, *invent lies to make other people feel better. Why can't I do it for myself?*

"Erin," she says again. "What did she look like? You didn't mention that when you told me about … the rest."

He spills it out so fast she wonders if he uses it as a prayer at night. "Small, about five-three. Dark hair, almost black, she kept it cut short. Big, brown spaniel eyes. A smile that could …"

Nothing like me, Beth realizes. "She had a beautiful name. Do you know what it means?"

"'From Ireland,'" he says.

"That's one meaning," Beth says. She looked it up that afternoon. "But in Gaelic, it means peace, too. I'll bet she'd want you to have that."

He looks at the coffee table. "When I can't sleep, sometimes I still see her face. She smiles at me and tells me things will be okay." She wants to cry for him. "But I can't see her so clearly anymore. She doesn't come as often."

Maybe that's her way of telling you to move on with your life, Greg. She catches herself before she says it out loud.

"Maybe that's why I write, so I can control things in my little imaginary worlds, make them work out."

She realizes she's going to tell him, the words pounding in her chest, fighting to get out. She's never told anyone real. "I could have controlled things in my own life better, but I didn't. I fucked up, and what happened was my own fault."

His eyes move out of himself and toward her. "What happened?"

"I was raped when I was in college." Saying the words brings all the terror rushing back. Her breath freezes in her chest, Rick's hands on her throat again, on her breasts. Ripping off her thong and spreading her. An icy fist grabs her stomach. She fights everything back down and tries to breathe. *This is why he's never gone to visit her grave*, she thinks.

"Did they catch the guy?"

"I never told anyone. I always felt like it was my fault."

"Bullshit, Beth. Did you tell him no?"

"Uh huh. I think so. Yes."

She feels her voice flatten like Molly's, and the room disappears into a fog while she tells about being drunk and wearing sexy little underwear that meant she really wanted it. The flames in the fireplace embrace another log.

"You see what I mean?" Her voice wobbles like Jell-O. "I did. I asked for it."

She feels his rage. "Do you know where the guy is now?"

"No." She feels the terror slowing down in her chest now that she's let it out. Greg Nines slowly reaches over and touches her cheek.

"It wasn't your fault."

"It was," she sniffles. "I set myself up."

"No, you were with people you trusted."

He's going to put his arms around me, she realizes, *and I'm not afraid. It's because he hurts, too. He's been hurt even worse than I have. I wish I could help him, too.*

"God, Beth. I'm so, so sorry."

He pulls her into his chest, and she feels the tears surging to the surface.

Nine

Outsiders and residents under the age of fifty refer to Simsbury, Connecticut, as Sims-boring. Neal Lexington grew up in the sedate—read wealthy—bedroom community northwest of Hartford wearing blazers and school ties before serving four terms in the State Legislature, voting against the income tax, inheritance tax, and busing in students from the underprivileged—read black—sections of Hartford.

His campaign office overlooks the town's main intersection, where Nines sees two desks with phones and computer workstations. Cheap wallboard conceals a back room that he suspects houses several more of each.

It's Saturday. Two earnest kids who must be majoring in political science answer the phones. The girl with the blue turtleneck gives him a we-have-to-save-the-world-right-now smile. She's sorry, but Mr. Lexington is in an important meeting, and she doesn't know when he'll be back. He settles for Mr. Fletcher, Lexington's campaign manager.

Nines's first read on Fletcher is a used car salesman in a better suit, and he exudes a caffeine rush that makes Nines look for the espresso drip. Fletcher's rolled sleeves show arms covered with thick black hair, and his tasteful red tie still holds a perfect knot.

"Welcome to Ground Zero." His handshake belongs in Washington, too. "You want some coffee?"

"No, thanks." The forty-cup urn barely dribbles liquid into Fletcher's mug, and nobody else is in sight.

"Mr. Lexington has a blue eye and a brown eye, doesn't he?"

"Sure," Fletcher said. "It's great for the campaign pictures. Nobody forgets who he is."

"His children would inherit that trait, too, wouldn't they? If he had children and wanted to acknowledge them."

"What are you getting at?" Fletcher eyes turn cold.

"Of course, if the mother wasn't his wife, it might be awkward explaining how two parents with no history of the trait could produce such a child, wouldn't it?"

Fletcher loses none of his energy, but his warmth fades by the second. "Paternity's where you're going with this, isn't it? Stories, stories, stories. Bullshit, bullshit, bullshit."

"How about the boy people claim Lexington fathered," Nines says, "the one who also has mismatched eyes?"

Fletcher seems to force his pulse rate down by sheer will power. He finishes his coffee in two swallows, and Nines waits for steam to come out his ears. "Hell, Kennedy fucked around, all of them did, and people said oh, my, my, but deep down, they thought it was great. Clinton, too. That whole cigar and blue dress with the come-stain hoohah didn't hurt him at all. Lots of people thought he was too much of an intellectual, but dipping his wick in strange made him human. Shit, a broad shoves it in your face, only an asshole won't go for it."

Nines doesn't like Buzz Fletcher but understands how he got the nickname.

Neal Lexington appears through the door in a cloud of testosterone, his bronzed god appearance suggesting that his important meeting took place in a tanning booth. He matches Nines's height, but he's twenty pounds heavier, just at that age, fortyish, when weight becomes harder to shed.

"I know a lot of people claim that I'm indiscreet, but it's all cr ... nonsense." His voice was made for sound bytes. "I admire women, but I'm happily married and have a handsome son and beautiful daughter."

"Do they have your mismatched eyes?"

Lexington gathers the mass of a small landslide without moving. Nines can actually feel the force.

"Chris does."

"I'm sure you've heard the story a thousand times and answered it all of them, but I'm trying to track down the original source. Do you remember when it started?"

Neal Lexington has enough political savvy to lie, shake hands, juggle statistics, and kiss babies all at once, but he looks like he's telling the truth.

"Mr. Nines, I'm a homebody, pure and simple. Have been ever since I met Julianne, and that was eleven years ago."

"Besides," Fletcher interjects. "Neal's the real goods. Even if he were still finding a little on the side, people around here wouldn't mind. Shit, he could even do a black girl, and nobody'd get too upset."

"That's enough, Buzz," Lexington says quickly.

Nines turns to Fletcher and lets the Bad Cop deadness come into his eyes.

"Thank you for not referring to that black woman in question as a nigger."

Fletcher opens his mouth, but Lexington speaks first. "Buzz, why don't you go find someone to make more coffee?" When Fletcher is gone, Lexington's smile slowly relaxes. "The guy's a good strategist, and he can crunch numbers with the best of them, but his attitudes are a little …"

"Neanderthal?" Nines suggests. "I'm surprised you let him out there with that college woman."

"He's not *that* Neanderthal. I'm really sorry about his outburst. He's been working long days trying to get our team and plans together."

"Uh huh. I'm sure the three gallons of coffee a day help, too."

Lexington sits on the edge of the desk. "You don't strike me as a lawyer. Your clothes are too casual, and you don't have that twitch most of the ambulance chasers have."

"Is Fletcher married?" Nines asks.

"Divorced. No more bitter than any other man with his mindset would be."

"Is he from around here?"

Lexington's lips form another smile, but it never reaches his eyes. "Let me try again. You're not a lawyer. So what are you?"

Nines shows his license. "I'm working with a client whose life has been threatened. Where were you Wednesday evening?"

"Um, Valentine's Day, right? Let's see, my wife and I had dinner reservations at eight, right here in town." Lexington plays with the mouse on the PC, and the screensaver blips off. "I'm sure you won't tell me your client's name."

"No," Nines says.

"Political? Male? Female?"

"No, no comment, and no comment."

Lexington repeats that mouth-only smile. "Not bad. I admire people who realize that knowledge is power only as long as no one else has it. You could go far in politics, Mr. Nines."

Nines would rather chew on jumper cables.

Snowflakes the size of butterflies hover in the air when he leaves the building. He dials Beth's cell, and she picks up on the third ring. The warmth in her voice surprises him but not as much as the warmth he feels in his own chest.

"Hello, Greg."

"Tally. Beth. I've just met Lexington and his campaign manager. We can talk about it when I come over."

"It's Saturday night." He understands the loneliness in her voice. "I figured you'd have plans."

"You had a break-in last Saturday." He doesn't expect it to happen again, but why tempt fate.

"Um, we're ordering Chinese in a few minutes. You want to join in?"

"You and Jim?"

"Molly's here, too, and Trish Pierce, my agent. She'd like to meet you to talk about how things are going, too."

"Figure forty-five minutes, maybe an hour if I hit all the red lights."

"Okay." Her voice gets lighter. "What do you like?"

"Nothing fancy. General T'sao's chicken and an egg roll is fine."

"Brown or white rice?"

"White. Steamed?"

"You got it, and Jim's brewing some of his secret herbal blend, too."

Beth wonders if Jim feels like the other half of Siamese twins. He sits at the far end of the dining room table listening to Molly and Trish rattle off sales figures and Web site hits and new tour dates. *Love Insane* is going through Borders and Barnes & Noble like coffee through her dad's kidneys. Amazon.com has sold eight hundred copies in the first two weeks of this month. Isadora Press is fielding offers to sell Taliesyn Holroyd to a bigger publisher who can keep up with the printing demand, and Trish is trying to get Isadora to record an audio book. She's pushing for Jennifer Jason Leigh to read it.

Jim's eyes dig through the cloud of words to meet Beth's. She knows how he feels from the other side. She's the blonde on the Web site, the woman in silk and leather at the readings who signs books and smiles when people say Taliesyn Holroyd is their favorite author. Isadora Press pays her two thousand dollars a month and the rent on her West Hartford apartment to embody the beautiful romance writer, but she hasn't been able to get ten good pages on paper since moving in.

Jim, on the other hand, pumps out twenty-five hundred words a day on the first draft of *Love in Pain,* but nobody will ever know that the cheerful guy in the flannel shirt is Taliesyn Holroyd.

"You should have seen her at Borders two nights ago," Molly tells Trish. "She left them for dead. Handled the questions like a pro, even gave them some humor, and made everyone from the manager to the cashiers to the readers fall in love with her. Sold about two hundred fifty copies, too."

"It went that well, then." Trish Pierce has a Noo Yawk whine, spiked reddish highlights, and ten extra pounds. She's forty trying to look thirty and almost pulling it off. She has four other best-selling romance writers in her stable, plus two mystery writers who have been nominated for awards in the last three years. "Beth, that your take on it too?"

"Well, I had a good time, and I think the people did, too. Jim picked a good mix for me to read." *It must really suck to have someone else claim she wrote your words,* she thinks. *Almost as much as knowing you're blocked for the first time in your life.* "I wish he could take the credit for it."

"I'm getting the money, Beth. You deserve more than we're giving you." Jim looks at her the way Tommy Fields did when he saw her in her prom gown. It was still fun to tease the boys back then. She and Tommy went beyond teasing.

"Any more trouble?" Trish asks. "I was hoping this high-powered bodyguard you've picked would be here so I could talk to him." She says *tawk.*

"He'll be back later," Beth says. Saturday night, and Greg Nines doesn't have a date either. Maybe he'll watch the UConn women play Pitt with her. "He's checking out the people I could think of who might want to hurt me."

"Can't be a very long list," Molly says. Her gold frames reflect the lamp in the corner. With the drapes drawn per Greg's orders, the fireplace makes the room feel like a make-out chamber.

Trish opens her mouth but closes it again, and Beth can feel the question, which she's fielded a million times before, often from guys who turn her stomach into a corkscrew. *How come a beautiful woman like you is alone?*

"I'll stick around for a while, if you think he's going to show up."

Molly looks at Beth again. "If Mr. Nines will come along, we should probably check out Binding Agreements tomorrow or Monday, get a feel for it before your reading Wednesday."

"Let's do it tomorrow," Beth says. Maybe getting out of the house again will loosen up the words. She's never been seriously blocked before, and it upsets her. Besides, she's discovered that she enjoys being onstage again, especially since she doesn't have to worry about dropping that baton.

Jim brings a menu back from the kitchen, and they discuss the merits of Chinese *versus* pizza. Beth's cell rings, and she checks the ID Greg Nines.

"Are you hungry?" she asks. "We're thinking of calling out to Jade Palace."

Greg arrives ten minutes after Molly leaves to pick the stuff up. Beth introduces Trish as "our agent" to lessen the sting for Jim. Trish looks Greg over with the practiced eye of the experienced divorcée, which she is, and he tells her about Drew Brennan, Neal Lexington, and Buzz Fletcher.

"I want to check Fletcher more carefully," he says. "Lexington has an alibi for Wednesday night."

"Fletcher doesn't?" Jim demands.

Greg shrugs, and Beth notices his shoulders. "He needs a short leash."

"Do you think they're behind this?" Trish asks. Her voice could scrape the ice off a windshield.

"Lexington doesn't seem to care about the book. I didn't use any names, and he didn't try to get any. Buzz doesn't like women, though. I'll tell Svet to check him out, too."

"Svet?" Trish asks. Jim perks up, and Beth feels a protective surge. If the bitch jokes about flirting with him, Beth will tear her eyes out.

"His researcher," Jim says. "Brilliant woman, and charming."

Oh shit, Beth thinks.

Molly knocks on the door, and Greg lets her in. Trish leaves. She has an hour-plus trip back to Fairfield County. Jim resets the alarm, and they regroup around the dining room table.

Molly reads the boxes.

"Beth." She puts mango shrimp on the plate, and Beth passes it to Jim. "Oops, sorry. I thought that was yours."

"I'm the phoenix."

"Oh, right. I'm the other mango, and Mr. Nines is the General T'sao, right?"

Beth sips her tea and wonders if Greg Nines likes basketball.

Jim and Molly scrape the dishes and fill the dishwasher. When Molly leaves, the remote control feels heavy in Beth's hands.

"Time for the basketball game. Want to join me?"

Greg looks around the room. "There's no clock in here, and you don't wear a watch."

"It's seven, isn't it?"

He checks his own watch. "Yeah. How did you know?"

"I just feel time. Ever since I was little. My sisters used to get pissed at me because I gave them grief when they started that are-we-there-yet riff."

He sinks onto the other end of the couch, and she wishes they had a bowl of popcorn so their fingers could brush each other.

They sit through two people who encourage them to become members of Connecticut Public Television to be sure that all this great programming stays available. Neither speaker has the energy of oatmeal, and the one Beth thinks of as Fashion Victim Number One tries to model the new promotional sweatshirt. She's wearing the one she got two years ago, or was it three? No, it was the first year the Lady Huskies didn't go to the championship after Diana Taurasi graduated.

UConn misses their first three shots, and Beth feels her fists clenching like back in high school. When the ref misses a foul on Pitt, she leans back in frustration.

"C'mon, ref. A moving screen's still illegal."

"You know basketball?" She's forgotten he's there. "Did you play?"

"Oh. Yeah. I mean, no. My brother was a forward in high school. He told me I was too much of a girly-girl. So I was a majorette."

"Do they go to basketball games? I don't think ours did. Football was about it."

"You're right, but I went to Mark's games. And I'd stand in the driveway so he could get used to shooting over a defender. I'd put my arms up over my head." She feels her face getting warm. She's forgotten all about that.

"What?" Pitt calls time out.

"I was just remembering once. Mark was going to be a senior, so I would have just turned sixteen. We were out there one Saturday afternoon, and I put my hands up to block him—he's six-four, so he shot over me anyway—and he stopped and looked at me funny. Then he blushed like a tomato. I asked him what was wrong, and he said 'Jeez, sis. It's a good thing none of the guys I play against look like you.'"

She looks at the TV again, the pledge number still on the screen. "I was the best dancer on our squad, but I developed late. When Mark said that, it was the first time that I realized I was finally getting ..."

She feels him looking at her, but he's not laughing. Even better, he's not leering.

"They gave me a little trouble at first," she says softly. "I had to learn to adjust."

"If you were a good dancer, you could have been a good athlete, too," he says, "but I'll bet the teams liked you cheering them on."

"It was fun." The Huskies steal an inbound and score a lay-up. Pitt calls another time out. "I liked it. Being the captain of the majorettes, everyone looking at us out there in the middle of the field at half time, flipping those batons up into the lights." *Once Mom and Dad got me contacts, I could see the baton well enough to try out.*

"I'll bet you could still do those routines, couldn't you?"

Suddenly, she feels old. "So much is different now. Maybe that's why being attacked threw me for such a loop."

"That would traumatize anyone, Beth."

She runs her fingers through her hair. "I still believed in the high school rah-rah thing. I was a majorette, right? Show them your legs and your pretty gold panties, shake your boobs, kick your tassels, and they love you. You're kind of sexy, but you're not a real person, so it's all safe.

It's like my playing Tally now. She's writing these R-rated fantasies, but she's not a real person either, so it's all right."

"Beth."

"I wasn't ready for it." She feels something spiraling out of control, and she can't stop it. "I liked the pretend so much I forgot I wasn't back on the football field anymore with all those other people around. I was shaking my ass and showing my tits and laughing at how much fun it was. No wonder guys thought I was coming on to them. But in high school, if you said no, guys believed you. This time, I was at a party, and everyone was even more wasted than I was, and I didn't understand that the rules were different."

His arms come around her, and she listens to his heart beating. The Lady Huskies go on a 12-2 run.

"No sports," he says finally.

"No." It's the week for confession, and this one is nothing like the other one. "I'm legally blind without my contacts."

"I wondered about that," he says. "Your eyes are so blue, I wondered if you wore tinted lenses."

"Lenses, yes, but they aren't tinted. These are my real eyes." She catches herself moving closer to him again, and their faces almost touch.

"They're beautiful, Beth."

They sit only inches apart while the world freezes in its tracks. Then Renee Montgomery hits a three, and the crowd roars. Beth forces herself to slide back to the safe end of the couch.

"Do you think your friend will find anything on Fletcher?" she asks when she's regained her composure.

"If there's anything to find, she's the one to do it. Have you thought of anyone else yet? An ex-boss, coworker, maybe someone in school?"

"Uh uh." She wishes she dared to look at him again. "I don't get around much anymore."

"Since 2003, you mean?"

I never should have married Drew Brennan.

They watch three more scoreless possessions while both teams forget how to shoot. "Um, your friend, Svetlana. I have to admit, she's not what I pictured when you called her your researcher. She looks like she left the Cat-O-Nine-Tails in her bedroom."

"She keeps a spare in her trunk," he says, and Beth hears herself.

"I'm really being catty, aren't I?"

"She read your books and told me to take your case."

"She remembered them?"

"No, she read them the night after you came to my office. Well, she read the first one and the hardcover, skimmed another one."

Beth feels her mouth sagging open. "That night?"

"She reads about three thousand words a minute in three languages, and she has eidetic memory."

"God." Beth feels dumb and useless. "What does she do for fun, plan to take over the world?"

"I don't think she's looked that far ahead. She's easily distracted."

"By?" Then Beth understands. "Oh, you mean men. I was ready to smack her this afternoon, watching her tease Jim."

Greg shakes his head. "She wasn't teasing, but she's not big on commitment. Except for her marriage, which didn't last long, I can't think of any real long-term relationships."

"What's her definition of long-term?"

"Breakfast the next morning."

UConn is up by sixteen with a minute left in the first half.

"Molly thinks we should go down to Chester tomorrow," Beth says. "Check out the place where I'm reading Wednesday."

"It'll do you good to get out of the house for a while. The weather's supposed to be decent. Maybe early afternoon? We can eat somewhere along the river."

They sit through more urgings to pledge, deciding whether they want a windbreaker, an umbrella, or a travel mug. The teams reappear for the second half, and she asks him how seriously he's going to check on Buzz Fletcher.

"I don't really have anywhere else to go," he says. "Your ex-husband's alibis check out, and you and Jim didn't give me anyone else."

"Do you think Fletcher is the one?"

"Just because I think he's a jerk doesn't mean he's a potential killer. I don't know how he or Lexington could be watching this place enough to know your writing schedule, either, but someone knew it well enough to hot-wire your upstairs."

Beth feels cold. "The alarm's on now, isn't it?"

"Uh huh." UConn puts in the subs and eventually wins by twenty-two points. Beth feels Greg's eyes on her. "Why don't you get some sleep? I'll take a quick turn around here, then take the couch."

"You have a room upstairs." The words come out before she can stop them. "Are you afraid I'll try to corner you?"

The look on his face makes her want to take it back. She whirls toward the stairs, but Jim's coming down, doubled over and his face the color of plaster.

"Jim?" She sees huge drops of sweat on his forehead before he drops to his knees. Greg bounds over to catch him before he lands on his face.

Ten

"Perhaps you are guarding the wrong person." Art Tomasiewicz leans against the wall near the reception desk while Beth—Nines has to remember to call her Tally in front of others—fills out the last of the paperwork. The waiting room smells of too many people in too little space, some of them with too little hygiene. The conversation around him is a rich stew of Spanish, Polish, and at least two other languages he's never gotten around to learning.

"Beginning to look like that, isn't it?" he says. They pumped Jim's stomach last night and think the shrimp may have been bad. He vomited and flushed most of them at home, so they don't have enough to test.

Jim appears through the doors in a wheelchair again, and Beth hugs him. Maybe they can give him a frequent visitor discount.

"The alarm never went off," Nines tells Art, "and he never left the house. The only people there were the three of us and Molly Pitkin, the webmaster. Oh, and Tally's agent, but she left before we ate."

"What did you eat?"

"Chinese from that takeout place on Columbus." Nines watches the nurse wheel Jim toward the entrance.

"Perhaps this was an accident," Art says. "Fluky, but everyone you are looking at is a man, and women are

more apt to use poison. Did anyone else eat the same thing
he did?"

Nines knows where he's going. If the food was
poisoned, it had to be Molly, who picked the stuff up.
Otherwise, their phone is tapped, too much Grand
Conspiracy for healthy people to contemplate, even if
bodyguards do develop a certain paranoia.

"I think Molly had the shrimp, too," he says. "You
want to look at the boxes?"

"Not worth it. You have lots of coincidences, so
perhaps the girl is just afraid of the dark. The only thing
hinky is that wiring job a few days ago. It's the only reason
I am even here."

"I know, but thanks for running those license plates."

"Sure." Art drives off while Beth and the nurse
maneuver Jim into the back seat. By the time they reach the
house, Svet's Mercedes crouches in the driveway.

"Is he all right?" are her first words when the others
emerge. She sees Jim, and an alien look flickers across her
face, something vaguely maternal. Nines watches her take
Jim's arm and guide him up the steps. "You frightened
me."

His reply fades when they vanish through the door.
Nines feels Beth's eyes on him.

"Men are one of her basic food groups," he tells her,
"but she usually enjoys the hunt more than the actual
catch." He hears Beth clamp her teeth shut.

Svet settles Jim on the couch with his feet on the coffee
table. "Would you like tea? That is good for an unsettled
stomach." She bustles off. When she returns to sit next to
Jim, Nines feels the chill between her and Beth.

"Andrew Brennan seems to have recovered from his heartbreak and moved on." Svet never looks toward Beth. "He is living within his means and occasionally has a beer with a few colleagues after school on a Friday. His wife has a realtor's license and sold three houses last year, all in Hamden. They have a few friends and often attend high school athletic events. They chaperoned the Christmas formal this year."

"Does he cheat?"

Svet folds her legs into a full lotus.

"He appears to be a devoted husband. He also carries out his duties as a teacher competently, if not brilliantly. The only times his name shows up in legal records are his marriage certificates and his divorce." She finally faces Beth, and the chill becomes more pronounced. "I get no sense that he was either unfaithful or abusive during your marriage. Was there something else?"

"We just didn't work out." Beth's voice is even colder than Svet's.

"You do not talk to him now?"

"Not since he sent the last alimony payment. I didn't even know he'd remarried until Greg told me."

Nines answers a knock, and Molly enters, her face a greenish-gray.

"You okay?" he asks.

"Not dead yet," she says. "I was up most of last night."

"Jim, too. We just got back from the hospital."

Molly's eyes flicker to the couple holding hands on the couch, and she stands more upright while Nines takes her coat. She sinks into the chair near the TV and assures Beth that she's probably going to live, but she's written out her will on toilet paper.

"I have nothing new on Neil Lexington," Svet says quietly. "He attends most committee meetings and responds to constituents' calls promptly. His voting record in the State Legislature would do a Klansman proud, but he has never been mentioned for any malfeasance."

"No more catting around?" Nines asks.

"James here may have contacts that I do not." She squeezes his hand, and he perks up. "But he seems to have curtailed such activities when he married. Perhaps he found the love of his life."

Beth crosses her legs five feet away, and the denim looks so warm Nines wants to lay his cheek against her thighs and take a nap. The idea catches him off guard, and he almost loses track of what he's saying. "He told me he wouldn't mind voters thinking he loved women, and Buzz even said they wouldn't care, as long as the women were white."

"I'm liking this guy more and more by the minute," Beth says.

"I still need to look at Mr. Fletcher more carefully." Svet moves even closer to Jim. "I have found an arrest for assault several years ago, but no details. It was contemporaneous with his divorce, so that may have been a factor."

Nines watches her and Jim telepathically make out on the couch and realizes Beth and Molly are watching in amazement. Svet turns to Beth.

"I have read several of your stories now. *The Kansas Review, the New Yorker*, a few others. I enjoyed them."

"Oh. Thank you." Beth struggles to shift gears. "They're pretty different from Taliesyn's stuff."

"Yes. The voice and rhythms differ radically, and the women are much more complex. So are the images. You use many tactile references in your short stories, but the Taliesyn Holroyd novels rely heavily on visuals."

"It's a different way of thinking," Beth says. "Readers are used to it."

"But the sense of touch can be such a powerful stimulus for erotic scenes," Svet points out, "and in one story, you use an aroma to trigger a flashback. That is very well done, and it would work in the novels, too. It could be a powerful way to deliver backstory, for example, and smell in a sex scene could be ..."

"Porn," Beth says.

She answers so quickly that Nines understands where Svet's going. "Touch and smell are more female orientations, aren't they?"

"Yes," Svet agrees, "like Chopin in *The Awakening*. She uses round objects like fruit, and they are warmed by the sun. She is, of course, suggesting breasts." She and Beth stare at each other for so long that Nines wonders whose move it is. Then Beth's eyes shift to Jim, and he nods.

"Okay," she sighs. "You're right."

"James writes the Taliesyn Holroyd novels, doesn't he?"

Beth's eyes fill with tears when she looks at Nines. "I'm sorry. Romance readers expect a female writer, and Jim doesn't quite fit. I look the part, and I've published, so I can handle questions at the readings."

"You're not writing anything now, are you?" Nines asks. "I saw your computer the other day, lines of *I can't write anything*."

"It must be very strange for both of you," Svet says. "James, you have written four novels for which you can take no public credit, and you, Elizabeth, are being lionized—is there a feminine verb for that? I cannot think of one—for stories in which you have taken no part."

Jim and Beth look at each other again, and Nines feels the tension between Beth and Svet lessen slightly.

"It's like I'm still learning who I am," Beth says softly. "Molly and I came up with that bogus bio, but I had to memorize it in case someone asks me about it at a reading. Jim's prepped me for hours on the other books and how he wrote them. He and I talk about *Love in Pain* as he's writing it so I can give people a little preview."

"Is Grusha correct about your own writing?" Svet's voice is professionally soft.

Beth blinks. "It's never happened before, but I'm completely stuck. I've lost my voice or something."

Jim looks like he wants to reach out to her. "You never told me, Beth. Is there anything I can do?"

"No," she snaps. "Sorry, that didn't come out the way I wanted it to. It's just … I'll work through it."

Svet speaks up again. "That means perhaps James here is the target, not you."

"But they tried to run me down a week ago," Beth says.

"Your photographs are on the Web site," Svet says. "Perhaps the person is after the mythical Taliesyn and not Elizabeth Shepard. Besides, James here was electrocuted. And poisoned."

"If it's the food last night, I got it, too," Molly points out. She's sipping a ginger ale from the kitchen and looks like she can only last about one more inning.

"That is true." Svet squeezes Jim's hand. "James, you should be in bed."

She escorts him up the stairs. Nines realizes the most beautiful woman he's seen in years sits five feet away with her mouth hanging open the way he suspects his is, too.

Beth picks up the TV remote and starts channel surfing, Sunday morning fare.

"You look like you could use some rest, too, Beth," Nines says.

"Were you two up with Jim all night?" Molly asks.

"I napped at the hospital a little," Beth says. Nines remembers her face, soft as a kitten's when she snuggled against his shoulder. He wanted to bury his face in her hair. "Was I heavy?"

Four consecutive channels have commercials.

"No," he says, "but Molly's right. You could use a nap."

"I'm too wired. It's Sunday. Jim doesn't write on Sunday, and I'm sick of pretending." She tries ten more channels, then switches the TV off again and drops the remote back on the coffee table. "Can we do something, get out of here for a while?"

Molly puts her glass on the table. Her face still has the pallor of a cabbage.

"You could check out that bookstore in Chester," she says. "Binding Agreements."

"Are you up to it, Molly?" Beth looks the brunette over. "We can find the place."

"Okay, fuck nobility. I'm going back home."

"Why don't you just crash here?"

Molly looks at the stairs. "Actually, that sounds good."

Svet appears again, her braid undone and her chestnut hair floating loosely across her shoulders. When she realizes the other two women are watching, she gives her hips just the slightest undulation on her way down the stairs before she bends over to pick up her coat from the couch. She twirls her scarf around her neck and turns to Nines.

"James is resting." It has the same fuzzy J-sound she gives *Zherry*. "He tells me he can think of no one who would want to harm him, but I will check his background anyway. I think there is still something in the books that is dangerous to Taliesyn Holroyd." She glances at Beth again. "I will continue to investigate Mr. Fletcher, too. Will you be here if I find something, Grusha?"

"Beth and I are going down to Chester in a few minutes," he says, "maybe do some shopping and lunch, check out the place she's reading Wednesday."

"Would you like me to follow you to Route 9? See if you attract attention?"

"Never mind." Nines is dying to ask her why she took so long upstairs.

Molly eases her way up stairs made of eggshells and disappears around the landing. Beth follows, returning in a clean, white shirt and crisp jeans.

"Tally Lite," she says.

Nines holds her coat and smells her scent on the collar. Her fingers brush her long hair over it.

"Can I drive?" she says. "I feel like I'm a prisoner."

"Sure," he says. "Do you know where the place is?"

"Yeah, only a few blocks off the Chester exit on Route 9. Easy as falling in love." She stops suddenly.

The sun is high but does little good. The frigid air nips at their faces when they go through the back door, and Nines resets the alarm before closing it. Molly and Jim can sleep until they come back. An icy crust crackles under their feet when they walk to the garage, and the door squeaks when Beth raises it.

"No Stanley garage door opener?" Nines asks.

"I think it's another one of Jim's projects for down the road," she tells him. The cold brings color to her cheeks, and her eyes sparkle like a TV commercial. "You don't mind me driving, do you? I just need to take a little control for a change. This is getting to me."

"I don't blame you, but we'll find the guy. Maybe when we get back, you can write about the store or something."

"What are you, a creativity consultant?"

"No," he says, "but Svet's got a double major. Lit and a master's in psych."

"I wondered about that." Beth digs in her purse for her car keys. "She really shook me up when she whipped out that stuff about imagery. Does she write?"

"She thought about it, but she doesn't like most of the really literary stuff. She's a little more … concrete."

Beth stops. "Concrete. That's one word for it. I'll bet she needs orgasms like I swill coffee. I don't believe what I'm seeing with her and Jim."

"I don't either," Nines says. "To tell you the truth, the cops who checked out your break-in last week weren't sure he was straight."

"I never even thought about it," Beth says. "He just projects niceness. I think she did him when she took him upstairs, don't you?"

She turns to Nines, and her hip brushes her car door. He hears a snap like a broken twig, and she stiffens. Her eyes roll back in her head, her legs buckle, and he leaps forward to catch her head before it slams the cement. When he puts a hand to her neck, he can't feel a pulse. He licks his hand before holding it under her nostrils. Nothing.

He digs into his pocket for his cell and dials 911, then unzips her jacket. He straddles her hips with his knees and presses the heel of his hand against her chest, searching for the tip of her breastbone. Her breasts are firm mounds on each side, and he pushes hard, one, two, three, four, five times, his weight behind it and his elbows locked. Beth's whole body recoils under his weight, but he doesn't feel a heartbeat.

He unbuttons her blouse, and her lacy blue bra makes him catch his breath. He hasn't even thought about touching a woman since Erin, and this is completely different. But Beth isn't breathing either, just like Erin, and he needs to save her. He tries five more thrusts, then crawls up to lift her head, prying her lips open and making sure her tongue doesn't block her air passage. He clamps her nostrils shut, covers her mouth with his, and blows as much air as he can hold into her mouth. He does it twice more, then moves back to her chest.

"Come on, Beth. Help me." His heart races in his chest, and he knows he's an eyelash away from panic. *Erin died because you weren't there, but you're with Beth, and it has to be different this time. You have to see her breathe, feel a pulse under that still warm flesh. She's so beautiful, so young. It's not right. Erin was even younger, and you couldn't save her,* a voice from deep inside reminds him, *or your child.*

He locks his arms on Beth's chest again, his whole body ramming into her heart. Three cycles of five, then he moves to her face again. How long has she gone without oxygen? He draws air into his chest and tastes her lips again, slowly blowing into her mouth. His hands hold her face tightly to his so nothing escapes. He tilts his head back for another breath.

A sigh drifts from between her lips, and he stops for a second. Yes, her chest moves, and he knows she's back. He finds her hand and squeezes it, then slides a hand under her head and pulls her into him.

"It's okay, Beth," he whispers. "I'm here."

When she moans, his eyes burn. In the distance, a siren grows louder.

Eleven

The people in the ER look like the same ones from last night, and Nines wonders where the hell else everyone should be on a Sunday afternoon. His car keys dig into his butt, and the public address announcements drill into his back teeth. He's still trying to make his hands stop shaking, and all that keeps him from flying apart is the taste of Beth Shepard's lips on his. His hands still remember her breasts when he got her heart going again, too, and he wraps the sensations around him to stifle the fear. She's alive. He didn't lose her, even though he still remembers telling himself that first day that he should check out the garage, anyone could just walk in. Then he got so busy looking at her, he forgot. Asshole.

An EMT with red eyes comes out and finds him. Nines doesn't want the guy working on him, not until he's had about twelve hours of sleep, but that doesn't look like a possibility.

Art's striding toward him again, too. "This is becoming a really bad habit," he says. "What happened this time?"

"Someone gimmicked her car. Lucky for us, she backed into it. If she'd grabbed the door handle, she'd be dead now."

"How is she?"

"They're bringing her out in a few minutes. She's going to be groggy the rest of the day, but she can sleep home as well as she can here." Molly Pitkin's already dropped off clean clothes and gone back to bed. He called her, and she stumbled in, still looking like someone should be warming up in the bullpen.

Art's eyes seem to line up a tricky putt. "This does not sound like one guy. Hit and run, electricity, maybe poison. How many people can hate her?"

"I'm beginning to wonder. You want to check out the car? It's the blue Honda in the garage. Just for the hell of it, maybe see if the other one's rigged, too."

"Any idea when the guy did it?"

"Neither car's been driven in a few days, and nobody was home while we had Jim over here getting his stomach pumped. Maybe he went in then."

"That means he knew you weren't home, like he knew the food was poisoned."

"But how?" Nines asks. "He can't be at the restaurant, too, even if he's listening to their phone."

Art plows through the people on the plastic chairs and vanishes. Then they wheel Beth Shepard out, her eyes rolling aimlessly around the room until they find Nines. He sees her hands tighten on the arms of the wheelchair.

"Stay down," he tells her. When they move her from the wheelchair into his car, she sags against him before he fastens her seatbelt. He pulls into the driveway a few minutes later and sees two cops in the garage. Art approaches again.

"Both cars are clean," he says, "but there are marks on the hood. The guy must have cleaned them up when you left."

"Tomorrow, I'm getting someone to put an alarm on the garage, too," Nines tells him.

He escorts Beth into the house, where Molly and Jim sit on the couch, both barely upright.

"Fuck the tour," Molly says. "I'm calling Trish and telling her to pull the plug. This isn't worth your life, Beth."

Jim doesn't say anything, but Nines can read his mind.

"I need to do it," Beth says, but the words simply drop out of her mouth and splat on the rug. Nines is impressed that she can make coherent conversation. "You've paid me for two months. I haven't done anywhere near enough."

"Someone's trying to kill you," Molly says. "We didn't know we were putting you in danger."

"You don't even know it yet, Molly," Nines says. Her face is still pasty, but her eyes have more focus. "The police think both cars were rigged, so we still don't know for sure who the guy's after."

"God," Molly says. He watches her try to think, but that's too much to ask yet.

"Why don't all three of you go to bed?" he says. He helps Beth up the stairs and can't help noticing how warm her body is when she leans against him. When they reach her room, she sags onto her bed.

"Beth, you need to rest."

"Rest." She doesn't move. "Okay."

"Beth?"

Suddenly, tears spill down her cheeks, and her fingers dig into his shoulder blades.

"Oh my God, oh my God, oh my God. What happened out there? All I remember is lying on a table ... light flashing in my eyes and a nurse. Then they said you'd gotten my heart going again. Did I die? I needed clean clothes, I let them throw away my jeans and my underwear. I messed myself."

He holds her even tighter.

"I'm going to find this guy," he says.

"I'm so afraid. How did I get into this?"

"I don't know. You need to lie down, Beth. Get some sleep."

"I can't. I'm afraid to close my eyes."

"Shh," he says. "Get under the covers, and you'll be fine. I'll be right downstairs."

"This isn't my real bed. I wish I could be in my own bed. I feel like a little kid again, I want my mom and dad."

"I know, it's all right. I'm here." Something clogs in his chest. "I'm going to protect you, Beth."

"I know, but I'm still afraid."

"What do you need?"

"Don't leave?"

"You have to undress."

"No. I'll sleep in my clothes. Promise you won't leave."

"I'll stay in the chair over there so you can see me. All right?"

Beth closes her eyes, but she still feels Greg Nines ten feet away. No man has been in a bedroom with her since she left Drew five years ago. She doesn't count Jim Leslie, whom she decided was asexual until he started preening in front of Svetlana, the Ice Queen. She's not ready for a man to be with her now. Then she thinks about Greg Nines not being with her now. Fear slithers through her stomach and rattles its tail.

She told him about her rape so long ago that it feels like part of her DNA She's never told anyone else, not even her parents. His eyes swallowed her hurt and her shame, and when he wrapped his arms around her, she felt like she was back in her own safe bedroom with the Strawberry Shortcake bedspread.

She's missing a few hours. She was talking with him, then she woke up in the hospital, her muscles sore and her head aching. They told her she'd been electrocuted. They checked her heart and flashed a light in her eyes, and she thought they were going to keep her there, but she wanted to go home. People die in hospitals all the time. She remembers her grandfather, healthy until he picked up some kind of infection. Sure, he was eighty-seven, but still. There are probably others, but her memory's a little discombobulated right now. Discombobulated. A fun word. Maybe she can work it into a story, if she can write another story.

Molly said something about canceling the tour. Would they still need her then? Words have become bricks she can't force through the funnel, so she'd have to take another temp job. She hates temping. Men notice her so quickly, she feels like a kissing booth, and she's running out of ways to hold them at bay.

Greg Nines held her this morning and in the hospital, though, and he didn't scare her. Why, because he's just protecting her as a job, or because he's been hurt, too? God, what would it be like to have your wife and baby torn away like that? No wonder he drank, but now he's coming up on, what, three years sober? Does he have a girlfriend? Not if he's hanging around here on Valentine's Day and Saturday night. She doesn't remember him calling anyone to cancel. Of course, he wouldn't do that in front of her.

She thought he was sleeping with Svetlana-Something-Like-Cancer until the woman walked in and steamrolled Jim. No, Greg and Svet have never been lovers. Beth knows the look that you can't keep out of your eyes. Making love with a man means you understand each other on a different level, and you never completely lose it. She's sure that if she and Drew met somewhere now, she could tell how he felt just by seeing his face.

Greg Nines shifts in the chair. Beth keeps her eyes closed the way she used to when Mom and Dad told her it was late, but she'd read Nancy Drew under the covers with a flashlight. She didn't figure out until years later that they deliberately hit that squeaking board in the hall so she'd have time to turn off her light and look innocent again. They knew she loved to read. Is that why she became a writer?

The air moves in the room. Greg Nines closes the door softly behind him and she almost calls out for him to come back. She hears his voice and realizes he's on his cell, probably talking with Svetlana again.

Does Svetlana really like Jim, or is she just playing, the way a cat dribbles a mouse around after wounding it before snapping its spinal cord with those chisel fangs? The woman has a terrifying intelligence, and she moves like a pornographic clone, aware of every inch of that cat-like body. She projects absolute control, except those weird flashes with Jim, when it seems like she can't keep herself from touching him.

"No," she hears Greg say softly. "She's sleeping now. I'm hoping she'll sleep through the night. Look at Jim again. Art says both cars were wired. I don't know if that means they're both targets, or if our boy doesn't know who Taliesyn really is."

She doesn't want to cancel the tour. Jim needs it to keep selling books. She could use the money, too, at least until she can find her own voice again. Her voice dried up when she moved in here and became Taliesyn Holroyd. Will she have to move out and away from here to draw it back?

If she quits and goes away, will the killer still be after her, or will Jim be in the crosshairs? Either way, Greg Nines won't be around anymore, and that would really suck.

The alarm's on, and both doors are locked. Nines keeps his baby Maglite aimed at the steps and goes down to the basement to check the windows there, too. Jim's workbench looks cleaner than his own kitchen back in Newington. He checks the windows near the water heater and furnace, then the keyed dead bolt on the back door. He leaves the basement door six inches ajar so he'll feel a draft if someone manages to disable the alarm. Whoever is trying to kill Beth knows about electricity.

The refrigerator hums softly, and he jumps. He lays a kitchen chair on its side two steps inside the back door, legs pointing toward the opening. He makes sure to close the drapes in the dining room and lays a chair in the doorway from the kitchen, too. Then he rumples the carpet in the den, checks the dead bolt on the front door, and settles on the couch.

No one else in the house even woke for supper. Nines wonders if Beth knows that he unbuttoned her blouse to give her CPR He remembers his helpless terror when he couldn't feel a pulse, then the wave of joy when he saw her chest slowly rise and fall again. He wasn't there for Erin. Their wedding portrait back at the condo reminds him every night. But now he's met Beth Shepard—not Taliesyn Holroyd, who doesn't really exist—who has the beauty to stop traffic, and has humor, intelligence, and warmth on top of it. And fear.

Svet agrees that Jim might be the target, so she's going through his past, too. Nines hasn't asked her what's going on with them, but he can tell that she sets off both Beth and Molly. Well, Molly creeps him out a little, too. There's something too robotic about the woman who pulls Beth's alternate strings.

If Neil Lexington doesn't care about his past, should someone else? Maybe he should ask Jim if he knows about that tomorrow. Jim seems to have a hunger for facts but a perspective on them, too. He was probably a terrific teacher, but Nines sees his soul in the house he's rebuilding board by board.

Buzz Fletcher has a mean streak, and he definitely dislikes women, but that doesn't prove anything. He doesn't seem to know about Beth or Taliesyn Holroyd, and Nines doubts that he's devious enough to work this whole routine. He'd come in and yell at Beth, maybe even try to hit her, but he'd rather see the damage instead of setting a trap so he can be miles away when someone falls into it.

Tomorrow, they have to check out the place in Chester for Wednesday's reading, too. Nines admires Beth's reluctance to cancel the tour because she doesn't want to let Jim Leslie down. He tells himself that if they continue the tour and get her out of the state, she may be safe for a few weeks, but then she has to come back.

The wind's picking up. Nines steps over the chair in the kitchen and stares out the back door, then moves to the side of the house away from the driveway. He makes a pot of coffee and returns to the couch, where he sits with the lights off. He feels steam rising off the mug and slowly guides it to his mouth.

The wind thrashes the tree limbs outside, the rustling like an old woman whispering in the dark. He listens for the words, but they don't come. Erin's face is getting fainter and fainter in his head, and he worries that the day will come when he no longer sees her. But when he closes his eyes, Beth Shepard appears before him looking so real he can reach out and touch her.

Footsteps move above him. Beth is awake. He finishes his coffee, then pours another mug. When that's gone, it's after midnight. He checks the dead bolts and the alarm again, then drags himself upstairs. He spent last night in the hospital with Beth while they pumped Jim's stomach, and the lack of sleep is catching up with him.

Light slides under Beth's door. He moves carefully down the hall and listens. Keys clack swiftly, and he hopes Beth isn't still practicing *I can't think of anything to write*. After a few minutes, he eases the door open a few inches and looks in.

The light off her monitor turns her hair a silvery blue. Gold-rimmed glasses rest on her nose, so thick they distort the monitor when she turns her head. She's completely unaware of him, and her lack of self-consciousness makes her so beautiful that his chest hurts.

Her fingers fly over the keyboard, specks filling the monitor line by line. For the first time in weeks, Beth Shepard has found something to write.

Twelve

Molly has some whiny boy band on her CD player as they pass the sign announcing the exit for the Goodspeed Opera House on Route 9. In winter, the shoreline of the Connecticut River features glacial rock faces, shiny with ice. Thick, green woods and occasional rustic farmhouses offset them in summer, but now everything sulks in the gray palette, the slight drizzle that keeps the windshield wipers going adding to the gloom.

"If this freezes, driving back's going to be a bitch," Molly says.

Beth sits in the back seat with Greg. Warmth flows off him, and she replays his tucking her in yesterday afternoon. She woke up, and he was gone, but she heard him moving around the house and knew he was taking care of her. She felt like she'd found the first thread pointing the way out of her labyrinth and wrote nearly six pages, some of it actually English. It's only first draft junk, but it's more than she's produced in weeks.

"We probably won't need to stay long," Greg says. His voice makes Beth's ribs vibrate. "I just want to see where they put the seats and how traffic flows. It's a funky little shop in an artsy town, so I want to look at the windows and parking, too. Besides, don't you and Tally want to talk to the staff?"

"We should," Beth agrees. Molly's CD changes to Melissa Etheridge, and the rain lets up a little. It's about twenty-five miles from New Britain to Chester, home of Binding Agreements, most of it down Route 9, so traffic on a Monday afternoon is light.

"I sent this place and R. J. Julia pictures from the Borders gig last week." Molly passes an SUV crawling along at thirty miles per hour. "I don't know if I'll take more here or not, have to see what it looks like, but R. J. Julia is big-time. I'll definitely take shots there."

R. J. Julia in Madison hosts over two hundred writers annually and always wins the New Haven *Advocate's* Best-Of award for bookstores. Binding Agreements has only been open a year but aspires to the same kind of reputation. Maybe they think Taliesyn Holroyd will be the next Nora Roberts. Beth hopes they're right. Now that words are starting to trickle out, she can do more under her own name, too.

Molly swoops into a parking lot by a black-shingled two-story with a swinging sign. The bay window displays a poster promising Taliesyn Holroyd is coming, and her picture looks like she escaped from a '50s pulp novel cover. Beth feels herself blush. She knows what she's wearing under the red silk blouse and black leather pants. What would Greg say? Then she remembers that he gave her CPR yesterday, so he knows what she wears. He's touched her breasts, too. Unfortunately, she doesn't remember that part, because she was dead.

Kevin Sheehan looks like he's missing Freshman Orientation to show them around the store. Beth loves the smell of books and notices the cozy children's nook in the back corner, posters of the Pokey Little Puppy, Curious

George, Peter Rabbit, and Harry Potter on the walls and a big hooked rug on the floor. Just like naptime. Kevin gestures to a bay window.

"We usually set readers up right there," he says. "It's the sunny side of the building, when we have sun, and you can put extra books and stuff on the ledge. The light makes it feel nice and open."

"How many people do you think will be here?" Greg asks.

"We've got about seventy signed up so far, and most of them have copies of your books." Beth feels Kevin's eyes on her. When she smiles at him, his eyes almost glaze over. Molly's trim little butt disappears up the winding stairway. She's still pale from the food poisoning, but her stamina is definitely back. Beth knows she's already calculated the square footage downstairs and the ratio of space to patrons.

Kevin shows Greg where they'll set up the autograph table across from the kids' corner and far from the cash registers. Impulse buying is vital to a small place like this. Another poster of Taliesyn Holroyd smolders near the exit. Yes, they want her to sell well, and they want her back. The place gives off the warm comfort of a country kitchen. All it needs is that apple pie aroma. Beth suspects that Kevin's working on that, too.

Molly scurries down the stairs. "You've got to see this."

They follow her back up into a room with folio art books along the far wall and hardcover nonfiction to their left. To Beth's right, diffused light spreads over a gigantic coffee table covered with magazines and newspapers and surrounded by soft chairs and a couch that needs a puppy sleeping at one end. Beyond it, a woman who looks like she was born to wear cardigan sweaters and glasses on a chain leans over a counter with tea, coffee, and six flavors of scones.

"Jim would love this table," Greg says. "It has to be custom made."

"I'll bet the high school kids come here to do their homework and fool around," Beth says. Greg gives her a funny look. "Well, look at it," she continues. "Soft cushions, nice chairs, food. Throw in a little mood music, and you could score like Charlie Sheen."

"This is a great place for you to wait before you go on," Molly says.

"Yeah," Greg agrees, "but I'd better check it first."

When Beth looks out the bay window downstairs, the soft rain has become sleet with attitude. They thank Kevin, agree that they'll be back at four-thirty Wednesday, and hunch their shoulders back to the car. Molly starts up, and Beth feels the front wheels try to spin when she pulls out onto the street.

"Shit," Molly says. "It doesn't feel any colder, but this stuff is freezing."

"I think Jim said he was going to make beef stew tonight," Beth tells her. "You should stay over. No sense driving any more in this stuff than you have to."

Beth feels the car's front end try to drift toward the guard rail before Molly coaxes it back.

"Sounds like a plan to me," she says.

Molly needs nearly two hours to get them home, the sleet turning to hail, then back to sleet, then to something they can't even name, and her defroster blowing hot air that dries out everyone's sinuses and makes talking difficult. She turns into Jim's driveway a little faster than Nines would recommend, but he can tell that if she slows down, let alone stops, her inertia will leave her stuck where she is. She slides next to his car, and they let the sleet clack around them to the back door. Molly stops long enough to grab her overnighter from the trunk.

Jim Leslie has towels in his hands and coffee in the pot. A teakettle whistles on the stove.

"Good," he says when he sees Molly's bag. "I don't think you're going to get out again."

"Even I'm not that crazy," she tells him.

"I looked at the weather on the Internet." He moves over to stir the pot. "It's going to drop another ten degrees. Then this will change to snow, but it looks like it'll be solid ice underneath."

"Swell," Beth says. "Maybe we can tell ghost stories around the fireplace, what do you think?" She goes upstairs to change out of her sultry romance writer costume and returns in her usual sweatshirt and jeans. Fuzzy slippers cover her feet.

Leslie's stew fills them all with a rich, brown glow, then everyone else goes upstairs for a laptop assignation. Nines checks the locks, the basement, and the alarm, then settles on the couch with *Love in Maine*, the first Taliesyn Holroyd novel. He wonders if Beth Shepard has copies of her short stories around somewhere so he can compare the style. Svet's already told him what to notice.

A hundred pages and a hot make-out scene later, he realizes that Beth Shepard is coming down the stairs. Her hands wrestle with each other like pale snakes.

"Could you come up and look at something?"

The bedroom looks the way he remembered it, her Tally costume tucked in the closet and the rest of the room unadorned except for the comforter on the bed. She points to her laptop.

"I just checked the Tally Web site a few minutes ago," she says. "This was in the new messages."

Nines looks at the screen. The sender is IZonU, and the message is as succinct as the previous one: I CAN WAIT.

Even though the message came from miles away, Nines forces himself to keep his hands off the laptop. Beth's face crumples, and he draws her into his arms.

"Shit," she whispers. "Shit, shit, shit."

"I'm going to find him, Beth. He's not going to hurt you."

"I'm just so …"

Nines hears footsteps, and when he looks up, Leslie and Molly stand in the doorway. Molly's eyes narrow behind her lenses, and Nines realizes Beth's huddling into his chest.

"Um, is this a private party, or can anyone join in?" Molly says. Her voice holds no humor. Or much of anything else.

"Beth," Leslie says. "I just checked the Web site and saw …"

"We've got it," Nines says. "Beth came down to get me."

"It had to come in sometime today," Molly says. "I sorted the messages this morning before I picked you up."

"Can you check this one and see where it came from?" Greg asks.

"Probably West Haven again." She moves to Beth's chair, and Beth sinks to the bed. Leslie disappears and returns with a steaming mug of tea. Nines watches him brush his lips gently across Beth's forehead and retreat. He still comes across as a playful dog, but between Svet's reactions and the paternal care he shows Beth, Nines sees that the guy has the makings of a terrific father.

"Okay." Molly slides the chair back and turns to the others. "It's not West Haven. Since the sender's different, maybe it really is a different person."

"If it's not from West Haven, where did it come from?" Leslie asks.

Molly chews on her earpiece. "New Britain Public Library. Sent early this afternoon."

"Where's ...?" Nines starts to ask, but Leslie's already answering.

"Just a few blocks down West Main. In good weather, it's about a ten-minute walk."

Nines feels everyone's eyes on him.

"I wonder if this is really a different person, or if he's just using a different name to throw us off."

"Doesn't matter," Molly says. "He's getting closer."

Beth can't breathe, but she feels Greg's arms steering her downstairs to the couch. Something cool touches her fingers, and she opens them to discover Jim's replaced her tea with a large glass of pinot noir.

"Thank you," she manages. *Love in Maine* lies face down on the table.

"Okay," Greg says. "We know the guy's been watching, but he's not going to get in here tonight."

"That's for damn sure," Molly says. They hear the sleet lashing the windows. Beth's hands feel cold enough to freeze her wine, and she's telling herself this is really getting old.

Greg turns to Molly. "You say that e-mail was sent this afternoon?"

"Twelve forty-two." Beth feels Molly's eyes on her. She looks like she's doing a lab experiment back in high school biology.

"The library's only a few minutes from here. Jim, have you ever been in it?"

"A few times but not for a month or so. Why?"

"I'm just wondering if anyone saw you and knows who you are."

"Can't be," Molly says. "The guy's tried to kill Beth, too."

Beth realizes that her fingers are wrapped around Greg's hands tight as Band-Aids.

"You know," Jim says, "this is all crazy."

"Uh huh," Greg says, "and some crazy person wants to kill you or Beth."

"Which is it?" Molly demands. She's a good web designer, but her intensity creeps Beth out, especially now. She was hoping to do more writing tonight.

"I think the guy's still after the writer," Greg says. "The threats have come to the Web site instead of Beth's e-mail, and the house has been a target."

"What about the hit-and-run?" Beth asks.

"That's the exception," Greg admits, "but your picture's on the Web site."

Beth feels the dervish in her chest slow down as he takes control. Molly stops chewing her glasses. Jim never sits still, but even he slows down, too.

"Lexington couldn't care less about what you write, so he's low on the list. I think the Winsteads are, too. They're defending their son, but the stepfather is a lawyer. He knows you're changing the details enough so he couldn't prove malice even if he wanted to, and the mother's paperwork is solid enough so there's no reason for her to be upset except that she's heard this stuff over and over for years."

"What about Beth's ex?" Molly says. "The first e-mail came from West Haven. That's only a few minutes from Hamden."

"He's got an alibi," Greg says. "We'll keep digging. I don't think he's the one either, but Beth, it does suggest that the guy knows about your divorce. He's trying to make us look at Drew."

Beth feels the color draining from her face. All she wanted to do was help Jim and make a few bucks while she finished up a few more stories, thank you very much. Why does that make someone want to kill her?

Molly peeps through the drapes, then announces that the sleet has turned to snow, and she's going to bed. Jim and Greg discuss some Civil War battle, and Beth can't help staring.

"You know history?" She's never noticed that little gold fleck in Greg's brown eyes before.

"I liked English and history in school, but I wanted to be a cop like my father."

Beth refills her wineglass. She hates the groggy feeling the Seconal tablets give her in the morning, so she avoids them as much as she can. Besides, she only has six or eight of them left. When she returns from the kitchen, Jim's heading toward the stairs. He stops to hug her around her wine, then she continues on to the living room.

Nines is just picking up the paperback again when Beth sinks to the couch next to him, and he knows she doesn't want to be alone. He drops the book back on the coffee table.

"What do you really think?" she asks.

"I don't read much romance fiction." He knows she'd be playing with that phantom ring except that she's gripping the wineglass.

"You know that's not what I mean."

"Svet would call if she found anything."

"She's ... unusual," Beth says. He knows that *interesting* usually means something negative, but he's not certain about *unusual*.

"We've known each other almost half our lives," he says. "She's brilliant."

"She said she's divorced. How come she's not married again? More fun controlling lots of men?"

"She still takes her ex out to dinner on their anniversary. She tells me he's thinking of getting married again."

"How long have they been divorced?"

Svet and Jerry were separated when he asked to be a pallbearer at Erin's funeral, and that was five years ago this coming June, longer than their marriage. The thought burrows into his chest. "About four years."

"You ever think about ...?"

"No." His feet tap on the floor, and he knows that means he wants to run. "We're good friends, but we'd drive each other crazy in a week."

Beth sets her glass on the table and looks like she knows she's stepping over a line. "What do you do in your spare time, Greg? When you're not protecting damsels in distress?"

"I used to coach Little League," he tells her. "I was a decent center fielder when I was a kid. Carl Pavano came into the league in Southington the last year I played."

"I assume he's a good player? I don't follow baseball."

"He used to be with the Yankees."

"Did you ever play with him?"

"Maybe, but I don't remember him at all, and who knows what a ten-year-old will be in another six or eight years?"

"You don't coach anymore?"

"No," he says. "Not since …"

She looks at her glass. "I can put this away if it bothers you." He shakes his head. "Do you miss it? I mean baseball."

"Sometimes." He can't do it anymore because those boys remind him of the child he and Erin should be raising right now.

"My brother played basketball. I guess I told you that."

"Right, and you were a majorette."

"Yeah. You didn't have to know anything about the games, but you knew people were looking at you out there. I was a show-off in high school."

"Maybe you should have been a performer instead of a writer. A dancer, an actress."

"I don't like people looking at me anymore." Her eyes fill with tears, and he feels his own breath miss a beat. "I was such a tease."

"Nobody deserves what happened to you, Beth." As long as they talk, their voices will keep her demons at bay. He's got all night.

"Nobody deserves what you got either, Greg."

He wishes he'd lit a fire in the fireplace. The light would fall on her left side and make her a soft orange. With the snow blanketing the roof, all they'd need then would be a bearskin rug.

"I was wondering about your short stories," he goes on. "Svet says she likes them, and she wouldn't say that unless it's true."

"I've got copies at home."

"Which is where?"

"West Hartford." Beth runs her fingers down the stem of the glass. "One of these days, maybe I can go over and get some."

"I'd like to read them."

"Don't say it if you don't mean it. It won't hurt my feelings."

"No, I would."

He can feel her heat where her feet rest on the table almost touching his. Then they talk some more about their families. Her father was a judge, and his father was a cop, how coincidental. They run out of family material, and he watches her flailing for something else.

"How do you think the reading will go Wednesday?" she asks.

"If it's like last week, you'll be terrific."

She takes that in. "Do you think I should give them the hot sex scene again? Or is it too much?"

He hasn't touched a woman in five years, and he hasn't missed it until now.

"I didn't know romances got that sexy." Svet said Tally's heroines come like train wrecks.

"Jim's writing contemporary chick lit, so yeah, he can talk about tab A going into slot B, and the girl can even say *fuck*. Not too often, though, and the C-word only if she's really pissed at some other woman."

She stares at the paperback on the table. "This sucks for Jim, writing the books and me taking all the credit."

"But you're helping him."

"Yeah, but it just feels …" Beth runs her hands through that spun golden hair and shifts gears. "He should find some nice girl and settle down."

"You're a nice girl, but he thinks you're out of his league."

"No woman's out of a man's league if he pays attention to her. Jim listens, and he worries about me. I think he feels responsible for all this shit."

"Svet's looking into him, too, but she's not finding anything. That means it's either the books or you."

She shivers. "Does she always flirt with guys the way she did with Jim?"

"I think she's impressed with his mind."

"He's impressed with hers, too, among other things." She moves even closer to him. "Will you promise not to laugh?"

Her face is so serious, he finds himself crossing his heart like back in grade school.

"I saw her coming on to Jim, and I was jealous. I haven't felt anything about a man in so long, and I like Jim, and she came in and …"

"Svet's …"

"Let me finish, please. This is really hard and I feel stupid and scared."

He reaches down and finds her hand. It's shaking. "Beth?"

"When I see them together, it makes me realize that I want it, too. I want a man to look at me that way again. I've been so scared for years. You scared me at first, but you look at me and I ..." She stares at the fireplace, and her throat moves. "Have you been with a woman since your wife died?"

"A few blind dates." He doesn't want to cry, but he understands what she's afraid of. The same animal is galloping around in his chest, too. "Svet or Art set them up."

"How'd they go?"

"I think I made it through the evening once. I never called any of them again."

"They weren't Erin." It's not a question.

"No." The word has to fight its way free.

"Or what if they left you, too?"

"No." Beth's face blurs when he tries to look at her. "What if I couldn't make it safe for them either?"

"That wasn't your fault, Greg." Beth's hand squeezes his, and she brings it to her cheek. Her tears are cold on his knuckles. She swallows and turns to face him head-on. "I was dead yesterday, wasn't I? That's what they told me at the hospital, and you did CPR and brought me back."

"I ..."

"You brought me back from death." Her eyes are shiny, and he wants to tell her he couldn't do it with Erin.

"Both ways."

His mouth won't work.

"Last night, I woke up with an idea," she says softly. "I started playing around with it. I don't know if it will go anywhere, but it's the first thing I've written in weeks that didn't make me want to throw up. Jim's cranking out ten, twelve, fifteen pages a day, and I've been ready to sell my soul for a decent sentence. Just a subject and a verb, even." She puts her fingers to his lips before he can speak. "I wrote five more pages after dinner. While you were down here reading."

"More of the same thing?"

"The characters are us."

The snow silently falls to the roof and shuts out the entire world except for Beth Shepard trying to talk.

"Svet mentioned my images," she says, "touch and smell instead of visuals. I hadn't thought about it, but maybe I do write that way. Chopin certainly did."

"I don't know Chopin," he says.

Beth's sweatshirt swells and contracts, one, two, one, two, inhale, exhale.

"Yesterday, you must have touched my breasts when you gave me CPR"

"I'm not sure what you want me to say, Beth." Beautiful warm mounds under his fingers, that lacy blue bra.

"I wish I'd been awake to feel you touching me."

"You're the most beautiful woman I've ever known." He knows he can't take it back.

"I was writing about you," she whispers. "I don't know what you're really like, but I know what you are in my mind. Pretending's safer, but it's not enough anymore."

She stands, the light from upstairs a soft mango glow on her hair. His breath clogs in his chest.

"I want you to touch me again, Greg."

He's already moving toward her, wrapping her up at the bottom of the stairs. When his tongue slides gently along her lips, she opens her mouth, and her own tongue meets his. Then her arms are around his neck, her breath warm on his cheek, and he closes his eyes while a warm drone fills his head, and she presses herself into his chest. He cups her ass, and she rubs against him. He feels himself getting hard. His other hand slides under her sweatshirt, lifting it to reveal those beautiful breasts. He pushes her pink bra up and moves his lips down to taste her nipples.

"Yes, Baby," she whispers. She leans back against the wall. "Oh, yes." Her lips move to his neck.

He finds the fastener on her jeans first and runs his tongue between her breasts, then down across her navel, and she moans. Then he's pulling her jeans down, her pale tuft under a little pink thong. Her hands guide his face down, and he kisses that pink-covered thatch.

"Oh, Baby…"

His fingers push the fabric aside, and her breath whistles through her teeth when his tongue finds her. She grinds her hips against him, her fingers clutching his hair and her rhythm growing frantic as she leans back against the wall.

"Oh, that's so … oh, yes."

When he slides a finger into her, her orgasm is so fierce and sudden that it shocks them both. He realizes that they're half-dressed on the stairs of someone else's house, someone who could catch them with her legs wrapped around his head and her breasts glowing in the lamplight at any second.

"Greg," she whispers. "Oh, Greg."

"Beth." He wants her so much his knees shake.

She leans against him and holds him while they struggle for control. She pulls her jeans up without even bothering to adjust her thong, then she kisses him again.

"This is what I taste like?"

He still can't speak. They hear a click, and the upstairs fills with light. Beth's hand flies to the fastener on her jeans. She adjusts her bra, pulls her sweatshirt down, and starts up the stairs. Nines watches her blue hips sway and reminds himself to breathe.

"'Night, Molly." Her voice holds the innocence of a sixteen-year-old breaking curfew for the first time. He watches her disappear around the corner to her room, his loins full of the warm heaviness he hasn't experienced since high school.

Thirteen

He checks all the locks again and tries to kill the roaring in his ears. He can still feel Beth's body against him, and her taste fills his mouth. His heartbeat pounds between his legs, and he knows he's just narrowly avoided the stupidest mistake he's made since that drunk killed Erin. But it doesn't feel like a mistake.

When he closes his eyes, he can still see Beth's pale blonde hair under the lamp at the end of the couch, still see that sweatshirt rising and falling when she breathes. The hospital told her he brought her back to life, and now she's writing again, about him, or them. He wonders what she was saying when he looked in on her last night.

"Oh, yes, baby." Remembering her voice makes him sweat, even on a night that would give a polar bear chills. He remembers the way her skin ripples when he touches her, the way her tongue tastes against his, and that voice. Oh, God, that voice.

The wind howls around the house, drowning out everything but Beth's moans in his head.

He walks through the whole downstairs again, checking the doors and windows but really trying to leave Beth Shepard's voice in Jim Leslie's cellar. Or by the back door, in the kitchen, or on the stairs. Erin's voice seems to float out of the fireplace and harmonize with that keening wind.

"It's okay, honey, I'm okay. It doesn't hurt here. We

don't hurt, but we miss you. I'm sorry I'm not there to make you happy, but I'll wait forever for you."

He sinks to the couch. When he closes his eyes, he can visualize Erin standing in front of the bricks, her eyes level with the clock on the mantel. Next to her, he sees a taller woman, though, with glowing champagne hair and riveting blue eyes. Her moans are several notes lower than Erin's words, and when they blend, their harmony pulls him in two directions at once.

He shakes his head to drive the vision away. Beth Shepard is a client. You don't sleep with a client. It's unprofessional, and it's dangerous, but he hasn't been with a woman since Erin died. The last week has forced him to remember that every time he looks at Beth.

Through the slit in the drapes, he watches snow float down to halo a street light, big fluffy flakes covering everything so thick that he can scarcely make out the park across the street. An Eskimo would think twice about being out in this weather, even to go up the hill to the emergency room.

Back on the couch, he picks up *Love in Maine* again, but the words aren't Beth's voice. Why didn't he notice that before? They aren't Erin's voice either, just funny marks on paper, and he drops the book back on the coffee table.

Beth's wine glass stands there, too, curves like her hips, dark red dregs in the bottom, two shades darker than the lips he tasted half an hour ago. He takes it to the kitchen, splashes detergent, runs hot water, and scrubs like Lady Macbeth trying to sterilize the scene of the crime. From behind the refrigerator door, a half bottle of Merlot talks dirty to him.

It's after midnight, so today's February 20th. On
Saturday, the 24th, he'll be three years without a drink. The
light over the sink throws shadows that make the kitchen as
threadbare as a Dickens novel, and he feels his hands
shaking. That bottle is only six feet away, and he wants it
almost as badly as he wanted Beth Shepard on the stairs.

He manages to dry the glass without dropping it,
running the dish towel over those seductive curves until the
fabric squeaks against the glass. He puts it back in the
cupboard and his cell phone chirps.

"Hello?" He hears breathing at the other end, then the
voice slides slowly into his ear.

"Greg."

It's Beth Shepard.

Beth turns off her laptop, takes out her contacts, and slides
her big T-shirt over her head. The cold sheets give her
goose bumps, and the wind whistles through the branches
outside her window. Without her glasses, even the darkness
is fuzzy. She only knows there's a ceiling above her
because snow isn't falling on the bed. Even with the light
on, she wouldn't know where it was.

Her lips still tingle from Greg Nines's kiss. Her nipples
still feel hot from his tongue, and between her legs …

She closes her eyes, but all she can think of is how he
set her on fire. She felt the difference in him when they
met—was that a whole week ago?—and she latched onto
his pain like radar. Do hurt people attract each other like
alcoholics? All she knows is that by the time Jim guided
him around the house, she was studying how he walked and
how he stood and how she felt when he looked at her. The

night they helped Jim in the kitchen was the most fun she'd had in years.

Why did she tell him about her rape? She's never told anyone before. She still believes she asked for it, but he says no, and his eyes make her want to believe him. She wants to help him, too. No, that's not true, she wants to hold him, and she wants him to hold her.

Only a few hours ago, that same icy terror tried to choke her, but he held her and promised he'd take care of her. She remembers the heat rushing through her chest and remembers what she told him. "I want you to touch me again."

If Molly hadn't come out that damn door, she would have torn his clothes off and ridden him right on the bottom step. Christ, what if Molly had caught them?

She wants him in her bed, and that's crazy, especially with Molly and Jim here. Maybe if he finds the guy who wants to kill her, maybe if he's still interested after that, they can get together.

Maybe if he can forget his dead wife.

Oh, God. He's still mourning the woman who was carrying his baby when a drunk rammed her car. He beat the guy up and turned into a drunk himself and killed someone else and got canned. It all goes back to the woman he loved so much, the woman Beth is telling herself she can replace like one of Jim's happily-ever-after heroines.

Where is he now? Is he in bed, or is he on the couch, or is he in the kitchen checking the back door? Or is he in the basement cutting his throat with one of Jim's tools?

Whoa, girlfriend, she tells herself. *Let's not get crazy. Remember, he touched your boobs yesterday and didn't go nuts. Or is that part of the romance fantasy, too? You're*

*standing in for a romance writer, so you're a major babe, a
bodice ripper heroine, right?*

*Who are you kidding? You're a basket case who led this man
on because he saved your life yesterday — which is his job, by the
way — and now you're in bed hot and bothered, and he's probably
downstairs snickering at the sex scenes in Jim's first book.*

God, she wants him so much she's watching porn
flicks on her eyelids.

She doesn't dare go downstairs in her T-shirt. She's not
wearing anything under it, and he might misunderstand.

*Misunderstand? Exactly what do you want, Beth? Do you want
him to be okay, or do you want him to make love to you, or
what? Jesus, make a decision here, all right?*

She finds her glasses in the drawer and brings her
phone back to the bed. Maybe he'll come in and sit in the
chair and watch over her like he did yesterday afternoon.
Maybe she can make him hold her again. Maybe if she
touches him …

His phone rings twice. Three times.

"Hello?"

"Greg."

"Beth. What's the matter? Are you all right?"

All right. Outside, the wind howls like a bereft
banshee, and sleet peppers the roof like buckshot, and
someone wants to kill her. But she's safe and warm in bed
with the man who promised to protect her on the other end
of her phone. Only minutes ago, he kissed her and gave her
the first orgasm she's had since she was old enough to vote.

Only minutes ago. It already feels ancient, her pulse
slowing down, the heat inside fading like it never even
happened. Damn Molly for coming out of her room.

"Shit," she whispers.

"Beth?" She feels his concern and pictures him dashing up the stairs, muscles rippling and eyes flashing like one of Jim's fantasy hunks. But Greg Nines looks better than all of those cartoons put together and he's real. She knows he is. She can still taste him.

"Greg. When you kissed me, when you touched me, I'd forgotten how good it could be, and now I want it,you, again. I'm lying here so hot, I'll bet the snow's melting on the roof above me. I want you so much it's making me crazy. It scares me."

The pause is so long, she's afraid he's hung up on her.

"It's going to be all right, Beth. I'm going to take care of you."

She hears him reword what she said and wants to interpret it in more ways than he can probably imagine. Right now, they all sound pretty damn good. She closes her eyes and lets his voice wrap around her.

"Where are you now, Greg? Are you still down on the couch reading Jim's book?"

"Uh-huh. I can tell you didn't write it, though. The words don't feel right."

"How do you mean?" His voice slides into her ear so she can believe he's there with her.

"I don't know quite how to say it. I'm not a writer. Svet probably knows the words. Terms. Whatever."

Oh, please don't bring the Ice Queen into this.

"It just doesn't feel real."

"It isn't real, Greg. They're just stories. Jim made them up."

Just like I'm making up this fantastic fairy tale love between you and me, she thinks. *How pathetic is that?*

Then another voice answers, *how pathetic do you want to be?*

"Yeah. Well."

If she goes downstairs to sit with him on the couch, they can throw a log on the fire and tell ghost stories like when they were kids at summer camp, if he went to camp. Or love stories. Or maybe she could just peel off her pink tee shirt and climb onto him. *Whoa, Beth.*

"You should go to sleep, Beth. You need your rest."

"You should get some rest too, Greg."

"I will. In a while."

"Do you really think someone will try to get in here tonight?"

"I don't think even an SUV could navigate in this mess. Someone on foot would last about two minutes."

"So why not come up here to bed?" She hears the slip. "Your bed."

The pause before he replies feels long enough for her to file her nails.

"I'll stay down here a little longer."

"You said you think it's safe."

"Down here, yes."

Damn. She feels desire run his horny fingers down across her stomach.

"You really should go to sleep, Erin. Listen to the storm outside. It's like rain on a roof in the summertime, soothing."

Erin. A wrecking ball slams into Beth's chest, and she bites her lip so hard she tastes blood.

"It'll keep the bad guys away, too. It's helping us."

Her eyes burn, and she feels six years old again.

"Greg." She tells herself she's not going to cry, she's not going to cry, she's not going to cry.

"Lie back and close your eyes." She realizes he doesn't even know he said it. "It's going to be fine."

"Talk to me, Greg. Please. I need to hear your voice. I love your voice."

"Promise you'll sleep?"

Promise you won't call me Erin again. "Yes."

She feels him take that in, too. He actually listens to her. That's scary, too.

She listens to the soft murmur while she slides her glasses into the drawer and tucks the comforter under her chin, the glow from her phone just enough so she can see the purple blur keeping her warm like his voice in her ear. It sounds like a daddy voice, big, soft, and safe. Very safe.

She stops listening to the words and lets the timbre and rhythm fill her like warm milk. When her eyes feel heavy, she puts her phone on the nightstand and turns off the light. His voice has made her body so loose, someone could pour her into a bowl.

She tells herself he called her Erin because he loves her as much as he loved his dead wife. *Yeah, right.*

She closes her eyes.

Nines hears the silence in his ear and realizes that Beth has turned her phone off. He turns toward the stairs and listens, but nobody's stirring. Good. Another five minutes of that honey voice, and he would have mounted those stairs, walked through Beth's door, and climbed into her bed.

He switches off the lamp behind the couch. Then he licks his fingers and gives the hot bulb a half turn. He loosens the bulbs in the dining room chandelier and the

bulb over the sink in the kitchen, too. Beth's voice still
vibrates in his ears while he lays a chair on its side two
steps inside the back door.

"Why don't you come up here to bed?"

The refrigerator whirs in the dark behind him, and he
jumps. When he recognizes the sound, he relaxes again and
makes his way through the darkness back to the living
room.

If he can resist Beth Shepard, a bottle of wine in the
fridge is nothing, even less than a snowflake in the storm
outside.

He considers finishing *Love in Maine* but decides to
take advantage of the storm that allows him to sleep while
he knows it's safe.

He visualizes Binding Agreements in Chester again and
selects his best vantage point while Beth—he has to
remember to call her Tally in public—reads to her fans
Wednesday. The shop is small enough so he can see the
whole room if he hovers near the window across from those
stairs. Facing the audience means he can gauge their
reactions, too. He doesn't expect trouble, though. Whoever
their man is, he prefers stealth and booby traps to a frontal
assault, and he won't be able to tamper with the wiring in a
store that's been open and occupied for the previous eight
hours.

Nines counts his steps to the bottom of the stairs. This
is where he and Beth kissed. His hand touches the wall
where she leaned back against it while he pulled down her
jeans. He still sees her body, ripe as an orchard when she
opened herself to him. The memory is so powerful he
nearly tumbles ass-over-teakettle back down the stairs.

At the top of the stairs, he sees no light under Beth's door. Molly's and Jim's rooms seem to be dark, too. It's after midnight, so all good little writers lie snug in their beds while visions of best sellers dance in their heads.

The wind is dying down, but that's the only sound in the entire house. No clack of laptop keys drifts from Beth's room. Maybe she really has gone to sleep. Nines lingers by her door longer than he needs to before he forces himself to move on to his own room. When he peers out the window, snowflakes the size of golf balls float down around the street lights.

He undresses, tucks his Ruger under the pillow, and leaves his cell phone open on the night stand, the screen pointing away from him. He leaves his door six inches ajar so he can hear any noise outside before he slides under the blankets. He stares through the gloom toward Beth's door and says the words he resisted all the time they wrapped their voices around each other on their phones.

"I love you."

Finally, he closes his eyes.

Fourteen

When Nines walks into the kitchen the next morning, Molly already has coffee ready and pulls a mug out of the cupboard for him.

"It looks like we've got about six or seven inches," he comments.

"At least the sun's out now," she says. She's wearing a brown turtleneck and cords with functional boots.

He pours coffee. When he turns around, her eyes look colder than the ice coating the driveway.

"Are you fucking Tally?"

Something wrenches in his chest. "Her name is Beth."

"We're paying you seven-fifty a day to protect Tally." Molly rinses her own cup in the sink. "For that kind of money, you might want to remember the distinction." She yanks her coat from the hook and vanishes through the back door.

She's right, of course. She must have heard them last night. She's pissed off, and she's going to be a problem if he doesn't stay on the white squares. A lot of people looked the other way to get him a PI license and a pistol permit less than six months after he'd shot a man while drunk.

Powdery snow flies when he shovels, but the bottom two inches is ice, just as Jim Leslie predicted. The temperature dropped so quickly that the water changed over with no slushy mid-layer, and it's going to take a flame-thrower to clean the walks completely. Molly has shoveled a path to her car and brushed the snow off, but now she's chipping at the ice around her door handle. He finds a charcoal lighter in the garage and goes to help her.

"You said a relationship went bad in Massachusetts," he says. "That's why you came down here."

"Uh huh." Her cheeks glow with the exertion, and her eyes hide behind her fogged-up lenses. Cold becomes her.

"You could just pick up like that?"

"I was hurt very badly, Mr. Nines." A bowling ball seems more vulnerable than Molly Pitkin. "I lost someone dear, and I was really fucked up."

"I suppose if your business is on line, you can do it anywhere."

She runs the charcoal lighter up the edge of the door and the ice slowly congeals. "Right now, I have five accounts that aren't even in New England."

"How did you and Trish pick Beth Shepard to stand in for Jim?"

Molly brushes her short hair off her forehead. "Isadora Press and Trish both liked me for the web design, and I told them I'd need pictures of Taliesyn Holroyd. That's when Trish told me he was really a man. We put our heads together and came up with a wish list of what a double should look like. We agreed that she should be young and attractive."

"Why didn't you do it yourself?"

Molly's eyes narrow suspiciously. "I'm going to take that as a compliment. Thank you, but I'm not good with people, and I don't know enough about writing to handle questions. A few days after we talked, I saw this beautiful woman at Westfarms mall. I think she was coming out of Victoria's Secret."

"Beth?"

"Uh huh. I dashed across the center court and asked her what her name was, and did she need money, and could she meet someone. She must have thought I was coming on to her. She sort of backed up, and I slowed down when I realized I was scaring her."

"Then you found out she really was a writer."

"How perfect was that? It was like a sign from the gods." Molly's door handle moves a little when she throws her weight to it. "She said she was between temp jobs, so I brought her over to meet Jim and Trish, and they hit it off like they'd been friends for years."

"But she stayed separate at first, right? You just took pictures and stuck them on the site."

"She didn't need to be with Jim until Trish and I persuaded the publishers to kick in some bucks for the tour. Then we all realized she had to know the books cold. She moved in here about a month ago."

"Nobody was worried about hanky-panky with her and Jim."

Molly's eyes flicker. "Jim comes across like a kid with a new train set. Until your little Russian friend came over, I wasn't sure he had a Y-chromosome."

Okay, so he's not imagining anything. Svet lights Jim's oven. "The police who checked out the house when the alarm went off last week thought he was gay."

"I wasn't sure, but he's charming, and he cooks, and Beth seems to have this really weird phobia about men." Molly's drawbridge goes up again. "Except you."

"She had a bad time before," he says. "She's divorced."

"She's beautiful. She could be with some movie star, but if I didn't know she was divorced, I'd think she was still a virgin. Until I heard you two last night. Jesus, have a little class, will you?"

Nines's face feels hot. "I want to find whoever's trying to kill her. It would help if she could come up with more names."

"Shit, Mr. Nines, look at her. Her doing something to someone just doesn't compute, and if she did, she'd bust a gut to fix it. I'm surprised she and her ex don't still talk."

"He's remarried."

"Oh. That would explain it." Molly's car door opens in a shower of ice fragments. "So, where do you go from here?"

"I'm going to talk with Svet and my buddy on the New Britain PD, see if they have anything on the cars or the circuit breaker." He watches Molly turn her defroster on and grope in the back seat for her scraper. "Will you be back later?"

"I've got to catch up on my other jobs. I'll be back tomorrow afternoon to take you and Tally down to Chester again." Molly chips at a widening gap in the ice near the center of her windshield. "It's supposed to be warm and sunny the next few days, so maybe this shit will melt."

Nines watches her pull slowly out into the street. New Britain's plowing relies more on the spring thaw than motorists would like, especially in the hilly sections, but Molly maintains a steady pace up Ivy Street to a main thoroughfare that's presumably clearer. When her car vanishes, he cleans the front walk. New Britain has an on-street parking ban during snowstorms, and he can't recognize any strange cars in nearby driveways. He can't see anything but large, white blobs under the snow, anyway.

He stamps the snow off his shoes and finds Beth on the couch. Her hands wrap around a steaming mug, and her eyes grow even bigger when she sees him.

"Are you all right?"

"I'm fine." Actually, he isn't. In a sweatshirt, jeans, and no make-up, she's still the most beautiful woman he's ever seen, and her energy makes him dizzy. He catches himself wondering what color her underwear is today.

"Last night," she says. He can tell she's struggling to find exactly the right words again. "I wanted you to make love to me. That's so new it scared — scares me. I'm sorry."

"Molly heard us."

"Oh, shit." Beth's face turns pink. "That's bad, isn't it?"

"Well, it was pretty indiscreet of me, and unprofessional." Her face flickers, and he puts a finger against her lips. "I'm not sorry last night happened, Beth. Just the circumstances. When this is over ..."

Jim Leslie emerges from the kitchen with a file card in his hand.

"I'm going out in a while," Nines tells them both. "Do you need me to run any errands?"

"I'm getting stir crazy," Beth complains. "Can I go with you?"

"Not a good idea," he tells her. Actually, he'd love to take her back to his condo where they can be alone.

"Okay." Beth sighs, and he has to look away from the husky on her sweatshirt. "Um, I need some solution for my contacts. You can get it at any drugstore you go by."

"I didn't realize you wear contacts, Beth." Leslie's eyebrows drift upward. He hands Nines the file card: bread crumbs, eggs, orange marmalade.

"Yeah, I wear glasses for about one minute when I get out of bed in the morning and again when I'm getting back into bed at night. They're so I can find my way to and from the bathroom."

Nines studies Jim's shopping list.

Svet has her PC and her laptop open, minimized screen icons dotting the bottom of both monitors when she lets Nines in. The normal twenty-minute drive has taken him an hour. He drops his coat on the chair and scratches Arnold's ears.

"I think Daniel Fletcher is not our man." Nines belatedly recognizes Buzz's real name. "He is too busy chasing women around Avon, Simsbury, and Hartford to concern himself with Taliesyn Holroyd, and he has never purchased one of her books. Nor has his illustrious master. I checked their credit cards."

"Library, maybe?"

"Neither has a library card." Svet brushes her hands through her dark hair, and Nines realizes it hangs loose instead of her usual braid. "Fletcher received a year's probation and sixty hours of community service for the assault several years ago. Apparently, both he and the other participant were drinking, and neither remembered who made the original remark to which the other took exception. It involved a woman of some notoriety."

"Hooker?"

"Stripper. The Star Lounge in Hartford, just passing through, as one would say. She has a Web site and many oeuvres in her portfolio, along with a fetching collection of clit rings." Svet smiles slightly. "I approve of women who know how to accessorize."

Nines refuses to be distracted. "How about Drew Brennan?"

"I think whoever sent the e-mail deliberately went to West Haven to draw our attention to him. He appears sadder but wiser since divorcing Elizabeth Shepard and has had no communication with her since his last alimony payment in September of 2004."

Svet flicks the mouse, and her PC screen fills with data. "I have also been looking at James on the assumption that our killer is using the writer as a decoy. He has an MALS and CAS from Wesleyan University, taught for twelve years, and won five million dollars in the Connecticut Lottery in 2001. He purchased the house in New Britain soon after that."

"Quit teaching then?"

"At the end of that school year. As a teacher, he knew his subject matter, had high expectations for his students, and wrote a few recommendations for college applications. He occasionally chaperoned an activity but did not sponsor any clubs or coach any teams."

"Any divorces or relationships?" Svet goes motionless again.

"He is an only child, his mother lives in Rhode Island, and his father died of cancer ten years ago. He has dated occasionally, but no serious entanglements."

"Molly told me this morning that Beth moved in with him last month to prep for the tour. Apparently, once they met, she had no problem working with him."

"What is her issue, Grusha?" She looks through him, and he knows she sees something in his face.

"She was raped in college," he says. "She never reported it, but it's why she's still so skittish about men."

"She is not skittish about you, Darling, nor you of her." Svet continues before he can put in his disclaimer. "Do you know the name of the man who raped her?"

"I can ask."

Svet's face never leaves her monitor, but her expression softens. "I was prepared to dislike her. I pictured a shallow, conceited woman used to getting her way because of her beauty."

"She isn't like that at all."

"No, she is delightful and intelligent enough to be afraid of this predator." She faces Nines. "And of you." The floor shifts for an instant, then she continues. "You are attracted to each other." Arnold sits up and yawns.

Nines studies the monitor. "Yes."

"I am not your mother, Grusha. I will not disinherit you if you select a woman I don't like." She turns back to the laptop. "And I like her."

Svet never commented about his relationships until she introduced him to Erin.

"Her webmistress, on the other hand ..."

"She thinks I'm taking advantage of Beth," Nines says.

"Why would she care?"

"At James's house. Beth dislikes me because she thinks you and I are lovers. Please set her straight on that. But Molly Pitkin and I recognized a sameness that is repulsive."

Nines opens his mouth, but Svet continues, an unfamiliar passion flavoring her speech.

"The woman is a joyless automaton. She is what I could become if I no longer enjoyed sexual congress. I doubt that she has ever had a relationship in her life."

"She told me she broke up with someone last summer and moved down here."

"Really? My first guess would be that her appliance's batteries expired."

Nines waits for the room to warm up again. "She could be a lesbian."

"I don't recognize her vibe. She feels devoid of emotions." She taps her fingers on the desk, long fingers, blood-red nails and four rings, like a Gypsy fortune-teller. "If I spent much time with her, my piercings would rust."

Arnold trots toward the kitchen.

"The more we look at this, the more I suspect that the target is Elizabeth Shepard and not really Taliesyn Holroyd. You said her parents are retired?"

"Uh huh. She mentioned last night that her father was a judge in Massachusetts. We joked about how my father was a cop, and hers was a judge, so we should have met years ago."

"Criminal? Probate?"

"I don't know. I'll ask. Oh, and something else. Trivial as hell, but it's the only other thing I know. Beth wears contacts all the time. Without them, she's practically blind."

"I know she sometimes takes Seconal to sleep. Do you know if she has any other medical conditions? Allergies, asthma?"

"I doubt it. They use Jim's fireplace a lot."

Nines has been away from the house less than three hours, and he wants to hear Beth's voice again. "Do you have any of the magazines with her stories in them? I'd like to read them."

"They are very different from how James writes."

"We talked about her touch and taste." He almost has to sit down when the words penetrate. "I don't want to hurt her, Svet."

"Someone else already has. Get his name."

She watches Arnold hop back onto the couch. "Jerry called me last night. He asked the woman to marry him, and she said yes. He deserves to be happy."

"You deserve to be happy, too, Svet."

"I have always been too intelligent to believe in the validity of emotions, even during moments of physical intimacy."

"I don't think intelligence has anything to do with it," he says. "It just happens."

"I have never had the courage to give up control, Darling. This is certainly a first."

The verb tenses finally register. "Whoa. Are you saying …?"

"Jerry has found someone, so I must grow up and stop making the rules. Until Sunday, it has always been about climax."

When she looks at him again, he sags to the couch next to the cat. "You and Jim?"

Her eyes juggle happiness and something else he decides is fright. "James is not gay."

"How do you know?" It's like discovering that parallel lines really do intersect.

"Darling, I am a researcher. I only use primary sources."

At home, Nines empties the fliers, postcards, coupons, and an occasional bill from his mailbox. Most of it goes directly into the wastebasket. His answering machine stares blankly, too. He dumps his clothes into the washer and throws clean ones into his overnight bag.

He wonders if he wants to take an extra gun back to Jim Leslie's. His original plan to stash them in different places throughout the house seems less practical now that he knows the layout. Only the central area near the stairs is logical, and there's no cover there. Besides, his adversary prefers poison and electricity, not a frontal assault.

Jim's alarm is a mixed blessing. It warns that someone has breached the perimeter, but it won't stop them. Nines can easily fit through the windows facing the front porch, and there's still that vulnerable basement, which the guy has already entered once.

He studies the Sig Sauer in its case, then decides not to take it. It holds ten rounds instead of the five in his Ruger .357, but a semi-automatic takes an extra second to rack the slide, and that second could be crucial. Besides, he can't hide the larger gun under his coat.

He changes the sheets on his bed and wonders if he should bring Beth back here for safety tonight. Who is he kidding? He wants to see her body naked under his, hear her moans when he touches her. After so much time away from a woman, he may not be able to satisfy her.

That idea leaps from behind him, and he actually straightens up and stares at the light reflecting off a glass rectangle. It's Erin with her eyes glowing and her fingers locked around his arm. She wears her wedding gown and holds her corsage, her veil a halo above her glistening eyes.

He looks tall and stiff, awkward in a tux, but the boyish grin that he still had then tries to keep up with hers.

I told Svet the night after she introduced us that I was going to marry you, she said when he finally proposed six months after they met. I knew the second I felt your eyes on me that I was never going to be sad again.

Her parents loved him. He thought they deserved the Nobel Prize for giving the world Erin, with her soap-bubble laugh and her dancing eyes. The first time he kissed her, he had to fight to keep his feet on the ground. The first time they made love, it was like he'd never been with a woman before. The next morning, she climbed into one of his old T-shirts that fell below her knees and made coffee and brought it back to his bed on a tray.

I don't want to leave this bed again until you have to go to work, she told him, and they didn't.

When she told him they were going to have a baby, they lay awake all that night crying a little and kissing a lot while he ran his fingers over her small nose and her still flat belly. When he came home the next day, she showed him two books of baby names, and they tossed possibilities back and forth like popcorn at the movies until they agreed that if they had a girl, she would be Alicia Svetlana, after her grandmother and the woman who brought them together. A boy would be Edward Gregory after his father and mother. They wanted two more children after that one.

They didn't want an ultrasound, because they didn't care if the baby was a boy or a girl. Secretly, Nines hoped for a girl. The world needed all the wonderful women like Erin that it could hold. When he told her that, she nibbled on his ear lobe the way she did to drive him crazy.

*I don't ever want you to be unhappy, she said. If there's
something wrong, promise you'll tell me so we can fix it.*

You tell me, too.

Three months later, a drunk ran a traffic light.

What does he really know about Beth Shepard? She's
lovely and smart and empathetic, but she's a liar, too. She
isn't really writing the Taliesyn Holroyd novels, and she's
never told anyone except him about her rape.

Then he remembers how he feels when he pulls her
close and smells her hair. She told him because she trusts
him and wants him to protect him, and she wants to be
with him, too. That's not safe yet.

Erin's smile looks out at him from the gold frame.

It's never safe.

"I still love you, Erin," he whispers. The angel in the
picture seems to hear him. "But it's not enough anymore."
The more he stares at her, the farther away she seems to
be.

"I'm coming up on three years sober." Erin's smile
seems brighter, but it's like she's in a frame by herself now.

"Svet likes her, too." He's not sure why he says that.

He picks up Erin's picture from where she's watched
over him for four years and carries it downstairs to the
desk drawer.

Fifteen

Beth feels like she needs MapQuest to find her way back to the apartment she left in Amy's care a month before. Her cat tolerates Amy about as well as he tolerates anyone who fills his food dish and empties his litter box. Amy takes in the mail, too, which Beth hasn't picked up since that asshole tried to run her down ten days ago. The Visa's due, and she still has two queries out on a story.

Even under the snow, West Hartford projects old white collar money instead of old factory money like New Britain. Beth cruises through the center with its funky shops and funkier restaurants, including Fitzgerald's, where Greg Nines drank ginger ale, and turns down a side street with huge trees and driveways wide enough so neighbors can't see what you're having for dinner. Another turn and she's there. She recognizes Amy's Passat near the dumpster.

She knocks before unlocking the door. Sure, it's her place, but Amy's living there now, and she doesn't want to walk in and find her house sitter giving a boyfriend head on the sofa. Until last night, the idea of interrupting sex wouldn't even occur to her, but now she can't get it out of her mind. She considers writing a first draft when she gets back. Maybe she needs to do more research.

She should have told Greg she was coming over here, but he would have told her to wait until he could escort her. She wants to stay busy, activity burying the knowledge that someone is trying to kill her, even though she's still missing about two hours from Sunday afternoon. Knowing that Greg touched her breasts and locked his mouth on hers during those two hours, she feels like she lost something important.

Amy comes from the kitchen with a carrot stick in her hand. No sound of frantic dressing.

"Hey?" she says. Everything's a question with Amy. "I didn't know you were coming?"

"Me neither," Beth says. "I'm working on a story, but I needed a break. I figured I'd pick up the mail. How are you doing?"

The magazines on the coffee table are different, and an iPod rests on top of them.

"Okay, I guess. I worked all five days last week, two different places, and I'm going to be at some lawyer's office for a week starting tomorrow."

"Fine. Any problems? Heat, anything?" *Anyone try to kill you?*

"No, everything's good. Um, I could've picked up a little if I knew you were coming."

"Don't worry about it." Beth lets Amy put two cups into the microwave, and they have tea, sitting at the dining room table because the kitchen can only accommodate one adult. Amy's hair has blonde streaks Beth doesn't remember. Her bedroom door is closed, and she wishes she could crash here for a day or two. She misses her real bed. She took her own pillow and the comforter, but it isn't the same.

Amy's ring finger sparkles, and Beth realizes that's new. When she looks up again, Amy beams like a tanning lamp.

"Saturday night," she says. "Frank took me to Max Downtown, and we had champagne, and he actually got down on one knee in front of everyone and asked me."

"You told him you'd think about it, right?" Beth feels her arms going around Amy.

"Yeah, for about one nanosecond. Oh, God, Beth, I'm so happy."

"You've held out for the best, Amykins." Beth glances out the window and knows that the world still works. The sun still shines, and people still fall in love, and bills still come in the mail. Amy's joy vibrates her like a tuning fork.

"I knew he was going to ask, just not when. At first, I thought maybe Valentine's Day, but he didn't. We picked up the dress I wore that day, and he actually wanted to buy it for me a month ago, and he paid for it and said it makes me the most beautiful woman in the world, and he wanted me to wear it Saturday, and when he didn't ask Wednesday, I guess that's when I knew it was going to be then, so I was practicing all the ways I could say yes until he picked me up."

Amy doesn't take a breath during her whole speech.

"Maybe do him under the table?" Beth suggests.

"The tablecloths don't reach far enough to hide anyone, and I still think my butt's too big when I bend over."

Beth hugs her again. "When's the date?"

"We haven't set it yet, but I'm hoping in the fall sometime. God, Beth, you've got to be my maid of honor. Or matron. You've been married before. Whichever you want. God, I wish I was beautiful like you. You can wear any color ever and look so good."

"Fall." Beth sips her tea. *This shit will all be over by then, or she'll be dead.* "I'd love to. Thank you. Have you registered anywhere yet?"

"Uh uh, but we're going to Macy's this weekend and maybe Restoration Hardware. You know, in the mall?"

Amy Belanger's joy makes Beth feel like a majorette again, young, pure, and innocent. For an instant, she remembers why she agreed to marry Andrew Brennan, hoping that he would be the knight on the white charger dashing to the rescue. *Some first drafts don't work.*

"I've looked up that Web site," Amy says. "Your pictures look really hot. Do you get lots of e-mails?"

One guy last week said he wanted to kill me.

"The webmaster dumps most of them unless they've got an interesting question. I only see a few every couple of days."

"And the tour dates," Amy says. "That's like so cool pretending to be this writer. What's she really like, some little old lady who never leaves the house?"

"Something like that." *Part of the deal is that nobody finds out the real Taliesyn Holroyd is a man.* Trish, Molly, and Isadora press all insist on that. Beth thought she was going to have to drip blood on the contract and get a brand on her hip to seal the deal. *Her thong wouldn't hide it, though. Fortunately, nobody sees her ass. Except ...*

"Is Greg around?"

"Who?"

Beth feels her face heat up.

"Oh, Rufus. Greg's a character in a story I'm working on."

"He's probably on the bed." Sure enough, Amy pushes open the door, and Beth sees her black and gray tiger curled up by the pillow. He blinks at her placidly and puts his head down again.

"That's all the welcome I get?" Beth realizes that the room smells like Amy now, not like her. "Mom's been gone all this time, and you blink at me and go back to sleep? What a guy thing."

"He's dealing with the separation trauma really well," Amy says. "What's this story about, or can't you tell me yet? I know you don't like to talk them away."

It's about my bodyguard and how I came like an avalanche when he went down on me.

"I don't have it all worked out yet. I'm just working on the character, a man. He's a widower, his wife died in an accident a few years ago and he started drinking." She opens the battered wooden file cabinet she's lugged around since college and finds her contest-winner for *Glimmer Train*, then the ones from *Gettysburg Review*, *Tin House*, *Zoetrope*, and *The New Yorker*. A few of the others are more girly-girl than she wants Greg to read, and it surprises her how much his opinion matters to her. Rejection postcards build callous really quickly. If they don't, you go into retail.

"There's a woman, right? You write about women." Amy takes her cup back to the kitchen and returns with another carrot stick. "You want more tea?"

"No, thanks. I haven't worked the woman out yet. She keeps changing. Sometimes she's a lot like me, then it feels too … I don't know."

Beth's never had a real home since she left for college, a series of furnished rooms before the apartment with Drew, then more apartments later. Their anonymity blends into a non-life. All she has at Jim's are the Tally costumes and jeans, her iPod and laptop. She wants a real home with a kitchen she can move around in, a bedroom with her own furniture, a warm blue comforter, and Greg's smell on the pillow after they make love. She catches herself and focuses on Amy's words again.

"You meet the man, or did he just come to you?"

Almost on me, Beth thinks. "Um, he's based on a man I met. When I go to these readings, they've got someone doing security. You know, directing traffic when I'm signing autographs, stuff like that."

"You get that many people?" Amy looks impressed. "I wanted to come to the one last week, but I didn't want to make you nervous. You have any more around here?"

"Chester tomorrow, R. J. Julia in Madison next week. Bishop's Corner, too," Beth says. "I don't remember the dates. They're on the Web site, though."

"Bishop's Corner. I can swing by there if it's after work." She looks at Beth more closely. "You look a little tired. Maybe you're staring at a computer screen too much."

"I'm writing a lot," Beth agrees. "You look great. Frank's definitely good for you."

Amy chews on her lip, and the carrot looks like a cigar stub. "You're not telling me something, Beth. Is the writing really going okay? This tour thing probably really messed up your rhythms, didn't it? Maybe you should get to the gym a little. Or a massage? I can call Sara. She can get you in, I'll bet."

"No, I'm fine. I was blocked for a while when I moved, but I've worked through it. I needed a break, so I figured

I'd come over today, grab the mail, see Rufe, I didn't think you'd be home, but you are, and we're talking, and that's …" She can't stop. She finally clamps her teeth together and feels Amy's eyes on her.

"Beth?"

"Amy, you get any weird phone calls in the last couple of weeks or see any strange cars in the lot or anything?"

Amy stops chewing her carrot. "Beth, are you in trouble?"

"No, of course not. Who'd want to kill me?" *Shit, she didn't mean to say that. Now Amy's really looking worried.* "Uh, that's not what I …"

"Jesus, Beth. What's going on?"

She feels her eyes tearing up and that animal racing in her chest again. "Someone tried to kill me."

Amy's hands clamp onto hers. "Oh, my God. Who is it?"

"I don't know. That's why I've got the security. He's staying at Tally's place with us."

"Why would anyone want to kill you?" Amy's eyes flicker to the deadbolt.

"I—we—don't know. We don't even know if he's after me or after the real Taliesyn. We've both almost been killed, and the cops don't have any ideas. Greg's trying to take care of me, but he doesn't have any leads either."

Amy pulls her to her feet and hugs her. Since Amy's only five-five, the wrong person gets most of the benefit, Beth's tears dripping onto her shoulder.

"Oh, my God, Beth. Is the guy following you?"

"I took a few wrong turns here, I haven't been out alone in a week, and I was going crazy. I had to be by myself and come back here for a few minutes. I feel like I'm in some weird alternate universe. I fucking hate it."

She realizes for the first time that it's true. She can't write, she has to live somewhere else, she can't even have her cat with her because Jim's allergic, and she isn't supposed to go anywhere without a chaperone. She's given up her whole life, and now someone wants to take it away from her anyway. The world sucks.

"You can quit," Amy says softly. Beth loves the way Amy hugs her and knows she's going to be a terrific mom.

"Yeah," she says, "but now we're not sure if the guy wants the writer or me. If it's really me, it doesn't matter if I quit or not."

"Shit, Beth." When she feels better, Amy walks her down to the parking lot with her cell in her hand. "Beth?" she says. "If I were you, I'd bag this writer and look for a serious boyfriend?"

Beth takes about fifty extra turns, and nobody seems to be following her. Then she cuts over to I-84, to 72, then the downtown New Britain exit. She's never gone this way before, but now she's learning to be careful. Fear does that.

Three golf balls surround the practice cup on Art's worn carpet. Nines never figured out the appeal of golf. If you want to walk a couple of miles, you don't need to carry an overpriced bag of sticks with you to make it real exercise, do you?

"The cars were clean," Art tells him. "There were smudges on both hoods and a couple of fresh scratches on the girl's battery but no prints."

"If this is the same guy that diddled the circuit breakers, he knows his stuff," Nines says. "It wouldn't have taken him long."

"No." Art taps the balls back to the other side of his desk and takes his putting stance again. He looks like a grizzly bear with a matchstick.

"He could have done it any time," Nines thinks out loud. "Hell, neither of them have driven in days. He could have even set it up when he did the basement."

"But he was around to see you leave," Art points out. "He went in again to clean up while you had the girl at the hospital."

"I know." *So many businesses in the area, nobody would notice a strange car. The list of cars and plates I made a few days ago is useless.*

"I've even checked with realtors and landlords," Art says. "Nobody's bought a house in the area since before Christmas, and nobody worth checking out has moved into any of those apartments on West Main. Nobody within a good mile and a half of Ivy Street."

"What a shock." Nines feels the futility making him crazy.

"You have any more possibilities?" Art retrieves the balls and takes his stance again. "The girl's ex-husband has not been in the area, and this still does not sound to me like Lexington."

"I don't think his buddy Fletcher has the patience, either. I've got Svet looking at Jim Leslie, too."

Nines hopes Jim has the rough draft of the next book far enough along so Beth can finish it, different style or not. If Svet really has the hots for him, she'll turn him to a pile of ashes in under a week.

"If Lexington is clear, perhaps the boy with the weird eyes?"

"There's solid paper on the real father," Nines says. "He died in New Hampshire when the kid was still an infant. His mother was up there then, so how did she and Lexington ever meet? I don't even see why the story has legs."

"If the woman had actually grabbed the door handle, she would be dead now," Art says. "She can only get lucky so often."

"What worries me is since the guy's missed when he's not there, he may try something more direct pretty soon."

"I don't know." Art still hasn't sunk a putt. "It does not sound like his style, and maybe that hit-and-run in West Hartford really is not connected."

"Maybe not. He can't keep coming back into the neighborhood forever, though. Somebody's going to spot him. All he has to do is look at the Web site and know Tally's going to be at a lot of bookstores in the next two weeks. I can only watch so many people and ask Molly if she'd mind sitting in the car so the guy can't fiddle with it again."

"Bag the signings."

"I don't think so. The last book was her first big seller, and both her publisher and agent want to ride it for all they can. They cancel, she's yesterday's pizza."

"Let her take off her clothes for one of the skin mags. Put a naked photo on the Web site. Guys will buy the mag, and maybe their girlfriends or wives can buy the books."

"You think like an agent, Art." Nines remembers Beth Shepard in that little pink thong. "Or a high-class pimp."

"We are a high-class outfit."

Nines remembers the itinerary. "She's going out of state in March. We're hitting the Southwest, then the West Coast. Be gone for about three weeks."

"Maybe this asshole will lose interest."

"Or maybe it means he's got to work fast."

"How long will you be with the woman?"

"I don't know how much longer they'll be willing to pay me." The thought of Beth thousands of miles away makes his stomach clench. "There's a good chance they won't want to send me along with her."

"You think he will try something at the airport?"

"Too much security. I think he's running out of time."

Art shoves the golf balls into the corner and stands his putter next to them.

"That means you are, too."

Nobody's bothered to leave a message at Nines's office. He flips through the mail, writes two checks, and realizes he has to buy Jim's groceries and Beth's contact lens solution before he goes back. He dials Svet again, and her voicemail picks up. She recognizes his voice and cuts in.

"Grusha. There are three Judge Shepards in Massachusetts. Find out which one is Elizabeth's father, can you?"

"I'm going back in an hour or so. I'll call you."

"Good. And see if Elizabeth can recall the name of the man who violated her in college, unless you have a better idea."

"No," he admits. His results with Art Tomasiewicz leave her underwhelmed.

"This man is very clever."

"That means this whole thing has logic to it," he says. "All we have to do is find the reason. You're sure Jim's not the target."

"Not as himself. I think less and less that the book is an issue. Tomorrow, perhaps we can interview him and Elizabeth together and find something. I will come over."

"Are you packing a bag?" he asks innocently.

"I travel light, darling."

"You really like Jim, don't you?"

"Like. Such an innocuous word. Yes, I do. I need to let go of the past."

"Maybe we all do."

"That has layers, Grusha."

Beth Shepard is less than ten miles away, and he can see her face when he stares out the window at the melting snow and ice. "I need to pick up a few things and go over there again. Tally's got another signing down in Chester tomorrow. I want to be rested."

"Sleep can be very therapeutic." Svet adds no punchline.

Sixteen

That upstairs nook at Binding Agreements gives Beth room to pace, and she's making the most of it, Trish and Molly fussing over her and Greg sitting where he can see anyone coming up the stairs. Molly prepped her stuff on that ledge by the bay window twenty minutes ago, and Kevin probably won't take his eyes off it until she sweeps down the stairs. She wonders if the store has a sound system that can play a trumpet fanfare, or maybe her high school's fight song. She wishes she still had those cool white boots with the tassels for her majorette routine, but she doesn't have a baton, either. Besides, the ceiling's too low.

She sips tea and locks her mind on becoming Literary Barbie. She's wearing those same leather boots she wore to Greg Nines's office, so she's six feet tall, and the leather skirt and crimson blouse match the poster downstairs. She's wearing her lucky underwear, too, the pink nothings Greg saw Monday night, but that's her own little secret. She catches herself playing with the gold chain that falls to her breasts.

"Fifteen minutes," Trish says. She's counted down every minute since they came up here, so Beth knows she'll hear it fourteen more times. Her fingers move to the Tally ring.

"Isn't five-thirty an odd time?" Greg asks. "I would have expected seven-thirty or eight. This feels like it'll cut into people's suppertime."

Molly shakes her head. "A book club usually meets here at eight on Wednesdays anyway." She wears a dark sweater and slacks so nobody will notice her shooting pictures while Beth fills the spotlight.

"Besides," she adds, "they figure people will buy Tally's books and check them out while she's signing autographs. They've got eighty-four people signed up for this, and most of them have reserved a copy of *Love Insane*."

"That doesn't suck," Trish says. She's starting to fidget, and Beth can feel it getting to her, too.

"Trish," she says. "You look like you need a cigarette."

"I'm out," Trish says. "I forgot to get more on the way down."

"I can run out and get you some," Molly offers, and Beth flashes her a silent thank you. "There's got to be a drugstore around here somewhere. Why don't we go down and find out where it is?"

Molly leads Trish out of sight, and Beth feels Greg looking at her. "You're going to be great," he tells her. His voice feels full of smile, but she knows he's wearing a gun.

"I'm going to go hotter than I did at Borders," she says, "unless the crowd has lots of white hair." She's been thinking a lot more about sex scenes since the other night.

"Maybe they'd like it anyway," Greg says, "get the blood flowing a little." He looks down the stairs. "When I go down, I'll stay at the bottom of the stairs and check people out, then I'll move over to the window when you come down. Kevin'll be at the bottom to run interference for you, too. Give him a smile. I think he's in love."

Beth practices her smile. "I don't want him to wet on the rug."

"Good point." Greg chuckles, and it feels like hot cocoa on a winter night.

Trish appears and looks at her watch again. "Four minutes."

"No cigarettes?" Beth asks. She was hoping Trish would stay the heck down there. Her boots feel a hundred pounds each, and her hands are getting cold. She puts her empty teacup back on the counter. Does she have time to pee again before they start?

"There's a CVS three blocks down the street," Trish says. "Molly's on her way."

Beth flutters her hands to get the blood flowing. Where's the band? She needs to hear the drum major's whistle. *C'mon, team.*

"You look terrific," Greg says. He looks like the center fielder he used to be, ready to take a bat and move to home plate. He disappears down the steps, and Beth wonders how many home runs he hit.

Then she hears a murmur from below that she recognizes as Kevin the Golden Retriever summarizing the lies from the Web site. Trish leaps to her feet, and Beth moves behind her down the steps, suddenly steep and narrow, into a room full of people in windbreakers and coats and an occasional ski cap. The colors remind her of a child's quilt. Greg parts them gently but firmly on his way to the window. His shoulders are loose, and his head turns easily, but she counts steps, left, right, left, right, and feels the Tally smile stretching her face. Polite applause washes over her, and a woman to her right says "Oh, she's even more beautiful than her picture."

Yeah, I'm taller than Jim, too.

Kevin moves toward the cash registers, and all the clerks in their perky cardigan vests clap, too. Greg moves between the window and the door. The dark window reflects an Amazon in red with almost white hair tumbling over her shoulders. She gets bigger and bigger, and Beth realizes with a shock that it's her. The lights eat her up, and the people are still clapping when she eases behind the lectern. Her copy of *Love Insane* lies ready with the bookmarks she put in it earlier: green for the description scene, blue for the character stuff, then two bright pink slips for hot sex. If the crowd doesn't feel right after the first one, she's got another mark for more character stuff, yellow in case she chickens out.

"Thank you very much," she says. She can feel the love filling the room and eighty pairs of eyes watching her sip the cup of water Kevin's set by the book. She draws air into her diaphragm and finds the green mark.

A car backfires outside. Glass shatters, and cold swarms over her. Something fluffs her hair, and she feels a prick under her ear. Greg Nines wraps his arms around her and pulls her down, rolling so he takes the impact then flipping on top of her and driving the air from her chest. People scream and drop to the floor, then Greg's hand is warm on her cheek.

"Are you all right?"

"Yes, I'm—" He's already on his feet and picking his way through the pile of listeners toward the door. His hand reaches behind his back and reappears with what she has time to see is a gun before he disappears through the entrance of Binding Agreements and leaps into the darkness outside.

Red taillights disappear around a corner two blocks down and a woman trots toward Nines with something in her hand. When she sees him, she speeds up. Short, dark hair, but he can't make out her face. Erin? But Erin's ... He centers his gun on her chest, and she stops dead with her hands over her head.

"No! It's me, Molly." *Jesus!* He lowers his gun, and his eyes sweep the street. Nobody else in sight. Molly comes closer, and he sees that the object in her hand is a cell phone. Sweat pops out all over his body. *Christ, he almost shot Molly Pitkin.*

"I saw them," she pants. "That car, I didn't get a good look, but I've already called 911." When she gets closer, her eyes are wide behind her lenses.

"Them?" he says.

"I'm not sure, but the driver would be on the other side of the car, wouldn't he? They just slowed down by the store and fired. Is Beth ...?"

"She's okay," he tells her. "How good a look did you get at the car?"

"It's a blue compact. I wasn't paying attention until they shot. I think a Connecticut license."

She steps back to the end of the alley and picks up a plastic bag with a CVS logo. "Trish's friggin' cigarettes. If service were better, I'd have been right in front of the bookstore again. I could have gotten a better look."

"And maybe been shot, too." Nines slides his gun back into the holster and feels his adrenaline rush fade.

"Oh, sweet Jesus," Molly says weakly. "Are you sure Beth is okay?"

"Come on," he says. "Let's go make sure."

Beth's chanting her new mantra, "I'm not going to wet myself," and Trish's face is the color of paste when Greg appears in the doorway, Molly a step behind him. He doesn't have flesh hanging from his teeth, which means that the guy got away. Molly throws herself into Beth's chest.

"Omigod, omigod, omigod. I heard the shots and I saw the window break and I ..."

"I'm okay." Her voice doesn't even shake. Well, only a little. Well, not too much. Well, she doesn't throw up. Kevin wobbles over to her, his freckles huge in a pasty face.

"Ms. Holroyd ... I ... Jesus. Are you hurt?" His eyes move to her left ear. She puts a finger to the pinprick and comes away with a drop of blood. Before the floor can lurch, Greg Nines shoves through the others and wraps his arms around her.

"Kevin, get back by the door." It's a cop's listen-to-me-and-do-it-now voice. "Nobody leaves. The police are on their way, and they'll want to talk to everyone. Maybe someone saw the car."

"Car?" *That's right, she heard backfiring. No, that must have been the shots.*

"Keep them here? Are you out of your mind? They're scared shitless. Hell, *I'm* scared shitless."

"Put in for overtime, Kevin, along with the rest of your crew. Break out the coffee and cookies from upstairs, make the time pass." He pulls back Beth's hair and looks at the wound, then lets out a sigh.

"I can still read," Beth says. The words amaze her when they come out of her mouth. Her knees are shaking, and she's still locking her thighs together so she doesn't feel anything trickle down them. Greg's arms still hold her tight, and she realizes again that in these boots she's eye to eye with him. His eyes are the color of Jim's brownies. "I can. It'll calm people down."

"Bullshit," Trish says. "We're getting you out of here, right now."

"Can't do it, Trish," Greg tells her. "We're all witnesses, even if we didn't see anything." He finds a napkin on the window ledge, shakes broken glass off it, and dabs gently at Beth's cut.

"Let me read," Beth says again. *Let me hide in the book so I don't have to think about this shit. I want to go home and tuck the covers over my head, but I don't have a home, and my mom and dad are thousands of miles away.*

"Are you sure you're okay?" Greg says.

"Yeah. Just hold me for a minute, um, 'til I get my breath back?" He seems to think that's a pretty good idea, too. He tells Kevin to move the lectern over to the corner out of the cold draft, and Kevin announces that Taliesyn Holroyd will read until the police come to take everyone's statements. His voice only cracks once.

"I'll sign the books, too," Beth hears herself say. "If people want to leave, I'll autograph the copies they've ordered, and you can hold them until they come back to pick them up."

She hears a murmur fill the room and realizes everyone's hearing the whole conversation. She's so wired she's almost yelling. Two clerks appear with a huge poster they tape over the broken window, and Kevin moves the lectern. Greg's arm guides her over behind it.

For the next forty-five minutes, she just follows the dancing letters in front of her until she feels herself running down and takes questions. She's heard them before and doesn't even come out of default mode. A state trooper appears and starts talking to people one at a time. Some of them disappear through the door when he's done, but even more stay to listen.

I don't use real people, but something I see in a real person may give me an idea. The way he walks, or the way she wears her hair. Anything can do it.

I try to write my first draft as quickly as I can. Then when I go back to it, I've had time to do the research on stuff I didn't know I'd need until I tried to write it. Really bad parts show up better when you've had time away from them. It's like meeting an old boyfriend again and remembering exactly why you broke up with him.

Are there any of those cookies left? Are they as good as Jim's?

A young girl in the back waves her hand. Beth likes the kids because they're not afraid to ask what grown-ups think is stupid.

How old were you when you decided you wanted to be a writer?

"About your age," Beth tells her. She forces a smile that elicits murmurs throughout the crowd. "I knew things weren't always perfect in real life, but I could write stories where they worked out that way."

How do you handle criticism?

"Usually, I cry a lot," she says, "but I have to admit, this town is a little tougher than I'm used to."

When the words sink in, her knees turn to rubber bands.

Two monoliths of books stand on the table. She opens the top one and writes Taliesyn Holroyd on the title page, concentrating on that cool flourish she's practiced. Then again, a few people are asking her to write their names, too. Molly finds a Band-Aid in her purse and presses it over the cut on her neck. About forty people stick around for the free coffee and pastries, but Beth signs every single copy of *Love Insane*, *Love in Maine*, *Love in Vain*, and *Love's A Game* before her hand cramps into an arthritic claw.

You wanted to write stories and sell lots of books, she tells herself. *Now you're doing a book tour and signing your name. Everyone at this store is looking at you like you're Xena the Warrior Princess, and people will tell their friends and neighbors and families about this day. Mom and Dad will be so proud, and Mark, Tina and Tori, too. I'm autographing these books a man wrote, we can't tell anyone the truth, and my own stuff doesn't sell enough copies to fill a wastebasket. What's wrong with this picture? I really, really need to pee.*

She tells the State Trooper that she had her back to the window and didn't see anything. She thought she heard a car backfiring until the window shattered behind her. Then she was on the floor under her big hunky bodyguard. When they finally let her go into the bathroom, she avoids the mirror.

When she comes out, Greg escorts her toward the car with one hand under his coat. Trish and Molly stand at the bottom of the steps in a cloud of cigarette smoke thick enough to carve, butts dotting the pavement around their feet.

"Molly," Beth says. "I didn't know you smoked."

"I just started. It seemed like a good idea."

They pile into Molly's car, Trish riding shotgun—what a joke—and Greg cradling her against his chest.

"I went back to my real place this afternoon," she says softly. "I got some of my short stories, if you still want to read them."

"You did what?" His eyes widen. "Jesus, Beth. You should have told me, and I would have gone with you. Don't you know how dangerous that was?"

"Hey," she says. "Nobody shot at me."

I'm so brave. I'm so tough.

Just as long as Greg Nines holds her.

As soon as they reach the house, Beth dashes upstairs and throws up. When she stops sweating and shaking, she throws the Tally costume across the bed and slips a flannel shirt over a turtleneck and jeans, nothing that needs buttons, because her hands still shake too much to fasten them.

She can feel the tension downstairs but needs to get her stomach settled and her brains back in place before she can talk. She returns to the bathroom, where a pale face stares out of the mirror. She finds some antiseptic cream and puts a dab on the cut below her ear. She tries to brush her hair, too, shaking hands and all, but it doesn't help.

She thinks Molly and Trish mentioned bagging the tour on the drive back, but she was too busy hiding in Greg's chest to pay much attention. The only thing she remembers clearly is his hands stroking her hair and his voice, something in it she hasn't heard before but making her glad he's on her side.

"Nobody is going to hurt you. I'm going to find him. You're not going to have to be afraid, Beth. Never again." Never afraid again. She hasn't stopped being afraid for ten years. It gnaws inside like a small rodent.

She stares at the Tally blouse and skirt splayed across her coverlet. Who knew that playing dress-up could be so dangerous? She closes the door behind her and forces her feet to carry her down the steps to where the others are waiting for her.

Molly and Trish sit in the chairs around the coffee table, Greg next to the open spot at the end of the couch. Jim sits at the other end. Far too close to him, almost in his lap for God's sake, sits Svetlana the Ice Queen.

"Do you want anything, Beth?" Jim asks. "Some wine, maybe?"

She shakes her head. "How did you — ?"

"Grusha called me," Svetlana says. "We must find out who is doing this. He and I together can think of more questions than either of us alone."

"I don't have any answers."

"Yes, you do, or James, but we must find the right question."

"Screw questions," Trish says. "We're canceling the rest of the signings and readings, Beth. It's too dangerous."

"Ms. Pierce," Greg says, "I'm not sure that Beth is the target. Maybe someone thinks she really is Taliesyn Holroyd and wants the writer dead, or maybe he really wants Jim. Or maybe it's Beth herself. Until we can figure that out, I don't know if canceling the tour will change anything."

"The e-mails went to the Web site," Molly says, "not to Beth."

"That may simply mean the sender wanted everyone to see it." When Svetlana speaks to Molly, her voice could chill champagne. Molly's return gaze is equally cold.

"Beth?" Jim says. "It's your call. You're the one who almost got shot."

Beth realizes again what a kind man Jim Leslie is. If she backs out, he loses a truckload of sales, and they have to find someone else to do the Web site if they want to continue. Where would they find someone if the word gets out that she'd be a target? She can stay on as the web girl if they bag the tour, but they'll lose the sales that her appearances will generate. Jim's willing to give it all up to keep her safe, but will she be safe if she quits? What if the guy really does want her instead of Jim? Thinking is hard. All she wants right now is to go away and find her own writing again.

"If we keep going, maybe leaving town for a few weeks will give the police time to find the guy," Greg says. "I can't believe he'd follow us. It would be too obvious."

"I don't know," Molly says. "He's tried four or five times already, and we still don't have the slightest idea who he is. Christ, he could end up sitting next to Beth on the plane before we even knew he was there."

"That is highly unlikely, Ms. Pitkin." The Ice Queen looks across the coffee table, and Molly's back goes up again. "If he were to do anything on an airplane, he could not escape undetected."

Trish looks like she needs another cigarette. Beth wonders if she and Molly smoked the whole pack in Chester.

"Let us move on," Svetlana continues. "Why does someone want to harm either of you? James, forgive me, but I have gone through your entire life, and I find nothing damaging to anyone. Nothing convinces me that Messrs. Lexington or Fletcher are involved either. They have verifiable alibis for the times of the earlier attempts. Elizabeth, as soon as Grusha called me tonight, I called your ex-husband, and he answered himself. He could not possibly have reached Hamden from Chester in that amount of time."

"How about Terry Winstead?" Jim asks. "You thought maybe his parents want to stop the book."

"No," Greg says. "They didn't even know Taliesyn Holroyd was writing a book."

Beth feels five sets of eyes turning back to her and tries to shrink into the couch. Svetlana turns to her, and her face looks ageless. Beth wonders if the Oracle at Delphi looked like that.

"I'm afraid it revolves around you, Elizabeth. I have tried to research your family. You mentioned that your father was a judge, but there have been four judges in New England over the past thirty years named Shepard. What is your father's first name?"

"Julian," she says, "but he and Mom moved to Arizona two years ago."

"Were there any jilted men in your past? A broken engagement, perhaps? A harassing employer? I know you answered these questions before, but we have missed someone."

Beth shakes her head helplessly. "I don't know. I can't think." She wants to go to bed, maybe take a Seconal and curl under the covers before she unravels before their eyes.

"Perhaps at graduate school," Svetlana purrs, "or in college?" Something in her eyes tells Beth that she knows.

"I ..." She feels Greg's hand holding hers.

"I mentioned it to her, Beth. I'm sorry, but we need to check it out."

"What?" Jim asks. Trish's mouth tightens into a raisin. Beth feels her stomach start to roll again, but there can't be anything left to throw up. Molly, Trish, and Jim look at her. She wants to tell them to go away, but it's Jim's house.

"Would you like the others to leave, Elizabeth?" Svetlana's voice wraps around her. "Perhaps you would feel more comfortable talking with a woman."

"No. I mean, it's not that." She feels herself starting to shake. The Ice Queen moves over and puts her arms around her, and suddenly she feels huge, choking sobs tear loose from her chest. Svetlana is warm, not really ice. She holds her and rocks her until the words finally break through the pain.

"I was raped. In c-college. I never t-told ..."

"It was not your fault, my dear," Svetlana murmurs in her ear. "Men always tell a woman it was her fault. She gave them a sexy look, she led them on, she dressed too provocatively. It is never true."

"But I d-d-did," Beth sobs. She swallows a lump the size of the coffee table and wipes her eyes.

"Grusha." Svetlana's voice takes command. "Please escort our friends to the kitchen."

Beth hears footsteps fade. When she opens her eyes, Svetlana folds her legs under her on the couch and takes Beth's hands.

"Elizabeth ... Elzbieta ... Beth?" Beth bites her lips and nods. "Take your time."

Ten years crumble around her and she tells about Rick Gorman licking her beer-soaked T-shirt, then discovering her Little Betty Tease bra. Then ripping off her jeans.

She's still sobbing, and Svetlana is still rocking her when Molly and Trish leave an hour later. Jim leaves a glass of wine on the table and goes upstairs. Greg stands across the room.

"I'm going upstairs, too, Svet."

"No," she tells him. "Stay down here and ascertain that the house is secure. Beth and I will go upstairs. You and I will talk later."

Svetlana hangs up the Tally costume and watches Beth take out her contacts. Beth wonders if she'll have to brush each tooth ten times before she can slip under the covers. She pulls the bottle of pills from the bathroom cabinet.

"Seconal." Svetlana reads the label. "Has this masquerade agitated you so much, Beth?"

"I've had the prescription for years."

"Do you always take them?"

"Maybe once a week. But tonight ..."

"You have earned one."

Beth almost expects Svetlana to kiss her on the lips before she leaves, but the woman merely touches her cheek for a second and closes the door softly behind her. It's only when Beth's eyes begin to close that she realizes the footsteps went beyond the stairs and into Jim's bedroom.

Seventeen

Nines is choosing a fourth story from the stack on the coffee table when Svet glides down the stairs and sinks next to him on the couch. Her long hair flows loosely over her shoulders, and even in the dim lamplight, her face has more color than usual. She picks up one of the stories long enough to read the title before dropping it back on the table.

"Well," he says. "Did we have a nice time?"

"Prissiness does not become you, Darling." Nines waits for her to purr and lick her crotch. Then he wonders if that's already taken care of.

"Elizabeth gave me the name of the man who raped her. If he attended the University of Connecticut, they will have his Social Security number, and I will find him in minutes."

"Unless he doesn't want to be found."

"That will tell us all we need to know by itself, won't it?" She holds up another story. "Have you read this one yet? I rather enjoyed it."

Nines takes the pages from her and puts them back on the table. "That was a little embarrassing, you know."

"For whom? Nobody saw except you and James, and he does not object. You have been my dearest friend for years. This new moral streak in you is disconcerting. Is it because you are falling in love with Beth, too?"

He has to draw a breath, which gives her time to continue.

"She is a beautiful woman, but her normal existence has sheltered her from many unpleasant things. She has never encountered true evil before, something so banal and irrational, and it leaves her terrified. Since she is impersonating someone who does not exist, her whole world lacks order now, so who can blame her?"

"I'm afraid, too."

When Svet brushes her hair back, the lamplight gives it copper highlights.

"Of your feelings for her?"

Her hand moves toward his and he squeezes it.

"We base our lives on the assumption that things make sense. Man is a thinking creature, so that is his strength, but it also blinds him to other possibilities."

"This is a helluva time to discuss philosophy, Svet."

"But we must. Love is irrational, but lust is a chemical reaction given to us to guarantee the continuance of the species. We look at a physically attractive person. Beth is certainly beautiful, and you are attracted to her. We make rules of logic to control the irrational, our emotions. But hatred is an emotion, too. Like love, it grows from a small seed, perhaps physical appearance. Skin color or gender, for example, or perhaps from a small act done that we perceive as harmful."

"A grudge."

"In today's society, small issues often escalate to violence. A simple argument over a sports event or one's place in line. A love affair, a drug deal, road rage. Scientists argue about data, but the truth is that some people simply have a lower threshold of tolerance. I believe we seek a person who perceives that Elizabeth Shepard did something with malicious intent toward him."

"That's crazy."

"So is the fact that I am falling in love with James Leslie."

Nines feels like he's just lost a fly ball in bright sunlight. "You what?"

Svet's voice slows even more.

"My intelligence has always been my greatest asset and my excuse. Smart people intellectualize their feelings to maintain control, and I have always done it well. Jerry and I had great sex, but we simply used each other to satisfy our own needs."

"You still take him out on his birthday," Nines says.

"Perhaps that has been my way of maintaining a safe status quo, just as you worship Erin."

He remembers putting her picture in the drawer, but Svet's purr continues.

"James has a terrifying intellect, but knowledge excites him. For him, a fact is like a new toy a child finds under the Christmas tree. He examines it and loves it for its simple being. He may be able to use it in a book, but that is secondary. He loves simply learning it, as he loves learning to know me."

"I'll bet you've taught him a lot." Nines feels ashamed the instant he says it.

"I have not sought such a teacher-student role. Besides, I am a terrible lover."

"What?" Nines feels like that fly ball has caromed off his forehead.

"It is true," she says. "Dozens of men and women would call me a brilliant lay, but I have never allowed myself to go beyond noting what another person does to give me pleasure and vice versa."

Too much information, Svet. Way too much information. Before he can say it, he notices that her eyes have filled with tears.

"I told James," she whispers. "He knows of my ... affinity for sport-fucking, and he doesn't care. We talk research and computers and arcane facts, and then he holds me and I feel ... I find myself not worrying about technique or lasting or anything else. I love being with him."

He's never seen Svet play with her hair before, and he realizes just how upset she is. "It will not last. I am far too selfish to handle something like this. It frightens me too much."

"That's why Beth avoids men," he says. "She remembers being raped."

"Yes, a stupid, malevolent act. The man then tried to justify it so he would not feel guilty. The beautiful woman wore sexy underwear. She told me she still does so to remind herself that she has the power to drive men wild. It helps her maintain an illusion of control."

"That's crazy."

"Yes, but she functions. She can drive a car and purchase items in stores and write fiction. We all have our little rituals to keep fear at bay, but we have no idea if this attacker views Beth as a sexual being or something else."

"I'm going to find him, Svet."

"Yes, partly because that is the job you rationally know how to do."

"'Partly?'"

"She loves you, too, Darling. When I moved between the two of you earlier, I could feel the warmth." She reaches over and links her fingers with his again. "When this is over, perhaps you should visit Erin's grave."

"I know she's dead, Svet."

"You have stopped drinking. You can leave Erin behind, too."

He almost tells her about moving their wedding picture, but his voice fails him.

"I will locate Richard Gorman, and I will investigate Judge Julian Shepard's record in Massachusetts. If I find anything promising, I will call you immediately. Have you any plans for tomorrow?"

"I want to talk to Art again. I wish Molly got a better look at the car."

"It was dark, and she had no reason to expect the attack." Svet riffles through Beth's stories on the coffee table. "Here. When you have finished, show this one to James, too. It may help him to understand a woman's orgasms better."

"I thought he was getting a pretty good course in that."

Svet gives him the nasty smile that means she's back in control. "It would make me blush to discuss such personal matters."

Seconal always turns Beth's brain to moss, but she needed a night of sleep free from the nightmares that gambol around her like demons. She gropes in the drawer for her glasses, then goes into the bathroom to put in her contacts. She takes a long shower, the water turning her hair to thick hemp while she shampoos it. She wraps it in a towel and leaves the bathroom door open while she slides into jeans and a T-shirt. The steam evaporates from the mirror by the time she's tossed a flannel on the bed, so she studies herself more critically than usual. Yes, she has nice hair and a great body, but what does she have that Greg Nines might treasure when those assets depreciate?

The smell of hazelnut coffee fills the kitchen, and Jim's making an omelet. He stands differently, and Beth remembers that Svet went to his bed after tucking her in.

"It's going to be all right, Beth." He gives her a gentle hug and his lips brush her cheek. "We're on your side."

"I know." Greg is nowhere in sight and she wonders what time he finally went to bed last night.

"If you want to talk about last night … or anything…"

She pours coffee. "Thank you. Is Greg still asleep?"

"No. He said he wanted to see a few people, and Svetlana's looking up more stuff for him."

Jim's face picks up light when he says her name. Beth remembers the way the woman held her and let the pain come out, one jagged knot at a time, until she could cry most of it away. She likes Svetlana Melanova Thirst a lot more than she did yesterday.

"I hope they find something soon." She's tired of being scared. The writing is flowing a little, but it's nothing she can publish, mostly erotic fantasies involving a woman who's suspiciously like her making love with a man who's even more suspiciously like Greg Nines. She remembers the look in his eyes when he thought she'd been shot, then curling safely into his arms in the car.

"Me, too." Jim pulls something from the freezer and puts it on the counter to thaw. "It feels like a meat loaf kind of night."

"Can I do anything to help?"

"Can you sprinkle seasoning on vegetables?"

"Are you serious?" She bets she's a helluva lot more domestic than Svetlana. "Um, what time did the Ice— Svetlana—leave last night?"

"Late." Jim studies the breadcrumbs in his hand like he's not sure why he's holding them. Beth wonders if his research is going to show up in the sex scenes. He's working by a formula, so his sex scenes are hot but kind of generic. She's never felt she has the right to discuss that with him. It would be like asking her brother how to give her boyfriend a really good blowjob.

She refills her coffee and goes back upstairs.

"No luck on the car," Art says. "Well, the girl did not see enough to help. He could have gone around the block, and you probably would not have known, right?"

"I only saw taillights two blocks away," Nines agrees. "He was heading toward Route 9, but yeah, you're right, he could have stayed in the area."

Across the street, a garbage truck empties the Dumpster from the apartments. There's a package store half a block down that probably wasn't thrilled about a police substation opening nearby. Now they actually have to look at people's ID

Art nods at the phone. "I talked with the trooper from Chester. He says they dug three slugs out of the place, one in the window frame, and the others in the ceiling. Was the window high?"

"About ten feet above street level," Nines remembers. "The guy would have been shooting at an angle, not to mention hitting the glass at an angle, too."

"The slugs are from a .22."

Nines feels his eyes widen. "Who the hell uses a .22 now?"

"Good question." Art looks like he wants to practice putting some more. "Most all we get around here is gang shit. Everyone and his brother has a semiautomatic or worse."

Nines tries to pace, but the room's only the size of his kitchen. "A real pro? Around here? But who'd hire a pro to kill Beth?"

"Maybe it is not a pro," Art says. "The asshole has tried booby traps before. Maybe he is becoming desperate and had to find a gun in a hurry."

"A .22," Nines says again. "Maybe he's not used to guns and needed something he thought he could handle. Revolver?"

"They did not find any casings in the street, but they might have fallen in the car. They're scouring the area, and I told the cop to look through the database for any .22s that have been bought or stolen recently, but if our man has had it for years, we are out of luck."

"Do Brennan or Lexington own a gun?"

"I have not yet had time to check." Art glances at the pile of paper on his desk. "Is the woman all right?"

"Yeah." Nines remembers the smell of Beth Shepard's hair when she buried her head in his chest on the way home. "She gave us a couple more possibilities last night. Svet's checking them out."

"Anything worth passing on?"

"A guy named Richard Gorman, for one. He raped her at UConn ten years ago, but she never reported it. Svet's looking for him. And her father was a judge in

Massachusetts. Maybe there's someone going after his daughter."

"Is he still on the bench?"

"He retired a few years ago," Nines says. "He and his wife moved out to Tucson." He feels Art's next question and beats him to it. "I know, it's crazy. If someone's pissed off at the judge, why wait so long?"

Art watches his screensaver. "The guy has a gun now, which means he wants to finish it. I would love to give you a couple of men to help guard the girl, but I cannot pry anyone loose, even if we had the money for overtime."

"I know. If the guy's rushed, maybe he'll get sloppy, and we can find him."

"He has not been sloppy yet. I have told the patrols to go by Ivy Street a few extra times at night, but we still have no description, and he will not knock on the front door with an ax."

Art picks up his putter.

"What are you carrying now?"

"Ruger .357. It's easier to hide than my Sig."

"Not going to jam, either."

"No."

Art lines up a putt. "I have many questions for this asshole. I would really like to bring him in alive."

Nines remembers the last time he drew a weapon. He still sees it some nights, but not as often now that Erin doesn't visit. "Best case scenario, of course."

"Of course." Art's first putt is six inches short.

Eighteen

Words pirouette across Beth's monitor like a swarm of bees, so fast she can almost hear them buzzing. She hasn't been in the zone for over a month, afraid she'd never find it again, but now ideas zoom through her head so quickly that she can only get the basics down before they fly out of sight. Round, juicy adjectives shimmy before her. She'll cut them later when there's time to revise.

She's never used her own name for a character, but it feels right this time. The woman is really her, no denying it, tall, blonde, and alone. The ruby-nippled breasts will have to go away in the rewrite, though. That's too much like Jim's stuff.

He's shown her another ten pages, and the new female character has more dimensions than he usually gives them. She knows Ivetta is really Svetlana Melanova Thirst, hot as hell and twice as horny. She wonders exactly how much of the detail is real.

An hour later, she types "The End" and hits Save. Fourteen pages in one day, a new personal record. Give it a week, then print it out and go through it line by line. The ending feels a little contrived, but all it needs is some detail earlier to set it up. She can do that.

The aroma of Jim's meatloaf tiptoes up the stairs to tickle her nose, but it's still just teasing. She opens the Web site and answers the three questions Molly's passed on to her, then looks again at her pictures. Molly was going to take some at Binding Agreements, but that didn't happen for obvious reasons. She's left an e-mail saying she'd like to take some at the house tomorrow if it's okay. Beth replies, "Works for me," then closes up and lets Jim's cooking smell draw her down to the kitchen. She remembers that she promised to nuke the veggies.

Jim's puppy routine has slowed so he feels like a hunting dog at point. Svetlana must be changing his metabolism. His eyes flick to her, then to Greg holding the Pyrex top so she can sprinkle parsley on the carrots like someone who's in the right place to catch her after a flip, but only the captain of the majorettes gets to do flips. Everyone else just smiles and grinds.

Greg pours coffee. All of them like it strong and black, enough caffeine wafting through the kitchen to keep them awake until the weekend. Then the microwave tweets, and Jim pulls the meatloaf from the oven, his own secret marinade coating it the shiny brown of a new shoe. Beth thinks it relies on a combination of orange juice, A-1, wine, and something else she can't name.

Jim puts slices on all three plates, and the first mouthful makes Beth warm all over. She's cutting her second when the phone rings.

Jim wrinkles his face. "Let the machine take it."

Beth sips her coffee while Jim's monotone plays out. Then, "God damn it, Beth, pick up the fucking phone. What is all this shit with people checking up on me? I don't need it, and it better stop right now, or you're talking to my lawyer."

Beth's appetite vanishes.

"Drew?"

"Beth, what the hell is going on? Jesus Christ, phone calls last night, and a cop shows up at school today and asks if I own a gun. Do you have any idea how that looks in front of the kids?"

"Drew." Someone's standing on her chest. "Drew."

"What's happening, Beth? I don't need this kind of harassment. Joanie's upset, too."

Beth feels Greg crossing the room and waves him off. She's not afraid. She really isn't, but a question slams into her brain.

"Drew, how did you get this phone number?"

"You left me that text message last night, remember? I called your apartment. I didn't even know you'd—"

"I didn't send you a text message, Drew."

"Bullshit. Someone sent me a message, and it had your name on it. About eight last night. I was grading papers, had my phone off, didn't notice it until a little while ago. What the fuck is going on?"

She feels a chair materialize under her, and Greg mouths, *who?* She mouths back, *my ex* and overwhelms the voice chewing on her ear.

"Someone tried to shoot me yesterday. They're checking out everyone who might have a reason."

"Good God, Beth." Drew's voice modulates into the one she remembers. "What happened? When did this start? Are you all right?"

Greg pulls the phone out of her hand. "Mr. Brennan, this is Greg Nines. We talked a few days ago."

Jim leads Beth back to the table, but her knees don't work anymore. He holds her chair, but now the food might as well be sand. Greg's voice doesn't get any louder, but she feels it roughen until she could file her fingernails on it. His words slow down, then a little more.

"Now, do I need to make anything else clear to you? Tell me now. You may hear from me or my associates again. If you do, a smile goes a long way."

He hangs up, and suddenly it's too much. Beth feels the walls caving in around her.

"Shit, I can't do this anymore. I really can't." She pushes back from the table and stumbles into the hall, her tears blinding her to everything except the light at the foot of the stairs.

"Beth."

She seizes the banister and pulls herself up so she can storm into her room and slam the door. She flops on the bed and buries her face in her pillow and wishes she still had a teddy bear.

When someone taps on the door two hours later, her nose feels like a big red ball, and her eyes burn like she's been reading acid. She blows that big ball twice and finds a voice that doesn't shake too much.

"Who is it?"

"Greg." Well, she had a fifty-fifty chance of guessing that, didn't she? She opens the door but can't look above his feet planted on the floor about shoulder width. He's wearing jeans above them, just like she is.

"I know you're not okay, Beth. I don't blame you, but come on downstairs. We can get you a little food, and I'll tell you what's happening now."

"I'm not hungry."

"Okay. Come on down anyway, just walk a little. Get the tension out."

"I'm ..."

"Here. Let me help you."

His arms wrap around her, and she clumps down the steps on rigid knees. Then they're in the kitchen, and he cuts her a slice of meatloaf and pours her a glass of wine.

"Do you want me to stick it in the microwave?"

"Please."

She listens to the time-temperature-start song: *this is the meat loaf, reheat* like the old "shave and a haircut." The whirring ends in a high peeping, and Greg escorts her to the dining room table. She forces herself to taste the first piece, which melts on her tongue.

"Drew Brennan doesn't have a gun," he tells her, "at least, not legally. Svet's checked that, and Art has confirmed that he was in Hamden when someone shot at us last night. My guess is the shooter sent a text message after that just to draw our attention."

"Who sent the message?"

"His phone didn't show a number for it."

The meatloaf disappears before Beth's eyes. And the carrots. And the glass of wine. Greg's hand is inches from hers.

"The man left slugs we can trace, and that's a big break. We're narrowing down alibis, and you've given us more names. Svet's checking them out, too."

He looks at her empty plate.

"Do you want more?"

"No. Thank you."

They wash the dishes, and Greg escorts her to the living room couch with another glass of wine and a glass of ginger ale for himself. Her stories cover the coffee table, and she's surprised that he's actually reading them, how much it matters to her that he likes them.

"I actually finished a first draft this afternoon. First one in months."

His eyes make her stop shivering, even more than Jim's meatloaf. "You're going to write a lot more, Beth."

She forces herself not to look at the stories, but the only other place to look is at Greg Nines, and that's too dangerous. She sips her wine and puts it on the table. He puts his ginger ale next to it.

"I like these," he says. "Svet liked this one, too. She thinks you really captured the woman."

The Ice Queen likes her work. No, she's not really ice. She's strong and tough, but there's something underneath that Beth never would have imagined until the woman held her and made it safe to let everything out.

"Tell her thank you. She's ... unusual. That's not much of a word, is it?"

"Colorful, maybe?" Greg's voice warms her ear, and she tilts her head toward him.

"She doesn't really mind that I hated her at first, does she? I don't anymore."

"It's okay."

"I was jealous about Jim. Well, that's wrong, too. Jim's sweet as hell."

"You're sweet."

She forges on. "I mean, he's ... he comes across as kind of a kid, I know that. Innocent, naïve. Like a very smart little boy. Precocious, but not?"

"He really likes you, too. He's worried, and he doesn't know how to help."

"I know. I was worried that…Svetlana is just…playing with him, but now I'm not sure."

"Svet's got enough playmates already," Greg says. She hears something she can't quite identify.

"She's really with him, isn't she? It's like something out of an alternate universe. But he's bubbling over with stuff. More vitality, more humor, even more dimensions. I was afraid she'd just make a fool of him and go away laughing her head off, but I don't think that's going to happen."

"Me neither." Greg's eyes slide past her toward the pool of light at the top of the stairs. "She and I talked about it last night. After she, um…"

"I know she went to his room after she tucked me in."

"When she came down here, she said it's new for her."

"Jim and I talked about her this afternoon. He told me that Svet told him something." Beth's face feels like a forest fire and she reaches for her wine again. "She said that God must truly love women, or He wouldn't have let us have multiple orgasms."

"I'm sure she's speaking from experience," he says, "or research, if you prefer."

"Oh, I'm sure." Beth puts her glass down before she spills it all over herself. "What's she doing to my baby?"

"She's falling in love with him."

The words tumble across the carpet, warm, fuzzy pastels. Greg sips his ginger ale and realizes he's still holding a story. He puts it down and picks up another. "This one. I hear you talking in it."

"Oh?"

"Yeah. I'm not a very fast reader. There's some PhD term for it, I guess, but it means I can only read as fast as I hear a voice saying the words. The woman in this story talks like you, your rhythms. She even has your timbre."

"Is that good?"

"Your voice is beautiful." She can't look at him. "But it has such pain in it. It's tough to read sometimes."

"I guess it's true that you write what's inside you. You try to invent things, but they have to start somewhere. I'm my own mother lode. Whatever's happened to me ..."

His hand finds hers, but he doesn't say anything.

"I want to invent a world that's safe," she tells him, "a world where things can work out better." She realizes it for the first time as she says it.

"Your characters don't find it, though."

"No. I ...they won't take that last chance, the giant step or something. I don't know."

"They're afraid," he says softly.

"So am I," she whispers.

"We all are, Beth."

We aren't talking about my stories anymore, are we, Greg?

"No matter how bad it is, it's familiar. You think you know what's coming and what the rules are, so you hold onto it."

"I want to move on, Greg. I really do."

"I do, too."

He's standing in front of her, so tall, so warm. He pulls her gently to her feet. His arms slide around her and she tilts her head up to find his mouth.

He kisses her for hours, his tongue gently brushing hers, his arms holding her tightly against him. She digs her fingers into his back.

I'm asking for this, she tells herself. *I want this man's arms around me, and I want to feel him inside me, and I want to make him so happy he doesn't remember that life really sucks. Maybe it doesn't really, but I'm so afraid. No, I'm not afraid, damn it. I'm asking for this.*

Her hands slide up around his neck, and she tilts her head and kisses him again. There's a roaring in her head and her heart feels ready to burst through her chest. She moves against him and feels him getting hard. She feels her own wanting, that warm bubbling desire she hasn't felt in so long.

I'm asking for this, she tells herself again. *I want his mouth on my breasts and I want...*

He pulls back and looks into her eyes. She pulls his hand back to cup her ass and pull her tight against him. Then she finds his other hand and moves it to her breast. He strokes her softly, and she feels her nipple turn to a diamond.

When he kisses her again, she tastes his loneliness and his terror and his wanting.

"I'm not the man who hurt you," he whispers.

She kisses him back. She knows that things are never going to be the way they were for either of them, no matter what happens.

"I'm not Erin."

They kiss again on the stairs, then again at the top, and then once more when they reach her bedroom.

Beth closes the door behind them and switches on the lamp to bathe the whole room in a soft honey glow before he buries his face in her hair and runs his fingers down her back then looks into her eyes, so close to his own height. He brings a hand up to touch her cheek and her own hand holds it there until she flicks her tongue across his palm, and his knees almost give out.

"I won't do anything you don't want me to do," he whispers.

"There's nothing I don't want you to do," she whispers back.

He eases her flannel down over her shoulders to puddle on the floor. She does the same to his jacket. He slides his hand under her turtleneck and feels her stomach ripple before he guides the cloth over her head and drops it next to her shirt. Her hair is a pale halo floating around her face, and he brushes her lips with his own. Her bra barely contains breasts that make him catch his breath, and he kisses the cleavage between soft blue cups. Her moan comes from deep inside her.

"If you want to stop …"

"Never," she whispers again. It sounds like a prayer.

She pulls his T-shirt up, too. When he drops it behind him, her tongue flicks across his chest, and he feels himself shivering. She kicks off her moccasins while he unties his sneakers, then he unbuckles her belt and pulls down her jeans. She steps out of them and sinks to her knees to kiss his belt buckle before she unfastens it. She slides his own jeans down, her lips making him hard under his briefs. He feels dizzy.

Beth stands again, a blue thong barely covering her champagne tuft, and he slides his hand inside. She moans again and pushes against his fingers, already wet.

"Greg."

He unfastens her bra, and his tongue traces her nipples, slowly moving lower, her hands guiding him to her navel, then lower still.

"Let's get on the bed."

She slides his briefs down, then runs her tongue up his shaft. He catches his breath, and she takes him in her mouth. "If you do that, I'm going to come in about ten seconds."

"Next time around, maybe?" She pulls away to lie back, and he grabs his jeans to find the condoms he bought at the drug store. They take their time kissing and learning each other's bodies. Her breasts fill his hands, her nipples hard beneath his fingers. She directs his hand to the wetness between her legs, sliding his finger into her, mewing softly, guiding him to where her juices soak him. Her other hand strokes him until he feels his entire soul nestling in her touch.

"Oh, right there."

She moves against him while her own hand brings him along, too, her mouth giving him one more gentle lick before she rolls onto her back and arches against him, one hand coming up to touch his face, her other hand finding his with the packet, unrolling the condom onto him. She guides him into her, and the whole world shifts.

He wants to last forever but he knows he can't, her legs wrapping around his thighs, arching to meet his thrusts, both of them trying to hold back.

"Oh. Oh, yes." Her words are hot against his cheek. "Oh, hold me tight."

He loses the rhythm.

She arches to pull him even deeper. "Come with me, baby, please." He finds it again and tries to hold back, but it's been so long.

"I'm almost there…Oh, hold me…I'm so afraid…"

She pulls his mouth to hers, and he tastes her moan. Her insides clench, and he plunges into her, his own release only seconds after hers while she rocks under him, the whole room roaring.

They lie together until that roar fades to a soft hum, his hand caressing her cheek. He starts to move away, but she pulls him close again. It takes him a minute to realize that she's crying.

"You feel so good inside me."

He floats on the smell of her hair and tries to remember what it was like with Erin. It was wonderful and exciting, but they're only words. He can't remember what it felt like at all. He tries to remember any of it, her taste, the little mewling sound when she came, anything, but it's gone. So is the agony when they told him she was dead.

Beth flicks a tongue across his ear. "I need to take out my contacts. Stay here in case I can't find my way back?"

She slides off the bed and bends over her drawer to find her glasses. He's never seen her legs before, and they're even more beautiful than he imagined. He watches her rear disappear into the bathroom and tries to remember Erin again. Her voice was higher, but what does that mean, exactly? And she always murmured, "Greg, Greg, Gregory" after they made love, and she smelled like flowers, but he can't remember any of it except as words. Even the joy that he felt mere minutes ago with Beth is fading like smoke in a strong breeze, and he doesn't want to lose it so quickly. It isn't fair that pleasure should be just a concept, but it's the same with pain, so maybe it balances out.

Beth emerges from the bathroom wearing gold frames with lenses that turn her deep blue eyes into poker chips.

She's so beautiful, he's afraid he's going to cry, too. He tells her so, and her eyes soften.

"It's the glasses, isn't it?" She tucks them into her drawer again. "Don't tell me I don't know how to accessorize."

"Actually, I was talking about your kneecap." He rolls over to brush his lips across her leg.

"Nobody's ever mentioned my kneecap before."

He kisses his way up her thigh. "Maybe I meant your navel." He slides his tongue between her legs, and her breath whistles through her teeth.

"That's not my navel, Mister."

"Guys don't ask for directions. I'll get there, okay?"

"Let me help."

She turns off the light, then slides under the covers with him to guide his head back between her legs. "There's no hurry," she murmurs. Then her breathing speeds up a little. "Oh, no, there's no hurry at all."

A few minutes later, she arches her hips, and he feels her coming again. And then again. She stops biting the pillow to muffle her cries and moves closer to put her arms around him. They lie quietly and get used to the feel of not lying in bed alone. Just when he thinks she's asleep, her voice warms his ear.

"Have you been with a woman since ...?"

"No," he whispers. "How about you?"

"It's been almost five years for me, too."

He wonders if he should leave. He doesn't want to. Besides, what's Jim Leslie going to say?

"Don't even dream of making me wait five more years for you to love me again," she tells him.

"I won't." Neither of them remarks on her using the word *love*. Her slow breathing warms the hollow by his collarbone, then he's asleep.

The curtains are drawn, but he sees light outside when Beth's mouth finds him again. He tries to hold back while her tongue slides up and down, then her lips close around him, the whole room turning pink and loud.

"Beth. Oh ..."

She straddles him, and they fuck like teenagers who are just discovering sex, pure hunger driving them until she collapses on his chest, and he feels more tears on his cheeks, but this time he's crying, too.

When he closes his eyes, he can't see Erin anymore. If he loses Beth, he'll be all alone.

Nineteen

Roberta Winstead's face dims when she opens the door. She looks at Nines's car like her driveway has just depreciated fifty per cent.

"I thought I told you to stay away," she greets him. He decides that means no coffee and cookies. "Do I have to call my husband?"

"Actually, I figured I'd call on him later, Ms. Winstead." She lets him into the house but doesn't invite him to sit.

"Which one of you practices target shooting, you or your husband?"

Her eyes narrow. "I beg your pardon?"

"Shooting. The trophies on the mantel. Are they yours or your husband's?"

"Um. Harold's. He's a member of a gun club, but what does that have to—?"

"Does he use a .22?"

"I don't know anything about guns. What business is it of yours, anyway?"

"Someone shot at my client, and the police have identified the weapon as a .22 pistol. Does your husband keep the gun here?"

"Mr. Nines, leave this house at once." Roberta Winstead draws a cell from her purse.

"Ms. Winstead, the police will ask to see the gun, too, and they'll have a warrant."

"Then let them do their job. I'm calling my husband."

When she slams the door behind him, he dials Art's number. The sun is high, and he hears melting snow dripping through the gutters.

"Art? Harold Winstead in Glastonbury owns a .22 pistol, and his wife won't let me see it. She just kicked me out of the house."

"Is the gun in the house?"

"She wouldn't tell me. The husband's a lawyer, so you'd probably better ask the Glastonbury PD to look into it. They'll need a search warrant."

"Christ, I'm not sure we can convince a judge we have probable cause."

"I just remembered that when I talked to her last week, she referred to Taliesyn as a man. She knows Jim Leslie's really the writer. See if that helps."

"All right, but it still may be difficult. The best thing is to send cops to talk to the lawyer, too. You have his office address?"

Nines gives it to him and shuts down.

When he reaches Svet's house, Arnold takes one look at him and goes out to the kitchen. You can always tell who your real friends are. Svet's eyes search his face, and he tries to look innocent, but he knows his eyes are different now because the world looks different. It has a little glow he doesn't remember.

"Ah." She sits cross-legged before her monitor. "Richard Gorman is now an architect in Indianapolis. He has lived there for six years. He earned a master's degree at Northwestern in Chicago, then returned to Indianapolis, where he was born. He has not been in New England in nearly three years."

"Harold Winstead owns a .22 pistol," he tells her, "like the one that was used to shoot at Beth, and the woman knows that Tally's really a man. I've sicced Art and the Glastonbury cops on them."

Svet blinks once as she assimilates the new data. "Has he an alibi for Wednesday evening?"

"They'll check that out, too. Anything on Beth's family?"

She moves the mouse and her monitor flashes to life.

"Judge Julian Shepard heard criminal cases for over twenty years," she continues. "About seventy percent ended in convictions. I have no idea if that is a typical percentage, and it doesn't really matter. About forty cases went to appeal, and most of them were upheld. I searched as many of them as I could find."

Nines tries to focus on Svet's screen, but his eyes still see Beth Shepard's glorious body open and vulnerable before he slips across the hall to shave and shower her scent off him. He still remembers it, a pale yellow, almost as light as her hair. If he could drink it, he could stay young forever.

"I tried to find other anomalies," Svet continues. "Challenging, since I couldn't find a way to phrase it for a search, but I found a handful of intriguing possibilities."

He moves to look over her shoulder, and she brushes his arm.

"I'm happy for you, Grusha." she murmurs.

"Is it that obvious?"

"You're almost floating, Darling." She turns back to the screen, and he sees four names with thumbnail biographies and photographs. The oldest is 1985, the newest 1998. "These four men all died incarcerated, two of them early in their sentences. This one interests me especially."

She clicks on the photograph of a man with brown hair and eyes. His forehead and chin seem to recede at the same rate.

"Jake Cowper, age thirty-six, arrested for robbing a liquor store in Springfield in the summer of 1992. He had a pistol and forced the clerk to lie on the floor while he emptied the till, taking about eight hundred dollars and a case of whiskey. The clerk and another patron, whose wallet was stolen, picked him out of a line-up three days later."

"If the cops had him in for a line-up, he must have been arrested before, right?"

"Yes. He served three years for a robbery in 1986. He maintained his innocence in this case but could come up with no alibi. He was sentenced to six years. Less than four months later, he was killed in a fight in prison. Apparently, someone else was the target, but he got involved."

"I'm still not seeing it, Svet."

"Eighteen months after Cowper was killed, another man confessed to the robbery for which he was jailed. This man resembled Cowper closely, and both witnesses identified him after the fact."

"Shit," Nines says. *A cop's worst nightmare, not to mention a DA's.*

"Yes. Cowper had a wife, an eleven-year-old son, and a twelve-year-old daughter when he was sentenced. The wife turned to drugs and was arrested five times for soliciting over the next eight years. She contracted AIDS and died in the summer of 2001."

Arnold returns to the couch. Svet's chilly drone continues. "The son has several juvenile arrests and dropped out of school at sixteen. The daughter was a brilliant science student but rebellious. She was often disciplined for truancy or insubordination."

"I still don't see where you're going with this, Svet."

"Jake Cowper had a trade when he was arrested, and Judge Shepard noted in his decision that he felt rehabilitation was very likely. He told the parole officer that if the man had a job lined up, he would be willing to reduce the sentence after two years. Alas, Cowper died before that."

"What trade?"

"He was a licensed electrician."

The kid learned from Dad, Nines realizes. *He would have been able to get past the alarm system to wire Jim Leslie's house and Beth's car.*

"Where is his son now?"

"I haven't had time to search. I only found this case an hour ago."

Nines feels that rush he used to get when a curve ball hung about belt-high, the sucker he could turn on and drill out of sight.

"He'd be what now, twenty-seven?" He tries to find the dates again, but Svet's scrolled beyond them.

"And his sister would be twenty-eight."

Then he might be in good shape, Nines thinks.

"Try to find them," he says.

"Leave your cell phone on, Darling."

He's pulling into the parking lot by his office fifteen minutes later when his cell rings. He flips it open without looking at the number.

"Darling, it's me again." Svet's voice. "Jake Cowper, Jr., is dead. He was killed trying to rob another package store in Springfield in July of last year, and his sister disappeared from her last known address, also near Springfield, four days later."

His stomach tightens. *A woman. They've never even thought about a woman.* "What does she look like? Any pictures?"

"Not yet. I'll keep looking."

"I just got back to my office. Let me know when you find something."

"I will call you. Then we should meet in New Britain."

"Maybe Art will have something on the Winsteads by then, one way or the other."

"If he is an attorney, he can fight a search warrant." Svet's voice has her thoughtful quality, and he can picture her sitting motionless like a Buddha. "Did you tell me that Mr. Winstead threatened you with legal action when you first met him?"

"Uh huh." He catches her drift. "So why would he bother to try killing Tally when he could tie the book up in court?"

"Precisely. He could take years, so much time and money that the publishers would abandon the project and tell James to write another book."

Nines logs onto the Internet and opens the white pages. Molly Pitkin's address and telephone number come up in Manchester, but there's no other Margaret, Mary, or Molly Pitkin anywhere in Connecticut. Her driver's license gives her age as twenty-eight.

"Svet, I'm going to talk to Beth's house sitter in West Hartford. Drew Brennan said she gave him Beth's number."

"I will call you when I find something."

He can't find a Margaret, Mary, or Molly Pitkin in Massachusetts either. Social Security lists thirteen Margaret Pitkins, none nearer than Pennsylvania, and that one is fifty-six years old. Eleven Mary Pitkins live on the East Coast, but the nearest one, in Providence, is four years old and African American.

Beth still feels warm even though Greg Nines slipped out of her bed nearly eight hours ago. She knows his scent is still on the other pillow, and she wants to go over and bury her face in it, but Molly is trying just one more picture. She's been saying that for the last half-hour, and a lot of them don't seem to be working, because Beth's mind is on other things.

She always enjoyed sex until Rich Gorman raped her. She didn't even remember why it was supposed to be such a big deal until Greg made her come on the stairs Monday night, but now all she can think of is last night when they carried each other up Mount Everest and across the whole Himalayan Range. And how much she wants to do it again.

"C'mon, Tally. Beth." Molly's digital camera looks as big as a pinball machine, and her eyes squint behind her gold frames. They don't distort her eyes at all, and Beth wonders if she really needs them. She's jealous. Without her contacts, she couldn't distinguish Molly from a telephone pole.

"You want a glass of wine?" Molly suggests. "Maybe relax a little?"

"Yeah. Okay, sure." She goes over to her laptop and opens the story she finished last night. It's too soon to start editing, but she scrolls through the words, and joy rushes through her chest. She's writing again. Okay, the characters are her and Greg Nines with a few details changed, but it's a whole damn story, the first one in months.

Molly knocks on Jim's door down the hall, and Beth hears voices, Jim thanking her for bringing him more coffee. Then she's back, the pinot noir sloshing in the glass. A big glass. Beth sips it and puts it next to the monitor.

"Um, maybe move it over here," Molly suggests. "We don't want a picture of you with alcohol."

"Probably not," she agrees. She's wearing Tally Togs, an emerald silk blouse open at the collar, her hair fluffed up, and a small pendant on a gold chain. The black leather skirt she's learned to love makes her legs long enough to mount a flag on, and the boots make her taller than Greg Nines. It's fun, but she'll never really be Taliesyn Holroyd. She doesn't write that way, and as often as she's practiced signing the name with a bravura flourish at the end, she's still Beth Shepard, Julian and Doreen's daughter, Greg Nines's lover.

That stops her for a second, and her eyes narrow just as Molly takes another picture.

"Shoot, Beth, what's wrong?" Molly snaps. "You're usually a lot more together. Didn't you sleep last night?"

Not much, she thinks. *Greg and I were too busy fucking each other's brains out. No, we weren't fucking, we were making love. I've never let myself go with a guy like I did with him.*

"Here." Molly hands her the glass again, and she takes a long sip. It's a little bitter. There's some sediment in it. Molly must have finished the bottle. She'll have to go out and get another one later. It's Friday night, maybe they should celebrate … something.

Molly guides her to the computer and tells her to chew on a pencil and pretend to proofread the papers in her hand. She seems to do that one all right. Molly moves to the other side of the room and takes a few more.

"Why don't you change to slacks and the turtleneck?" Molly suggests. "We can do a few of you answering letters on the Web site, then another one of you marking up your copy of the book for reading."

Beth starts to unbutton her blouse, then stops when she sees Molly looking at her.

"Um, why don't I leave you alone while you change? Here, I'll freshen up the wine a little."

Beth almost calls after her to say not to bother. The lack of sleep is catching up with her, and she's a little woozy. She hangs up the blouse and skirt and stands vaguely in her underwear. Then she remembers what she needs and finds the brown turtleneck in the drawer where she folded it this morning after Greg peeled it off her last night. She finds her favorite plaid flannel and leaves it unbuttoned over the turtleneck. L.L. Bean, look out. All she needs now is a golden retriever to complete the look, maybe an Adirondack chair in the background. Put Jim in the chair wearing sweats or something. She'd like to get him into a few pictures, pretend he's just some man. It's too bad he can't even tell anyone he's writing the books that are selling like Saturday night sin in Las Vegas. Price of fame. No, that doesn't make sense. How can you be famous when nobody recognizes you?

Molly hands her another glass of wine. Dark liquid almost splashes over the rim, and Beth's glad she's not driving anywhere. If she finishes the whole thing, she'll be ready to pour it over herself and ask Greg Nines to lick it off her. How would pinot noir nipples taste? That's an interesting image, maybe she can use it in a story. Should she write it down? No, it's weird enough so she won't forget it.

Don't use it in a story Mom might read, though. She sends her and Dad copies of all the magazines that print her stuff. Maybe one with pinot noir boobs will be the exception that proves the rule. Whatever that means.

Beth fights back a yawn. Molly's hands look white and shiny when she holds up the camera, and Beth almost stops to look at them again, but Molly's telling her to stand by the window. The park will show as a blurry bright background and put her in semi-silhouette. Molly will have to adjust the contrast, but that's what PhotoShop is for.

Molly takes six shots, Beth beaming at her and realizing she's having trouble keeping her smile crisp. She's starting to feel a little silly, and her legs are getting heavy. When Molly finishes, maybe she'll take a nap.

Amy Belanger's eyes scan Nines's license like she's looking for the pictures, but she finally lets him in and leads him to the living room, where she has a partial afghan spread on the couch and a crochet hook sticking from a skein of yarn.

The colors don't go with the apartment at all, and he decides the afghan is a present or for somewhere else.

Amy sways her hips around the coffee table, and he's not sure she's wearing anything under her gray sweatpants. She's definitely not wearing a bra.

"Um, I'm staying here while Beth writes her book?" she asks him.

"How long have you been staying here, Ms. Belanger?"

"About a month? Maybe six weeks. No, wait. Frank took me out for my birthday, and that was the eleventh, and I wasn't in here yet, and Beth talked to me a couple of days later, and I think I said okay, but I needed to tell the temp agency. Beth said I should just give them my cell number for contact so they wouldn't have to change everything, and I guess I did that."

Amy Belanger is sweet as a birthday cake, but somebody didn't light all her candles.

"He asked me to marry him last weekend," Amy continues. She picks up the crochet hook like it holds all her memory. For anyone else, Nines would call it a flash drive. For Amy, speed doesn't seem to be an option.

"I'm sorry?"

"Frank. My boyfriend." She shows him the diamond on her left hand. "My fiancé, now, right?"

"Right. Did you—?"

"I told Beth when she came over the other day. She was really happy about it, said she'd be my maid of honor—no, matron of honor—I always forget, she's been married. Of course she has, I was in her wedding, too. We were in this really nice blue, she picked out a color we all looked good in, not just her. That's Beth, she's so sweet. She never thinks about herself."

"Then you know her ex-husband?"

"Drew? Yeah, a little. I was really sorry when they split. He seemed like such a nice guy, but Beth was ..." Amy gropes for the word, but it eludes her grasp and disappears. Nines suspects it happens often.

"Have you talked to him lately?"

"Who?"

"Drew. Beth's ex-husband." Nines realizes the walls in the living room are a light blue that Beth probably loves. The room has a soft blue atmosphere to it, and he sees a pale yellow wall in the kitchen. Beth definitely lives here. The colors exude her warm energy, so subtle compared to the overpowering primary colors of Taliesyn Holroyd. He wonders about her bedroom.

"Oh. He called a few days ago. We talked for a couple of minutes."

"Do you remember what night that was?"

"Um, today's like, Friday, right?"

"Yes." Nines wants to shake her.

"Um, maybe ... last night. Yeah, Thursday."

"What time, do you remember?"

"Wow." Amy puts down her crocheting and Nines almost apologizes. He should have warned her there would be a quiz.

"Let's see, I guess I had just done Ruffie's box. That's Beth's cat. She calls him Rufe, short for Rufus, but I call him Ruffie 'cause he's a real sweetie. Anyway, I took his stuff and the bag from the kitchen out to the Dumpster, and when I came back, the phone was ringing. I usually let the machine in the bedroom pick it up. Usually they don't leave a message, but if they do, I call and see if there's something I should pass on to Beth."

"How often does that happen, that there's something you need to pass on?"

"Oh, like so far, never, but you never know." Amy finds her place again. "Uh, but Drew left his name, so I picked up the phone while he was still talking and said hi, and he said he was looking for Beth."

"Did you give him her number in New Britain?"

"Uh huh. He sounded really upset and said he needed to talk to her and it was really important. So I gave him the number, and he thanked me and hung up."

"What time was this, Amy? Can you remember?"

Amy runs her tongue over her lip, and Nines feels his hair turning gray.

"I think ... I had supper in the microwave ... and I took the stuff out, so I would have been eating at six. It was before that. Probably quarter to six, something like that?"

Drew called Beth at six, just as they were eating dinner. Nines remembers they all thought the call was a solicitor.

"Thank you, Amy."

"Did Drew find Beth, do you know?"

"Yes, he did. Thanks."

His phone rings again just as he sets foot onto the parking lot. He's still forcing his eyes to focus sharply after talking with Amy.

"This smells very funny," Art says with no preamble. "Two garbage collectors turned in a .22 revolver in Chester this morning. They found it in a trash can in an alley across the street from that bookstore."

Molly Pitkin stepped up on the curb as she ran toward him two nights ago. He realizes that now for the first time.

"The gun we want?"

"We won't know for a day or two, but three shots were fired." Nines hears rustling, Art's turning a page. "The gun was in a plastic bag, like a freezer bag, for food? The end of it was blown out. Our shooter had the gun inside a bag when he fired. Why the hell would he do that?"

"To keep from getting blowback on himself." Nines understands when he hears himself say it. "Art, I think Molly Pitkin's our shooter. Svet's found some stuff that means her real name may be Cowper. I'm on my way to Beth's now, and I'll call you when I get there, okay?"

"You got a description, I'll put out a BOLO for this Cowper woman."

"We don't have a picture, and her last address was Massachusetts. She dropped out of sight about six months ago." Nines pulls out of the parking lot.

That's why Molly missed. She couldn't aim well in the bag, and she probably isn't used to a gun anyway. He should have written down her address and told the Manchester Police to pick her up, but now he needs to warn Beth.

He battles red lights back to Farmington Avenue, then turns onto I-84 west. The midafternoon traffic is light except around West Farms Mall, where he has to fight the surge then cut over again for Route 9 South toward New Britain. He wonders whether to take the downtown exit at East Main over to High or go down to Corbin and backtrack. Then he remembers there's a McDonald's at Corbin and West Main, and nine million kids just got out of school. He settles into the right lane for Downtown New Britain, coming out by New Brite Plaza. Five traffic lights in three hundred yards, no matter how you turn. Naturally, they aren't synchronized.

His cell rings again. Svet's voice cranks at a level he's never heard before.

"Grusha. I have a photograph of Margaret Cowper. I finally tried the Motor Vehicles Department of Massachusetts."

"What does she look like?" He's afraid he knows, but maybe he's wrong. It's hard to drive and hold a cell phone with your fingers crossed.

"It is the webmaster, Molly Pitkin."

Molly's not in Manchester, he remembers. *Beth told me last night that she's taking more pictures for the Web site. She's probably there now, alone with Jim and Beth.*

"Call Art," he says. "Have him get a black-and-white to Beth's house as fast as he can and meet me over there."

He runs the light at Martin Luther King Drive and leans on his horn. An SUV lumbering down the overpass can't stop, and they both swerve, fortunately in opposite directions, and he guns through the light, horns blaring and fingers waving in his wake. Maybe it's good that he never learned Spanish. He flashes his lights and zigzags across Main, then screeches left onto High Street.

Cars line the curb in front of the library, shrinking the street to one-and-a-half lanes wide. A truck and an SUV block the intersection for West Main, and he's considering going over the curb when the light changes, and the SUV crawls ahead enough for him to squeeze by and turn right. Then he's on West Main, the curve to the park coming up.

He leans on his horn again. A wide-eyed woman slams on her brakes so he can cut in front of her and up the hill. The speed limit in the park is fifteen miles per hour, but he takes the turn at forty. Traffic is thin by the park, and he sees Jim's house ahead. Molly Pitkin's Nissan sits in front of the garage.

Molly's words swirl around in a cloud, and Beth wishes she would either slow down or shut up. Her head aches, and her stomach hurts. She wants lie down and take a nap until Greg comes back. She's finished the story, so she doesn't need another idea for a while. *No, that's wrong. I didn't want the idea for a story, it was for...whatever.*

"Beth, hold this a minute, will you?"

She takes her Seconal bottle and turns it over in her hand. *Why should I hold it now? It's empty. I don't need any pills anyway. If Molly would leave, I could curl up and fall asleep faster than Rufe back in my apartment. I wonder what Amy and Frank will pick out for their wedding. When will it be? I'll certainly be back from the tour by then.*

"Thanks." Molly takes the bottle back and puts it on the desk next to Beth's laptop. She should put it back in the bathroom. Otherwise, Beth will never find it. On the other hand, if she leaves it out, Beth will remember to refill her prescription.

Her eyelids sag, and she wonders when they got so heavy. *God, I can't stay up all night making love anymore. I must be getting old, or maybe Greg Nines just took me further than I'm used to. Well, it's been so long, I'm not used to anything.*

"You should lie down, now, Beth. I want to type a note on your laptop, okay?"

"Sure, okay." *Something funny here. Why doesn't Molly use her own laptop? She carries it everywhere with her, but Molly's already sitting at her desk.* Beth tries to look at her, but her head weighs a ton. Her stomach feels even worse and she wonders if she's getting flu. She doesn't want Molly to catch it, too, or Jim.

Molly taps out a message, the keys amazingly loud. *How does she type, with a hammer?* She mutters to herself and types a little more. Then her hand shakes Beth's shoulder, and the light fixture over the bed shimmies.

"You want a little more wine, Beth?"

"Okay." Her teeth feel gritty, and Molly helps her sit up and tilts the glass toward her lips. *Ugh. Why did I ever like pinot noir? This tastes like sand.* When Molly lets her go, her head flops back on the pillow, and her vision blurs even more.

She's lying on her back and staring at the ceiling, the same ceiling she saw last night when she guided Greg Nines between her legs, and she felt him moving inside her, and the warmth spread through her limbs until she came, her first real orgasm in years. No, he brought her off Monday, right there on the bottom step, and that was amazing. She almost screamed, it felt so good. Molly almost caught them. She hopes Molly leaves before Greg comes into her bed again. Maybe she should tell her that. No, maybe she'll get the hint when Greg comes in. *Too much thinking, Beth. Just go to sleep.*

Screaming fills her head, what the hell is it? A ululating howl, driving through her ears like it's going to blow out her forehead. If it doesn't stop soon, she's going to throw up. She hopes she can make it to the bathroom in time. At least she's got her contacts in so she can find her way. Maybe she should take them out if she's going to take a nap, but how can she sleep with all that damn' noise?

More pounding, even louder than Molly's typing. Then voices. Is that Greg? Why is he under water? Something about it's over, then Molly's voice saying put it on the floor and slide it over, or she'll kill Beth right now and take her chances. She's under water, too, and why would Molly want to kill her anyway? Beth tries to raise her arm to her forehead to check for a fever, but her arm is too heavy. Her vision's so blurry, all she sees is a big silver stripe shimmering in front of her face. It gets closer until the whole room explodes and she closes her eyes.

Nines sails by the museum and skids into Beth's driveway next to Molly's car. He dashes to the porch and finds the door locked. He should have told them to give him a key. He pounds on the door, praying that Jim or Beth will open it, but his gut tells him that they can't get there. He puts his face to the window. Nobody's in the living room, and he doesn't see movement on the stairs.

A siren howls behind him, then another, slightly out of synch, so they sound out of tune.

He turns his attention to the parlor window to his right. The living room is closer to the stairs, but the parlor means everything is to his left when he goes in, less area to watch while he's still ducking glass. He grabs a log from the pile on the porch and swings it through the pane just below the latch. Glass flies into the room, and Jim's alarm blares, an alternating wail that fills the whole neighborhood along with the sirens.

He knocks jagged stalagmites from the bottom of the window frame and squints inside. The room's empty, and the doors, one to the living room and one to the den, are both closed. Nines tosses the log behind him again and puts his right leg through the empty frame, following with his arm and torso, his gun aimed toward the doors. Forget subtlety. Molly knows damn well someone's coming in, and they aren't selling Girl Scout cookies.

He strides through the den and cuts left to come out under the stairs. He sweeps his gun toward the dining room to his right, but no one's there. He's sure the action is upstairs, if he's not too late. That thought turns his stomach to porridge, and he forces it back out of sight. The last time he went into a house, the subject was upstairs, too, but he and Davey had to be quiet then, and he was hung over.

The fireplace has logs and paper neatly arranged for a fire, and Beth's stories still lie on the coffee table where they left them last night. He only glances at the living room. It's beyond the stairs. The front windows frame the black-and-whites sliding to the curb in front, flashers blazing and sirens wailing. The cops can clear the living room and cover his back.

He mounts the stairs, flattening against the wall and remembering that they come out at the center of the second floor, rooms at all points of the compass. Jim's room lies straight ahead, the office to his left, his own room at about seven o'clock.

Beth's room is almost directly behind him, and he knows that's where she is. He knows Molly's there, too. If he can't save Beth …

Sharp knocking at the front door, and a stern command. "Open up in the house. This is the police." Sure, they have to say that before they come through the window he broke for them. They don't know the layout unless Art's with them, and how much time will he take giving them a tutorial? He hears more steps on the porch, sounds like the hippo ballet from that Disney cartoon, but it covers his own footfalls.

Wall rubbing his shoulders, his face and gun turned toward Beth's door. The only good thing about the arrangement is you have to come into the hall to get to another room. If Molly's in her own room or the office, she's going to be behind him, and he's seriously fucked. He sweeps behind him with his eyes, but his gun never wavers from Beth's door.

What if it's locked? Stupid, he doesn't remember if there's a latch or one of those pushbutton locks on the door. Did Jim change the hardware? Right now, the knob still looks old and funky. If the door's locked, it's secure enough to slow him down.

Then he remembers Jim's room has that big connecting bathroom. Maybe he can go through there. He slides down the wall toward Jim's room. Downstairs, footsteps fill the living room, and Art's voice gives orders he can't quite make out.

Jim's room still looks like a kid's closet, all the knick-knacks and books of an enthusiastic history buff spilling from the shelves, the brass headboard still with its lamp fastened over the pillow. No one's there.

Even though it's farther from Beth's room, Nines forces himself to check Jim's office.

Jim sprawls on the floor by his desk, his chair lying beside him. His face is pale, but Nines feels a pulse in his neck. His feet pick out the silent boards in the hall, and he returns to Jim's bedroom. Then he's at the bathroom door, modern knob, turning silently as he opens it an inch. Beth's door is closed, too. That means he can get closer before making his move.

His gun feels heavy, but it's only a five-shot magnum, not the fifteen-round Glock he used last time he was in this situation. Not the time when he shot too fast because he thought the woman was Erin. *Erin's dead,* he reminds himself. *Please, God, don't let Beth be dead, too. Stop thinking about that. Stay in the present.* No lights in the bathroom, either. He closes his eyes and grips the knob on Beth's side. Her room is the shady side of the building. It might be dim, so he gives his eyes three seconds to adjust, then twists and pushes.

Beth's door opens. He steps in and dodges to his left. Molly Pitkin stands by the bed. Her left hand clutches Beth's hair, and the right one points a knife at her throat. Latex gloves cover her hands.

"Stop right there, or I'll kill her." Her voice still has the emotion of someone asking for a match. Beth's face is even paler than usual. Nines thinks she's breathing, but he can't be sure.

"It's over, Molly." *If she's looking at me, she can't hurt Beth.* "We've found your picture, and we know about your family."

"Good for you, Cowboy, but you're too late. She's dying, and Jim's probably dead by now. If you behave, maybe you can save yourself."

"There are cops downstairs, Molly. You're stuck."

"Maybe, maybe not. Put your gun on the floor with the barrel toward you. Then push it over here with your foot, and put your hands behind your head."

"No." If he puts his gun down, what's going to stop her from killing Beth? Feet pound up the stairs.

"I'll cut her throat if you don't. Put it down. Shove it over here, and move over by the window."

He sees a pill bottle by Beth's laptop and knows it's her Seconal. He knows that it's empty, too. If he can take Molly down, they'll know what to tell the hospital. Her camera and glasses lie on the desk next to the bottle.

"What happened with the Chinese, Molly?" he says. "I have to admit, poisoning yourself too was smart. Otherwise, we would have known."

"I fucked up. I thought Beth ordered the shrimp, not Jim, but I ordered the same thing so everyone would think the food was bad."

"It made us look at Jim for a target again, too. Clever."

"Flattery will get you nowhere, Mr. Nines. Now put down the gun, and move over by the window. I won't tell you again."

He tries to keep his eyes on Molly's. The longer he can make her wait, the less likely she'll be able to react in time. He shifts his weight slowly to his left. If he moves in front of the window, maybe the backlight will shield his eyes in case he telegraphs something.

He bends his knees as if he's going to lay down his weapon. Now the light hits Molly's face at a different angle. Without those little gold frames, she's a short woman with short dark hair. Like someone else. He freezes for a second, and Molly sees his hesitation. Her shoulders whirl toward the bed.

The first shot comes from the right and catches Molly high in the chest. Nines brings his own gun up and fires a second later, red erupting from Molly's blouse, another shot coming from his right. Molly tumbles backward, the knife floating over the rug before her head slams the edge of the desk and she collapses in a heap. Art Tomasiewicz crosses to cover her, and Nines leaps to the bed. He finds a pulse in Beth's neck, but her breathing is labored.

"Seconal," he tells Art, "I think. Check that bottle on the desk."

Art squats without touching it. Blood is already soaking the rug under the remnants of Molly's chest.

"Yes." More footsteps fill the hall outside, and Art steps close enough to search Molly's neck for the pulse they both know has stopped.

"The front left room," Nines tells the first uniform through the door. "Jim Leslie's unconscious, too. It's Seconal poisoning." The guy vanishes, and Nines pulls Beth to a sitting position, where she flops against his shoulder. He drapes her arm around his neck and half-walks, half-carries her to the bathroom. Her legs are rubber, and she's dead weight. He sets her down with her face over the toilet, then puts one arm around her chest and pries open her mouth with the other. He clamps her tongue down, and sticks his fingers as far back in her throat as he can reach. He feels that little flap of skin hanging down and jiggles a finger beyond it.

"Beth, don't die on me." He fights to keep the panic out of his voice. He remembers the terror of last week in the garage. He saved her then, why should this be different? But he couldn't save Erin. She's gone forever. Someone shouts about an ambulance, and Art says fuck that, take the guy over in the car. He knows they'll have Beth there in three minutes, too, if he can make her puke. He jounces her a little, and sticks his fingers into her throat again.

"Beth, I'm begging you. Help me again, like last time. Please?"

He pulls his fingers out of her mouth, then slides them in again, deeper this time, her teeth scraping his knuckles, and he wiggles the tips against her palate. Her gag reflex comes to life and a thick purple and brown ribbon unspools into the toilet. He holds her hair back and waits until she finishes, then probes her again. Another purple spew erupts, and her shoulders wrench. Then she moans. It's the most beautiful sound he's ever heard.

Epilogue

Even in sneakers, Beth Shepard is almost Nines's height while they walk, fresh air painting her cheeks with a faint blush. She has the same slinky grace and the same vitality, but now she's not working at it and he feels the difference. She's shedding her fear.

Across Walnut Hill Park, a cruiser stands watch in front of Jim's house, a panel truck in the driveway while a glazier replaces the window Nines broke the day before. He and Beth look past the band shell, the sun warm on their faces and melting snow trickling in the storm drains.

"My own Seconal," Beth says. "How sick is that?"

"Creative, wasn't she?" Nines says. "When she couldn't shock you and couldn't shoot you, she decided to make it look like a suicide."

"Who'd have bought it?"

"The note's not bad. Maybe you really did love Jim, and maybe you really were jealous of Svet taking him away from you. You could have dumped a handful of pills into his coffee, then finished the rest in the wine. It might have played, especially since she typed it on your laptop with those rubber gloves on."

Jim Leslie is out of danger at New Britain General Hospital. If the Seconal had been in his system for another two or three hours, he would have slipped into a coma, but they pumped his stomach for the second time in a week, which is why he's still there. Lots of Jell-O and rest to get the G.I. tract back in shape. Svetlana Melanova Thirst hasn't let go of his hand in nearly twenty-four hours except when Beth took over so she could step into the hall and cry in Nines's arms. He's never seen her cry before.

"Except that you figured out who she was."

"Except that you only had five or six pills left."

It's too nice a day to think such thoughts. He watches the wind fluff that champagne hair and reaches over to brush it back off her ear. He has Svet's keys in his pocket. They'll go over and feed Arnold, then Svet will stay with Jim in New Britain tonight. Crime scene tape and Molly Cowper's blood still decorate Beth's room, but Art let her throw a few clothes into an overnight bag. Tonight, she'll sleep in Newington. Nines needs to learn how to sleep with a woman in the bed next to him again. Maybe they won't even make love. Maybe he'll just lie awake all night and get used to her warmth, her smell.

"Stupid of her to leave the bottle next to my wine glass so you knew what it was."

"Not really. If you were going to die, you wouldn't bother to keep it a secret."

Her fingers start to clutch the Tally ring, but she catches herself and reaches for his hand instead.

"Let's talk about something else."

They find a sun-warmed bench facing the band shell, and she snuggles against his shoulder. He feels lighter without a gun digging into his kidneys.

"I told Trish I'm still willing to play Tally, but now the truth is going to come out."

"Molly was after Beth Shepard, not Taliesyn Holroyd, so maybe you can diddle things a little. It's fantastic publicity."

"Yeah, but now who's going to put it on the Web site?"

Cars fill the parking spaces down near the museum. Someday, Nines tells himself, they should go there, but right now, they both need to be outside. His ears still ring from three shots in a small bedroom less than twenty-four hours ago. The police confiscated his gun, but Art fired first, so he doesn't expect any fallout.

"How did she find me, do you think?" Beth's voice sounds like she wants dad to tell her a story, but be sure it has a happy ending.

"When we look through her PC, we'll probably find lots of searches for your family, and eventually, for you. When her brother got killed last summer, that kicked her into high gear, but she probably already knew where you were. That's why she came in the first place."

"So it wasn't just a fluke that she ran into me at the mall."

"Uh uh," Nines says. "By then, I think she'd been following you and trying to figure out the best way to introduce herself. She's done enough web design to talk her way in as Jim's webmistress. We'll have to ask Trish who thought of a stand-in first." He's sure Molly found Beth's brother and sisters, too, but he doesn't mention that.

"So she already knew I was a writer."

"I'm pretty sure. A little cherry on the cupcake."

She nudges him. "Watch the double entendres, okay?"

Maybe they won't just sleep in his bed tonight.

"Do you think Svet will take over as webmaster?" she asks.

"She likes to try new things," he says innocently. "I heard her and Molly discussing DreamWeaver, so I guess she knows the stuff, and she's a fast learner."

"We'll need someone to take more pictures."

"Yeah, but one step at a time, okay?"

"When we get a new webmaster, Svet or whoever, I want to write something about my rape," Beth says. "I don't have to give all the gory details. I'm not ready for that yet, but I can warn women about making themselves too vulnerable."

"That's really brave of you, and it's a good idea."

"You think so?"

They meander toward the house, the sun making her hair into a halo above those beautiful eyes. A couple walking a pair of Labradors nods at them, and they nod back.

"Yes."

He stops, and when she turns to face him, he kisses her. He feels happy, and he's not even drinking. Three years today. He mentions that, and she gives him a smile that threatens to melt the rest of the snow. The War Monument looms at the top of the hill behind them.

"You won't need security anymore," he says, "but you'll need someone to carry your bags and check you in at the hotels now that Molly's gone, won't you?"

"You've got deep ulterior motives here, don't you, Mister?"

"It occurs to me that if I'm along already, I can meet your family when you stop for that reading in Tucson." Her face grows serious and her eyes stare at her hands. "I'm just thinking out loud."

"I'm really scared, but I'm waiting for you to tell me something else now."

"I love you, Beth." Her eyes move up to his, that wonderful deep blue he'd never seen before. "And I'm as scared as you are."

"We've only known each other two weeks. Not even."

She only wears a ring when she's Tally. It occurs to him that he should do something about that, too.

"I should go back into therapy," she says. "I need to finish cleaning up the stuff I've—we've—started." He can feel her strength flowing into him. "I want to get it right this time."

"I can go with you," he says.

"You don't have to."

"I want to. I want it to work this time, too." He takes a deep breath to drown out the roaring in his chest. "I have my own stuff to finish."

The glazier's truck pulls away. Nines sees the sticker on the shiny new pane of glass. He's not ready to go back into that house again, and he feels her hanging back, too. He turns toward his car. They can feed Svet's cat and swing back to his place. He feels another idea bubbling to the surface.

"I'm going to drive out to Litchfield tomorrow," he tells her.

It takes her only a few seconds to make the connection. "You sure?"

"I need to say good-bye to someone so I can be with someone else."

"Do you want me to go with you?"

"You don't have to."

"I know," she says. "I want to.

Meet Author Steve Liskow

Steve Liskow has published stories in three anthologies of New England crime writing and has twice won Honorable Mention for the Al Blanchard Story Award. "Stranglehold" won the Wolfe Pack's 2009 Black Orchid Novella Award and will appear *Alfred Hitchcock's Mystery Magazine* in the summer of 2010.

A member of the Mystery Writers of America and Sisters in Crime, he is working on a private eye series and a novel based on his previous life as an English teacher. He lives in Connecticut with his wife Barbara and two rescued cats. Visit his Web site at www.steveliskow.com.

Breinigsville, PA USA
09 May 2010
237621BV00001B/1/P